ENEMY DEAREST

WINTER RENSHAW

All Books Available here!

Free Content Available here!

I loved him. I lost him. And now he's back.

August Monreaux was a stormy sea of a man, the dark between the stars, an electric chill cutting through a crowded room—all wrapped into one wicked, beautiful package.

He was also off-limits.

My entire life, I was kept a safe distance from the notoriously virulent Monreauxs, banned from so much as breathing the same air. And like the good daughter I was, I obeyed those rules.

Until the one time I didn't ...

Only while I sampled him, he devoured me like the forbidden fruit that I was. And in the blink of an eye, my worst enemy became my first love. His poison became my antidote. His touch, my addiction.

After we went our separate ways and severed our ill-fated ties, I thought I'd never see him again ... until he crashed back into my life at the worst possible moment— and asked me to marry him.

But it wasn't that simple.

It never is.

It turns out marrying a wealthy powerhouse of a man comes with a price.

But walking away could cost me everything.

I was never anyone else's, not for a moment, not for a breath.
Before you, I was yours, but waiting;
all my life
I've been
waiting.

I know
nothing but peace,
understanding
this.

—Tyler Knott Gregson

CHAPTER ONE

Sheridan

I SINK to the bottom of the glimmering midnight pool, the cashmere-soft water swallowing me whole. With a lungful of sticky night air held tight in my lungs, I wait until my toes scrape the concrete bottom before floating to the surface.

My father always says, *"Nothing good ever happens after midnight."*

But it's 1 AM.

And this is divine.

I brush a ribbon of chlorine-soaked hair from my face, take a deep breath, and close my eyes, letting the full moon paint my body as I float on my back. Muscles liquid. Mind emptied of the day's worries. Naked as the day I was born and as free as a dove.

I could stay here forever—which is ironic because I shouldn't be here in the first place.

Technically, I'm trespassing.

Eyes shut, I inhale the distinct scent of pool water and nearby rose bushes, and try to imagine what it must feel like to be a Monreaux, growing up behind these privileged iron gates, a world away from us ordinary locals.

Not that there's anything wrong with being ordinary.

In fact, I'm quite content being a nobody.

There's more to life than having the world at your fingertips. It's okay to struggle, to want for things. Mama says it builds character; gives us the grit we need to get through the runaway rollercoaster that is life. Or maybe that's what she's had to tell herself all her life to get through the of inflictions God saw fit to gift her—a rare vagus nerve disorder that makes her body overreact to even the mildest stressors, a weak heart that makes everyday tasks feel like scaling Everest, and just this year he thought it'd be fun to throw in a bout with Guillain-Barre syndrome.

Mama also said no one every promised life would be fair for everyone. We all have our crosses to carry and comparing them doesn't do us any good. She also said that if all we have is each other, that would be enough. We don't have much in terms of money or possessions or bragging rights, but we have our loyalty and love, and for us, it's all we need to get through this life.

Squinting, I study the blanket of stars above, distracted by Cassiopeia's flickering constellation and the rich section of Milky Way that runs through her—until a light flips on near the back of the Monreaux estate.

A second later, a door slides open with a jarring slick before slamming shut with so much force the sound echoes off the water. My heart beat ricochets in my chest before whooshing in my ears so loud it drowns out my panicked thoughts.

Righting myself, I swim to the closest ledge, half-obscured by a manmade waterfall trickling over a boulder grotto.

Heavy footsteps pound the pavement, growing louder, closer.

I hold my breath—as if that could possibly make me invisible—and pinch my eyes shut.

"Show yourself," a man's voice booms over the trickling water splashing around me. "I know you're out here."

This morning I ran out for coffee for Mama and over-heard someone talking about how the Monreauxs were on their annual trip to St. Thomas this week—which was partly why I saw fit to scale their six-foot fence and dip my toes into these forbidden waters. That and it's been hot as Hades all week, and our air conditioner decided it'd be the perfect time to kick the can.

More footsteps.

I wince.

It has to be a property caretaker. Or maybe a house sitter. People like this don't just leave their massive homes sitting empty while they're snorkeling off some island in the Caribbean. Their staff doesn't take a vacation just because they do. I know that. I guess I figured whoever was here would be fast asleep this time of night ...

"You can't hide in there forever," he says with a voice too sharp, too young-sounding to be someone left to tend to a multi-million dollar estate in its owners' absence. He exhales, shoes shuffling closer. "Come on. I don't have time for this. Get your shit and get off my property."

He must've spotted my dress, bra, and panties, resting in a heap on one of the lounge chairs.

I swim out from behind the waterfall, keeping everything below my neck beneath the surface. Scanning the length of the mystery man, I start at his designer sneakers and trail up his ripped jeans before stopping for a brief detour at his broad shoulders, which are hardly contained in his gray t-shirt. Lastly, I arrive at his moonlit glare.

His dark brows angle in as he captures my stare, his expression unreadable. A warm breeze plays with his mussed, sandy blond waves and star-cast shadows frame his chiseled features.

He's beautiful, obscured in moonlight and all.

But his eyes glint, unamused.

And he doesn't smile.

I brace myself for a lecture or a cruel handful of words to be thrown in my direction, but the handsome figure simply takes a swig from the thick beer bottle in his hand, keeping his attention trained on me. My gaze falls to the complicated mess of tattoos covering the exposed skin of his left arm. And when I dare to meet his cold stare, I discover two small barbells piercing his right eyebrow.

This is a man who gives zero fucks.

"I'm sorry." I'm not above apologizing. I'm in the wrong. I shouldn't have come here tonight. Shouldn't have scaled his fence. Shouldn't have stripped out of my clothes and dove into his luxurious swimming pool like I owned the place. "If you'll let me get my things, I'll be out of here in two seconds. You'll never see me again. I promise."

His full mouth arches into a devilish smirk, and his silence sends a shiver down the back of my neck.

I've got less ground to stand on than a mouse who wandered into the den of a ravenous lion.

"You're August, aren't you?" I take a friendlier approach.

There are three Monreaux boys. Soren's the oldest and a bona fide rock God. I'd know his face anywhere thanks to the billboards all over town any time they tour through Missouri. Then there's Gannon. I've never seen him, but I know he's quite a bit older than me. August is the baby of the family, though if it's truly him standing before me, there's nothing infant-like about him.

He was only two when his mom died. She was jogging —near our house actually—when she was struck by a car and left to bleed out on the side of the road.

His father tried to blame *my* father for her death.

They have a history ...

A dark, rooted, tragic, ugly history that I don't dare discuss around him and Mama unless I want to see his eyes turn cloudy and send Mama off to the bedroom in a fit of tears. A history so shrouded, I don't even know the half of it —I only know that we don't talk about it.

If my parents knew I was here, they'd kill me. Figuratively, of course.

My entire life, it's been made abundantly clear that the Monreaux family is off-limits in every sense of the word. I'm not to go near them, not to breathe their toxic air. Not to so much as even whisper their name under our roof.

Being here, in these waters, on this property, is blasphemous to the Rose family name.

I didn't come here out of spite.

I didn't come to hurt anyone or to prove some kind of point.

But if my parents found out, they'd be devastated.

"I'm the one who should be asking questions, don't you think?" He takes another drink, his gaze all but penetrating my soul.

He isn't wrong.

This isn't the time to be friendly. Last thing I need is August telling his daddy that the Rose girl broke into their back yard and was skinny dipping in their pool. Word would get out. Phone calls would be made. Coronaries would be had. My parents probably wouldn't believe it anyway, but that's not a risk I'm willing to take.

Before I have a chance to utter a single word, August makes his way to a stone-covered cabana and returns with a fluffy white towel. Crouching by the ledge, he hands it to me. It's a simple exchange, yet the uneasy flutters in my chest do double-time when our fingers graze.

"So what name should I give the police when they arrive?" He rises, towering as he peers down. "You look like a ... Harper to me. Chloe. No. Addison. Definitely an Addison."

Pretty girl names ... or are they basic?

Is he trying to flatter or insult me?

I draw in a hard breath as I climb out of the water and quickly wrap my body in the soft warmth.

He tosses back another mouthful of beer, this one more generous than its predecessor.

"You're not going to give them *any* name." I keep my tone sweet as I tug my sundress off the chair, and then I turn my back to him and pull it over my damp body.

"What makes you so sure of that?" His words are subtly slurred. I imagine this isn't his first beer of the night.

I face him once more, hardening my confidence. "Because if you're who I think you are, you're not twenty-one. You're not going to be calling the cops with liquor on your breath."

His head cocks to one side, as if he's studying me from a new angle. "If I'm who you think I am, then you should know ... my family pretty much owns the cops. Sorry, Sugar Tits, but I've got nothing to be scared of in this scenario. You, on the other hand ..."

Either he's trying to get a rise out of me or he truly is as big of an asshole as they say ...

I may be known to keep sweet, but I'm not going to stand here and let someone objectify me because I made one bad decision.

"Sugar tits? I guess it's true what they say—money can't buy you class."

He laughs, unfazed, as if my insult merely ricocheted off his steely exterior.

"So what *should* I call you then?" His penetrating stare falls to my chest before skimming back to my eyes.

"You're seriously going to turn me in? I didn't steal. I didn't break anything. I didn't hurt anyone. I only went for a swim ..."

I fold my arms across my breasts, which I'm quite certain are standing at full attention, and toss him a frown.

"You trespassed on private grounds," he says. "Last I checked, the police don't take kindly to illegal activity in this part of town."

This part of town ...

Of course. The southwest quadrant Meredith Hills is the "rich" section of this godforsaken town. Anything south of LeGrand street and west of Sunderland avenue is *the* place to reside. It's an interesting layout too—the streets almost designed likes spokes in a wheel, all of them poking out from the Monreaux residence, as if it's the capitol complex of this great-and-powerful city.

I roll my eyes. "Spoken like a true Monreaux."

August chuffs. "What's that supposed to mean?"

I lift a shoulder. "You're your father's son. *That's* what that means."

I'm bluffing. I know nothing about his father besides the fact that he's a wealthy, powerful, and resourceful man and people tell stories and give warnings. I don't know what he's truly like behind closed doors—and I never intend to find that out.

August takes a step closer, though I attempt to pay him no mind. I also try to ignore the throbbing pulse in my ears and the nausea swelling in my belly. I have no idea what he's capable of, but I'd be wise not to put anything passed him.

I gather my bra and panties and stuff them into the pockets of my dress before sliding my feet into my faded flip flops. "Get over yourself. I said I was sorry and now I'm leaving."

Making my way toward the fence line, my steps falter—I'm going to look ridiculous climbing it in nothing but this soggy sun dress. But I force the thought from my head, ignoring the weight of his stare on my backside growing heavier with every step.

I don't care what he thinks.

The Monreauxs might own this town, but at the end of the day, August and I are nobody and nothing to each other. We've gone nearly two decades like two passing ships in the night. No reason we can't continue on that way.

"Hey ..." he calls after me, his voice cutting through the dark.

I keep going.

"Hey, I'm not done with you." His words are edgier this time, louder.

I pick up my pace, sprinting so fast I hardly feel the ground against my feet.

The fence is just a few meters away, almost in reach when the shattering of glass stops me in my tracks.

I glance over my shoulder as he collapses onto the edge of a pool chair, shards of his beer bottle broken at his feet.

Did he smash it ... on purpose?

A hundred Monreaux stories dance through my head all at once, rumors indistinguishable from facts swirling together in a sea of uncertainty. Most of the time people like to exaggerate for the sake of telling an interesting story, but Mama always says every lie is rooted in truth.

All I know is most people say that family is as dangerous as they are powerful, as unpredictable as the stormy sea. Dysfunctional yet loyal to a fault. And thick as thieves. Locals stay away from them for good reason.

I once overheard someone claiming that getting into bed with a Monreaux—figuratively or otherwise—is like playing a game of Russian roulette. Odds are you'll come out of it alive, but you'll never be the same after.

Unfortunately, those odds weren't in my Aunt Cynthia's favor when she dated August's father decades ago. She didn't come out of it alive—which is exactly the reason my parents forbid me from going anywhere near this family.

I steal one last glimpse of the wickedly handsome Monreaux boy, at his broad shoulders and chiseled jaw and messy hair, at the shiny fragments broken glass surrounding him, and I make a running leap for the fence.

Within seconds, I'm dashing home, to the side of town where people keep bars on their windows and police sirens double as bedtime lullabies. Where air conditioners break and water bills sometimes go unpaid. Where no one hires house sitters because vacations are the kind of thing you only do when you win a little bit of cash from a scratch-off

card or your tax refund is a little more than you were antici-
pating that year.

By the time I get to our little gray bungalow on North
Fifth Street, the soles of my feet are on fire, and my lungs
burn in sympathy. I toss my tattered flip flops in the garbage
can by the back door and sneak inside.

My father is working nights, and Mama's asleep in her
room, the TV blaring and ceiling fan whirring. They'll
never know about my little escapade tonight, thank
goodness.

On my way to my room, I catch my reflection in the
mirror in the hall, cringing at my blonde waves that have
dried into a frizzy lion's mane of a look. A second later, I
peel off the damp dress and toss it on the back of my
desk chair.

Tiptoeing to the kitchen, I fill a plastic cup with ice
water from the fridge and drink it all in one go. Returning to
my ninety-degree room, I crack a window, switch on a box
fan, and collapse on my lumpy mattress.

My breath eventually settles despite my adrenaline-
soaked blood, and the events of the past hour play in my
mind like a surreal fever dream.

Everything happened so fast.

Half asleep and semi delirious, I stare at the stained
ceiling above as a loopy grin claims my face. The whole
thing is kind of funny. Trespassing and skinny dipping is
the last sort of thing anyone would ever think I'm capable of
doing, Monreaux estate or otherwise. In fact, I can't think of
a single soul who'd believe any of this anyway.

Guess it'll have to be my little secret ...

And honestly, I've always wanted to see a Monreaux.
Maybe it was all those times my parents whispered about
them when they thought I wasn't listening. Or maybe it was

the way strangers always looked around the room before they'd start talking about them in public, like they had ears in every corner of this town. They were a mysterious enigma placed on the highest shelf, just out of reach.

At least now I can say that I saw one.

And if I'm lucky, I'll never see him again.

______

CHAPTER TWO

AUGUST

"WAY TO GO, asshole. Better clean this shit up before Dad and Cassandra get back." I'm awoken by a familiar voice in my ear followed with a sharp kick to the shin.

Gannon.

I sit up from the pool lounger chair, lifting a hand to my throbbing temple as my eyes adjust to the searing sun overhead. Instinctively I reach for my phone, only to find it in my brother's possession.

He waves it. "You can have your phone back when you grow the fuck up."

"Fuck you."

"You're pathetic, you know that?"

I smirk. "That's news to me."

"Maybe you should think about actually doing something with your life instead of chugging stolen beers and getting high by the pool."

I don't get high. I can't stand that head-in-the-clouds,

floating sensation. It's too *cheery* for me. But he can think what he wants to think. It's all the same.

"And hooking up with a different girl every night. You forgot that part," I add.

"You fucking wish."

If he only knew ...

I've gotten more ass this summer than Gannon's had in his entire life. And that's including the college-aged nanny he lost his virginity to at fourteen.

"Dad's going to be home in a few hours," he says. "Pick this shit up. Take a shower. Put on a clean shirt. Wash your damned hair. You look like you have fucking mange."

I've been called a heartless bastard more times than I can count, but put me next to Gannon and I'm a purring, milk-drunk kitten.

"At least I don't look like a corporate stock photo." I squint up at him, shielding my eyes from the glare of the sun. It's a Sunday afternoon, but he's dressed in designer slacks and an ironed polo with our country club's crest on the pocket. Ever since he graduated first in his class at Vanderbilt, the stick up his ass has grown exponentially. Just for fun, I add, "The discounted kind with dead eyes."

"You want your phone?" He waves it toward me. But before I can reach for it, he chucks it into the pool with a flick of his Rolex-covered wrist.

It lands with a pathetic splash, barely audible over the trickling waterfall feature my father's girlfriend insisted on adding last year.

I don't react.

I don't give him what he wants.

I never do—and I'm pretty sure he hates me for it.

"What do you think Mom would say if she saw us right now?" I ask.

The Mom card has always been Gannon's Achilles' heel. I was two when she died. I have zero recollection of her. But he was older. He still has memories. And he was the biggest fucking Mama's boy—at least that's what Soren tells me. I've seen it in some grainy home videos too. Gannon has always been ... *extra*. Our mother had the patience of a saint to put up with his constant neediness. "Bet she'd be real proud, don't you think? Watching us going at it like a couple of prideful jackasses."

Gannon remains impressively stone-faced, though uncharacteristically quiet for a minute.

"If Mom were here, pretty sure she'd be telling you to get your shit together," he finally responds. "But since she's not, someone's got to do it for her."

"You're doing the lord's work." I place my palms in a prayer position. "Saint Gannon."

My brother opens his smart mouth to respond, only to have his thunder stolen by our weekend housekeeper, Clarice. Gazing down, she toddles to the pool with a dust pan and broom in hand.

"Good morning," she says, crouching to sweep up my mess. Her knees crack and she stifles a moan as she bends. She's way too fucking old for this shit, but she's loyal and efficient so my father will keep her on until her dying day.

Once upon a time, she was our full-time grounds manager with a staff of fourteen hand-picked souls, but time caught up with her, as it does, and my father chose to keep her on weekends rather than put her out to pasture.

No one's ever accused Vincent Monreaux of having a soft spot, but he's good to those who are good to him.

Gannon pinches the bridge of his nose, giving me side-eye while Clarice does my dirty work.

I exhale. "Clarice, you don't have to do that. I've got it."

All of this fanfare over one fucking broken beer bottle—and none of this would've happened if it weren't for the naked chick swimming in my pool last night.

At first, I thought I was hallucinating. I'd had a few beers and I was heading back for more when I heard the splash outside. I shoved the living room curtains apart and peered toward the pool, which was pitch dark except for the faint glow of moonlight on the rippling water ... water that should have been still.

And then I saw her. Floating. Peaceful. Oblivious. *Naked.*

Clearly deranged.

Possibly high on drugs for all I knew.

Or dead.

I've never fashioned myself a hero by any stretch of the imagination, but I'd be lying if I said I wasn't preparing myself to fish a lifeless body out of the pool. But by the time I got out there, she was hiding in the grotto—like I wouldn't fucking find her.

Her clothes and sandals lay in a crumpled pile on a chair, and I yelled for her to show herself. When she finally emerged, it took all of two seconds for me to recognize that face.

She was a Rose.

Sheridan Rose, to be exact.

A vile, disgusting ... *beautiful* ... Rose.

I didn't know her, but I knew all about her—and her parents. So I'd kept a poker face and played dumb. I'd seen outdated pictures of her family before, from archived news articles. And I knew she'd dated a guy from my high school a couple years back. In tagged photos on social media, I'd studied her heart-shaped face for more hours than I'd ever admit to anyone ... because she wasn't just gorgeous, she was forbidden—and that made her unlike the rest.

For as long as I can remember, my father has been obsessed with the Roses and avenging the smear campaign they'd launched against him, his reputation, his business, and our family name a lifetime ago.

We'd almost lost *everything* because of them.

Not to mention my mother's death suspiciously occurred a block from their house, and the bastard who struck her and drove off was never found. To make matters worse, not only was my mother's life taken that day, but so was the life of my baby sister. Mom was twenty-two weeks along, carrying the little girl they'd so badly yearned for. A "sweet little angel" to round out our *perfect* family, as my father stated in a camera interview once.

Without warning, nearly everything my father had ever wanted was taken from him.

Forever.

He almost had it all.

To this day, my father is convinced it was one of the Roses. Someone who saw an opportunity and seized it. Someone with good reason to want to inflict the worst kind of pain and loss onto a Monreaux.

Someone like Rich Rose.

Last night, like a true coward and in true Rose fashion, the naked girl ran off before she had a chance to pay her penance. Like she could just wander in here and walk off like nothing happened ...

And then she had the audacity to ignore me when I called after her—that's when I smashed the beer bottle.

All I could think about was how the spawn of the family that destroyed mine dared to waltz her perfect peach-shaped ass onto our property like she owned the place.

The fucking *nerve* of that woman.

Clarice sweeps up the last fragment of glass, and Gannon heads into the house without a word—thank God. I wait until they're both out of sight before fishing my dead phone from the deep end with a leaf skimmer, and then I make my way inside to clean up. Not because Gannon told me to, but because I can't stop picturing the Rose girl's ripe tits and pouty mouth and I need to get my head straight with an ice-cold shower.

She was a sitting duck.

I knew *exactly* who she was.

I could have easily made her atone—in more ways than one.

She's lucky I didn't.

And if she's smart, she'll never set foot on these premises again.

Because I can't promise I won't seize the opportunity next time.

CHAPTER THREE

Sheridan

"I CAN CHECK you out over here, sir." I wave to a bearded customer Sunday afternoon who promptly deposits a pair of Air Pods and a wireless iPhone charger on the counter before all but tossing his credit card at me.

I scan his items, ignoring the weight of his gaze on my chest, choosing to believe he's reading my name tag instead of eyeing my covered cleavage. I've worked at this cell phone store six months now, and no amount of training could have prepared me for the assortment of general public creeps who come in. But I suppose it's to be expected. Par for the course or whatever. Everyone has a cell phone. "Two hundred four dollars and eighty-nine cents is your total today."

He sighs and nods as if the exorbitant price is my fault, and I slide his card through the reader and wait for the beep.

TRANSACTION FAILED.

"I'm so sorry, sir—" I say until he interrupts me.

"—try it again."

I run the card once more.

TRANSACTION FAILED.

"Is there another card you'd like me to try?" I force a friendly smile into my tone. These situations can be embarrassing, though something tells me this man has no pride and gives zero fucks.

Eyes glazing over my chest, he pushes a hard, stale coffee breath from his mouth before fishing a different card from his wallet.

The bells on the front door jangle, and my attention flicks in that direction. A tall figure fills the doorway, backlit by the sun. He takes two steps in, letting the door glide closed, and scans the store space.

Our eyes lock from across the room, and in a fraction of a second, my blood turns to ice water.

"Hello?!" The gruff man in front of me snaps in my face. "You still with me?"

His transaction goes through, and the machine spits out a receipt. I hand him a pen and clear my throat, keeping a close eye on August Monreaux with a lump in my throat.

"Welcome to Priority Cellular, how can I help you today?" My notoriously bubbly co-worker, Adriana, approaches him before I have a chance to warn her off so someone else can deal with him. Though what could I possibly say that hasn't already been conveyed by his ripped jeans, devil-may-care smirk, and the chilled glint in his eye?

Half-distracted, I place the Air Pods and charger in a bag with the man's receipt. He leaves before I can wish him a lovely afternoon.

From my periphery, I experience their exchange with voyeuristic curiosity. Adriana, forever oblivious, leads him to a display case of phones, plucking the most expensive model from its resting place and handing it off for August to inspect.

"I'll take it in black," he says, his voice carrying across the store. They discuss storage for a second before Adriana disappears into the stock room.

Our gazes catch again, and he won't let mine go. I'm not sure whether or not to care that he saw me naked less than twelve hours ago. I'm sure he's seen a million naked girls before. At some point, they all probably blend together.

I pull myself out of my own head and wave over the next customer in line. "Ma'am, I can help you over here, if you're ready."

Heat creeps up the back of my neck. I don't have to glance over to know he's staring at me with that piercing cold glare.

I ring up a purple car charger for a middle-aged woman in leopard-print Lululemons and a melting Starbucks iced latte in her hand. When we're finished, Adriana makes her way to my register, August in tow.

"Can you start his ticket, Sher? I just have to activate this. I'll be right back." Adriana brushes her hand against his arm. "You're in good hands. I'll just be a sec."

The silence is profound. Awkward. Intense. It's everything heavy, all at once, anchoring me to the floor and shortening my breath.

No one has ever done this to me before ...

I scan the empty box of his new phone and straighten my shoulders. "Can I have your number, please? To pull up your account?"

He shifts, jaw set as if he's attempting to stifle what he truly wants to say.

"Okay, I think we're good now." Adriana emerges after an endless moment and hands August his new phone. "Should just take a minute to load."

"Your number?" I ask again, fingers hovering over the keypad with the slightest tremble.

He hasn't taken his attention off of me for one second.

"Your brother is Gannon, right?" Adriana asks after he finally tells me his digits.

August arches a brow. "Maybe."

"He went to school with my cousin. I think they used to hang out back in the day," she says. To some people around here, running around with a Monreaux gives you bragging rights. "They got busted at a party out at the gravel pit off Highway 50."

"That doesn't sound anything like my brother," he says, monotone.

"Well maybe not *now*." Adriana's overfilled lips curl. "But back in the day, I hear he was quite the wild child."

August sniffs, gaze still trained on me. "Depends on your definition of wild."

"What's he up to these days, anyway?" Adriana continues, oblivious to the fact that he isn't interested in shooting the breeze about his older brother. "I see him riding around town in that electric sports car of his. The matte black one with the gunmetal-gray wheels."

I know the one. I've seen it dozens of times. But the windows have always been too dark to see who was seated behind the steering wheel.

Now I know.

"It's a piece of shit," he says, emotionless. "Pretty to look at. Nothing under the hood worth writing home about."

Damn. Bad blood?

I'd always heard Monreaux were thick as thieves, but I'd never considered they'd have an ounce of inner turmoil. Perhaps they're competitive with one another? Most brothers are.

Adriana and I exchange looks, and she gives an awkward chuckle. "Um, okay. So ... your total today is thirteen hundred dollars and fifty-two cents."

He slides a black card across the counter, equidistant between Adriana and myself. We both reach at the same time, hands colliding.

"Sorry, go ahead," I say to her. If ever there was a time to pray for a customer rush, it's now. But the store is dead. It's just the three of us now. The assistant manager is hiding in the back somewhere, as per usual.

She swipes the card, tapping her fingers to the beat of the pop song playing from ceiling speakers while we wait. "I heard your brother used to throw the most bomb parties at your house. My cousin has, like, the craziest stories." The register spits out a receipt and Adriana hands him a pen. "I think he said this one time, you brother—"

"—my brother's parties sucked," he says. "All those rumors you've heard, he probably started those himself. No one fucking likes Gannon."

Adriana bites her lip. "Damn. Okay."

"Speaking of parties, I'm having one this weekend. Friday." He signs his receipt, his silvery gaze flicking to mine. "You two should stop by."

My heart slams to my feet.

I'm not sure what his end game is here, but I have no desire to be part of it. Last night was a mistake. The kind of thing you do when you're young and dumb and delirious from a mild case of heat stroke.

My "no thanks" intersects with Adriana's "oh-my-god-yes."

She elbows me.

"I'm sorry," August says, turning to me. "I didn't quite catch that."

"I can't. But thank you," I say.

His head cocks, eyes narrowing into an incredulous squint. "You can't? Or you don't want to?"

"Sher, come on. It'll be fun," Adriana says. "Just tell your parents you're staying at my place."

August studies me.

"Seriously, it's not a big deal. And you don't even have to drink or anything ... I've always wanted to see the Monreaux mansion ... could be pretty epic ..." Adriana continues to try to sell me on something I refuse to buy. If working with her the past six months has taught me anything, it's that she's relentless when it comes to getting what she wants. It's why she's our top salesperson. She could convince the most discerning soul that the sky is glittering olive green, and they wouldn't bat a lash when she's done. "It would be a dream come true for me."

August smirks.

I'm glad he finds this entertaining.

"I will literally die if you don't go, Sher," Adriana continues. Half joking. Half not.

"You don't want that on your conscience, do you ... *Sher*?" August interjects. My name on his tongue is velvet smooth, sending shivers down my arm.

Ripping a piece of paper from a nearby note pad, August scribbles five numbers. "Party starts at nine. Here's the gate code for the night."

"Awesome." Adriana folds the note and places it in her

back pocket like it's the most precious thing in the world. "We'll definitely see you then ..."

August gives me a lingering glance before showing himself out, and the moment he's gone, I exhale the longest, hardest breath.

"Okay, what's up with you?" Adriana asks when we're alone. "Why are you acting so weird?"

"I was up late last night." I grab a bottle of Windex and a roll of paper towels and wipe the already flawless display case behind us. "Just ... tired."

"Too tired to realize we just got invited to the freaking Monreaux mansion?" If her brows were any higher they'd be in her hairline. "Do you realize how huge that is? And how epic that night will be? I mean, I've only heard stories, but, like ... all you can drink booze, weed, hot guys, good music, a pool ... it's the perfect summer party."

I toss a used paper towel in the trash. "Yeah, but that's not really my thing."

"Which is exactly why you should go."

"Feel free to go without me. Seriously. Go and have a good time. You can tell me all about it at work next weekend."

Lifting a hand to her hip, she exhales. "Okay, fine. I know it's not your scene, but will you at least go for me? This is literally a once-in-a-lifetime invite, and I want to have the time of my life. I want to get stupid wasted. And if I don't know anyone ... I need a safety buddy. Or something."

"A safety buddy?" I laugh.

"Just, someone to make sure no one slips me a roofie or whatever. Just follow me around like a shadow and make sure I don't do anything I'm going to regret the next day."

"No offense, but that sounds like a terrible time to me."

"Okay, then just go with me, and we'll grab a couple drinks, sit by the pool, and stare at all the hot people doing stupid shit." She shrugs like it's no big deal. "Just to be able to say we've been there, even if it's for an hour, would be amazing. It's literally on my bucket list."

"No it's not."

"It is now."

I chuckle, shaking my head and returning the Windex to the cabinet beneath the register. "Can I think about it?"

"No because I know you, and this is your way of buying time and hoping I drop it or forget about it or let it go," she speaks so fast I can hardly keep up. "But that's not going to happen."

"What about your friend ... what's her name? Molly? Can she go with you?"

"Molly's in Indiana this week visiting her grandma or some shit like that. And before you bring up anyone else, Christa's working Friday night, Harper's going to be with her boyfriend like she is every second of every freaking day, and Lydia and I are no longer on speaking terms as of last Thursday. Sorry, chica, but you're my only option."

"Adriana." I tuck my chin. "Please don't put this on me."

She clasps her hands. "I will get on my knees and beg if that's what it takes. I'll take any weekend shift you want. I'll pay you. I will give you my next paycheck in full."

"I don't want your money. And I need my shifts."

"Then what's the issue? Are you worried about what you're going to wear? Just come to my place and we'll get ready together. We can walk there, and I'll have my sister pick us up when she gets off work."

"Your sister who bartends?"

"Yeah."

I lift a brow. "Doesn't she work until three AM?"

"Fine. I'll see if my cousin can come get us. And if she can't, I'll break get us an Uber. Is that better? Then we can leave any time you want."

"Adriana ..."

She places her hands on my arms and gives them a gentle squeeze. "Please, Sher. Please. One hour of your life, that's all I ask for. I'll never ask you for anything else so long as I live. Promise."

The front door swings open, bells jingling, and a boisterous family of four barges in, ending our conversation.

"Please?" she mouths to me as she walks toward the customers.

She won't take 'no' for an answer. At the end of the day, I'm fighting a battle I won't win. As soon as we close up shop today, she'll start blowing up my phone. She's a little bit psychotic at times, but I also kind of love her. In the short time we've worked together, she's become one of my closest friends.

Maybe one hour wouldn't kill me ...

Lord knows she'd do anything for me.

I leave for college in six weeks. I've spent the last eighteen years trapped in the rusted cage my parents built for me the second I came into this world. If last night taught me anything, it's that freedom has a strange kick to it. Kind of like stepping into a foreign land for the first time. It's terrifying and exhilarating all at the same time.

My stomach furls at the thought of lying to my parents, but they can't keep me trapped inside their protective bubble forever.

Besides, I'm a responsible adult.

I can handle myself at a party.

Sucking in a long breath, I hold it. And then I let it go before settling on my decision. As soon as Adriana's finished, I'll share the good news ... if one can call it that.

It's one hour of one night of my life—what could possibly go wrong?

____

CHAPTER FOUR

Sheridan

ADRIANA HAS a power grip on my wrist as she leads me through a maze of beautiful people, people who clearly aren't from Meredith Hills because no one I've ever seen looks like this.

Outfits strategized to reveal taut, ripped bodies.

Glittery makeup accented by fluttery lashes.

Sun-bronzed, flawless complexions.

Shirtless guys with eight-pack abs worthy of big city billboards.

I'm a pale church mouse in comparison.

My little sunflower dress with the nineties scoop neck and t-shirt beneath was definitely the wrong choice for this party, but we're here and it's too late for regrets. Bless Adriana's heart for not saying anything, although she probably knew it wouldn't be in her best interest to give me any kind of reservations about coming here tonight.

A guy who looks questionably twenty-one(ish) stands

behind a fully stocked bar next to the cabana, mixing drinks and popping caps off beer bottles as he nods in time with the lounge exotica playing from hidden speakers around the pool.

The pool itself is glowing, the lights changing from turquoise to lavender to brilliant white and back. Everywhere I turn, people are making out—or more. Snapping pictures. Laughing. Chasing one another around the grounds.

While I was here less than a week ago, everything looks different all lit up and full of life.

Tonight, it's a whole new frontier.

A group of three guys with football player builds toss back shots of Lord knows what, one of them eyeing me up and down before his unfocused gaze lands on Adriana's backside.

"Come on," she leads me closer to the bar. "My sister says the best thing you can do at a party is walk in, look like you're making eye contact with someone in the far back corner, then walk like you're on a mission. Worst thing you can do is stand around looking all shy and awkward." We're almost to the dancing bartender. "We belong here just as much as anyone else."

"Two rum and cokes, please," Adriana orders our drinks a second later, shouting over the pulsating music.

I wasn't going to drink tonight, but I think maybe one could help take the tension out of my shoulders and wipe the amateur doe-eyed look from my face. Aside from making sure Adriana stays out of trouble, it wouldn't kill me to actually enjoy myself tonight.

"*Et voila.*" She hands me a clear plastic cup filled with fizzy brown soda and two skinny straws. "Cheers!"

I tap my drink against hers before taking a sip, and then

I wrestle the bitter wince off my face. My brain expected to taste sugary cola despite knowing damn well there'd be rum mixed in.

"It's good, right?" Adriana shouts over the music before downing a generous gulp.

I don't know about *good* ...

It's strong, for sure.

"Mm hm." I take a baby-sized sip. Rum doesn't taste how I thought it would. Then again, I don't know how I thought it would taste. Four liberal sips later, and it doesn't taste like much of anything anymore.

"Let's find somewhere to sit." Adriana takes my hand and pulls me toward a couple of empty lounge chairs. "I want to people watch."

I take another drink, my body growing warmer by the second, and I scan my surroundings. Between the lissome girls and chiseled guys, I've yet to spot a sign of August. As the host, I expected him to be making his rounds, handing out cold beers, and generally acting as the center of the universe.

On second thought, the man doesn't smile, and I'd hardly call him outgoing host material. He's probably hooking up with a pair of pretty best friends in some back room upstairs. I'm quite positive girls throw themselves at him, especially during an occasion such as this. You can't top those kind of bragging rights—it'd be like going to a party at the Playboy Mansion in the sixties and hooking up with Hugh Hefner himself.

"Hi." A shaggy-haired guy in a backwards baseball cap takes a seat across from us, his attention fixed on Adriana. "I'm Isaac."

He takes a pull from a green beer bottle.

"Adriana." She smiles, blinking her mascara-coated lashes before waving toward me. "That's Sheridan."

"You're new here," he says, solely speaking to her.

She leans back, shrugging a shoulder and dropping a wink. "How kind of you to take notice …"

"Think I'd remember seeing a face like yours around here." He takes another drink.

I stifle a laugh. This guy has no game and Adri is picking up every morsel he's dropping. But at least he's cute. I'll give him that. He looks like a twenty-year-old frat boy, but in a good way.

"Are you from Meredith Hills?" he asks.

She nods. "Born and raised. You?"

I scan the backyard for August again. All week I tried to imagine what our first interaction tonight would be like. Every time I drew blanks. The two times I've interacted with the man, he's been nothing short of aloof and unreadable. If I'm not mistaken, I think he's angry about the trespassing last weekend. But if he was truly that upset about it, why would he invite me here? He literally said "you two should come" when he invited us to his party. *You two*. Not just Adriana. Both of us.

My mind spins, dizzy with thoughts. Or maybe it's the rum and Coke. Adriana moves to Isaac's chair, completely engrossed in whatever he's prattling on about. I mind my own business because he reminds me of the kind of guy who's charming when he needs to be. Perfect hair. Laser-focused attention. Witty and charismatic. Too good to be true. But I won't rain on Adri's parade. She came here to have a good time. Who am I to stop her?

That said, I'm officially the third wheel.

Not that I mind, but it feels wrong to sit here and

twiddle my thumbs while the two of them look at each other with stars in their eyes and perma-smiles on their faces.

"Adri, you want another?" I rise and shake my empty cup.

She gives me a nod while listening intently to her frat boy, and I make a beeline for the bar. When I arrive, I'm third in line behind a girl ordering four mixed drinks for her and her besties and a guy who appears to be text-fighting with someone. A quick glance over my shoulder assures me Adriana's still doing fine without my babysitting services.

"Next," the bartender calls when it's my turn. I order two more rum and Cokes before spotting an overflowing tip jar on the ledge. Shit. Digging in my bag, I fish out two perfect singles and pray they're enough. He doesn't seem to pay attention one way or another. Too busy stepping to the beat as he pours and mixes. And when he's finished, he places our drinks on the counter and waves the next person up.

Drinks in hand, I turn to head back to Adriana—only to walk straight into some guy in a gray t-shirt and torn jeans.

The drinks spill down both of us—ice and all—before settling in a pool at our feet.

"Oh, lord. I'm so sorry." I clap my hand over my mouth, eyes flicking to his.

And then my stomach drops.

August.

He stands frozen. People around us begin to take notice, pointing, nudging. I'm sure he's used to being the center of attention, but not like this.

"I didn't see you," I say. To my left, someone trots toward the cabinet by the cabana to retrieve towels. The same towels August handed me last weekend when I emerged from his pool with nothing but my birthday suit on.

The kind attendee returns with two towels, but it only takes a second for me to ascertain that no amount of dabbing is going to salvage my dress or the giant cola stain running down the front.

Several yards away, Adriana and Isaac are in a world of their own. Still enraptured. We haven't even been here a half hour and she's just met a cute guy, there's no way I'd make her leave now.

"Come with me," August says, nodding toward the house.

"What?"

"Come with me," he repeats, though it wasn't that I didn't hear him the first time. I'm just confused.

Before I can protest, he's stalking toward the back patio in his wet t-shirt, crumpled towel in hand. I canter after him.

"You're really a man of few words, aren't you?" I try to joke with him.

He slides a door open and disappears into the darkness of the house, swallowed into a void. I step in after him. The scent of leather and cedarwood and time fills my lungs. This house is over a hundred and fifty years old. At least that's what the plaque said by the front gate.

Built in 1869.

It's been in the Monreaux family since the day someone dug a shovel into its earthy grounds. My house doesn't have much of a history. It was a tract home built by some fly-by-night builder in the seventies who was trying to cram as many entry-level houses onto one plot of land as he could—hence why I can hear with perfect clarity my neighbors fighting after dinner every night.

He leads me down a dark hallway, to a set of stairs so polished they shine in the dark, and once we reach the top landing, we take a left down another hall lit with hardwired sconces with flickering lights.

"I feel like I'm in a movie or something," I say, a slight nervous chuckle in my tone. I don't add that said movie would be a thriller. Something with ghosts and a haunted house. I don't want to offend him more than I already have.

Within seconds, we arrive at what I can only assume is his bedroom. Or at least it's *a* bedroom. There have got to be at least a dozen of them in this house, given its enormity.

August closes the door behind us before flicking on a lamp on a desk. The shades on his windows are pulled open and the moonlight and party from outside illuminates the surroundings. A bed. Two nightstands. A chest of drawers. I've yet to spot anything personal. Not a trophy or ribbon. Not a framed photograph or memento.

Strutting into his closet, he returns with a clean t-shirt and a white button down, both of which appear crisp and freshly starched.

"Here." He hands me the button down.

"Are you sure?"

He exhales. Annoyed, I think. I mean, it *is* a dumb question. He wouldn't have led me all the way inside and offered me clean clothes if he wasn't sure.

"Thank you." I tug the shirt over my head, unbutton the last few buttons and tie them at my waist. The stain on my dress is mostly covered—even if this outfit combo is insane.

His gaze drinks me in. I can't tell whether he approves nor can I tell why it suddenly matters to me ...

In one fluid movement, he rips his wet t-shirt off, tosses it on the bed, and tugs the clean one on. I force myself not to stare at his chiseled torso or the rippled abs that peek out from the fabric. Without breaking eye contact, he finger combs his messy waves into place.

"This is really kind of you." I smooth my hand along the front of the white dress shirt. "I'll have it cleaned and returned to you next week."

Somehow ...

I don't even know what dry cleaning costs. I've never owned clothes that couldn't be shoved in the washer with a scoop of Gain and hung on Mama's line.

"What would your parents say if they knew you were here?" He finally breaks the silence.

"I beg your pardon?"

"You're Rich Rose's girl." It isn't a question, and there's a finite layer of disgust in his tone, like muck and mire at the bottom of a sparkling pond.

I nod. "I am."

"Can't imagine your parents would be thrilled to know you were here," he says, adding, "with me."

"You're right. They wouldn't be."

Quietude hangs between us like a crystal chandelier.

"What about yours?" I ask, before I catch myself. He doesn't have parents. Plural. He has a parent. Singular. My cheeks burn hot in the dark. There's no fixing it now.

His gaze narrows. "My father would have his second coronary, that's for sure. He'd probably disown me. At the very least, disinherit me. And my mother, well, not really sure what she'd say since she isn't here to say anything ... and I think we both know why."

I cover my heart with a palm. "I'm so sorry. I wasn't thinking."

"Are you always so apologetic?" He leans on the foot-board of his bed, hands gripping the wood until the veins of his forearms bulge. "All you've done since you barged into my life is apologize for every little thing."

"Just trying to be polite," I say. "And you give me the impression that I'm bothersome to you. Or maybe you just make me nervous. I don't know. You have a very distinct ... vibe about you."

He squints. "And what kind of ... vibe ... would that be?"

I open my mouth to speak but nothing comes out. Lord help me if I unintentionally insult him again.

"Look," I say. "I shouldn't have gone for a swim the other night. It was wrong. I've never done anything like that before. You see, our AC broke last week and you know we're in the middle of this heat wave, and the public pool has been closed for maintenance all week and—"

He lifts a hand to silence me. "Please don't insult me with trying to justify what you did."

"Well, I'd apologize but you don't seem to like apologies, so ..."

"I don't like weak people. If you're going to be an asshole, own it."

"I'm not an asshole." I fold my arms across my chest, head cocked. "Kind of think it's the opposite of being a weak asshole when you're strong enough to admit when you're in the wrong."

He smirks. "Agree to disagree."

His attention skims past my shoulder as he checks on the party below.

"We should probably get back out there," I say. "I'm sure they're missing you."

He chuffs. "Doubtful."

Pushing himself away from the bed, he makes his way to a small cabinet in the corner of the room, which I quickly realize is some kind of fancy mini fridge disguised to look like a furniture piece. When he returns, he hands me an icy glass bottle with a skull on the label. *Misfit Meredith IPA*. I recognize the brand as the local brewery in town.

"Have a beer with me first," he says.

He doesn't want to go downstairs.

He wants to stay here, in this dark room, and drink with me.

I don't understand ...

Digging his keys from his pocket, he produces a small bottle opener to pop our tops.

"Drink up, Rose girl," he says. "The night is young."

Out of politeness, I take a sip. It's bitter on my tongue and smells like a more expensive version of the canned beer my father drinks after a weekend overtime shift.

"You sure you don't want to go back downstairs?" I ask.

He takes a sip. "Positive."

"Everyone's here to see you, you know."

He rolls his steel-gray eyes. "They're not here to see me. They're here because they want to know what it's like to be me ... if only for a night."

"Really?" I tease. "All of them? Every last person downstairs is here because they want to be you, August?"

"Yes. Even if they're too stupid to realize it." He doesn't flinch, doesn't miss a beat. Doesn't seem the least bit amused. "On the surface, they want free beer and some pictures they can post that makes them look cooler than they are. But deep down, they're curious. Maybe a little jealous. Completely unaware that they're in the midst of hitting their peak."

"That's no way to talk about your friends." I take a sip, letting the bubbles play on my tongue.

"Friends? I wouldn't know. Never had any." He tosses back a mouthful of beer, holding my gaze captive.

I roll my eyes. "Whatever. Weren't you, like, prom king at your school or something a couple years back? You can't tell me you don't have friends."

"They're void-fillers. Nothing more, nothing less." He captures my wrist in his hand, gentle. And his thumb circles my pulse, forcing it to quicken in response.

I pull away.

"Am I supposed to feel sorry for you? Poor little rich guy? Is that your schtick? Is that how you get ass?" I keep my words soft and light, but I very much mean every last one of them.

"Last thing I need is your sympathy. And I'm definitely not poor—or little. I don't have a ... schtick and even if I did, I wouldn't need to use it to get ass."

Without warning, he cups the side of my cheek. A tender move for someone so dark. I rake my teeth over my bottom lip—a protective move because I'm quite certain he's seconds from attempting to devour me.

I don't have a chance to tell him no though, because the second he leans in, the bedroom door flings open and Adriana appears in the doorway.

"Oh, my god. I've been looking all over for you," she says, oblivious to what this looks like. "I thought you left or something.'"

"What's up?" I ask.

August takes a step back, raking his hand through his hair and exhaling.

"That Isaac guy is a douche. I want to leave." She pulls out her phone, the screen lighting her face in the dim room. "My cousin is on her way to get us. She'll be here in twenty. You ready?"

August and I lock eyes, and I swear there's a silent plea for me to stay. But even if I wanted to, I couldn't. I came here with Adriana. I'm leaving with Adriana. But more important than that, I would never so much as think about staying for a Monreaux.

"She'll meet you out front in a second," August tells her, though he's looking at me.

Adri's dark brows rise, as if she's finally realizing we were up here along together, separated by mere inches before she barged in.

"Oh," she says. "*Oh*. Um, okay …"

"I'll be down in a sec," I promise her. "It's fine."

Adriana disappears, closing the door behind her.

"You're not actually leaving, are you?" he asks.

"Of course I am …"

"I can get you a ride home." He takes a sip of his beer.

"It's not about that."

He releases a hard breath, his stare narrowing and his full mouth pressing flat.

"Well, that's too bad," he says. The moonlight from the window behind me paints soft shadows on his face. In this light, he doesn't look so intimidating. "Was hoping I could get to know you a little more."

"Really? You wanted to get to know me?" I laugh, using air quotes and rolling my eyes. "Because something tells me you were looking to score," I continue. "And you and I both know that'll never happen in a million years."

"Why not?"

"Because you're you and I'm me. I don't think I need to elaborate." I place the barely-touched beer bottle on top of a nightstand and head for the door. "It's nothing personal."

"Don't insult my intelligence, Rose girl."

"I'm just stating the facts. We can't help the family

we're born into. We have no control over what our parents did or didn't do."

"So why should we suffer the consequences?" he asks.

He has a good question. I pause for a second. "Because we love our parents. And we respect their wishes."

I reach for the door knob when he comes closer.

"Must be hell," he says.

"What?" I stop in my tracks.

"Living by other people's rules all the time. Never doing what you want. What a fucking waste." He takes a drink, letting his tongue caress the bottle mouth for a split second.

"Adriana's waiting."

"Give me your phone."

"What? Why?"

"Give me your phone, Rose girl." He holds out his palm.

"I'm sorry, but no. I have no need for your number. I have no reason to ever text you. I'm flattered by your confidence and your drive to defy authority or whatever you're going for with this, but this is me kindly passing," I say.

"For the shirt," he says, his words staccato'd. "If you could text me when it's ready, I'll arrange to pick it up."

Oh. Right.

"It's a four hundred dollar Baccarin," he adds. I can't help but feel it's his bruised ego's way of making me feel like an expensive shirt matters more to him than seeing me again. "And I'd like it back."

Without another protest, I dig my phone from my bag and hand it over. When he returns it, I discover he's programmed his name as ENEMY DEAREST.

"There," he says. "Now your parents will never know."

My stomach somersaults—this isn't about the damn shirt.

But my resolve hardens to steel.

I can't get caught up in flattery. I can't lose myself in the temptation of the forbidden. I can't sacrifice my loyalty in the name of curiosity or cheap rebellion.

"I'll get you your shirt back," I say. And then I leave, navigating the dark hallways and shiny staircase and floating toward the sound of the party until I'm bathed in fresh, humid night air.

A minute later, I find Adriana waiting by the gate.

"Everything okay?" she asks.

"I should ask you the same thing," I change the subject.

Her cousin's silver Honda rolls up and we climb in. And for the rest of the ride home, she tells me how Isaac was only using her to make his ex-girlfriend jealous, how the second she showed up, Adri became chopped liver. And then her cousin drove us around town for a solid hour, blasting music as she chain smoked Pall Malls with all four windows down.

But I couldn't even appreciate the distraction—because all I could think about ... was August—a forbidden enigma of a man with a penchant for defiance and unapologetic honesty.

He's different.

And I can't stop wondering what might have happened had Adriana not busted into the room at that precise moment.

Would he have kissed me?

Would I have enjoyed it?

And then what?

I shake the thoughts from my head and focus on the sappy breakup music blaring from the tinny speakers behind me. Entertaining these curiosities is frivolous and reckless. No good can come from playing the "what if" game.

No good will ever come from a Rose and a Monreaux in the same room together. We were born into two opposing forces. Sharp against soft. Dark against light. Love against fear. We were raised in completely different worlds, with differing priorities and a distinct belief system instilled into us from day one.

It won't happen again—the two of us alone together. Drinking. Flirting. Getting caught up.

I won't do that to my parents, to my family's tragic history, or to my heart.

I have too much to lose.

CHAPTER FIVE

I'VE PLANTED myself near the grotto, vision fading as I finish yet another beer. Two girls make out, tongues and all, but I can't even appreciate it because all I can think about is Sheridan.

I'd consider tonight a disappointment, but I'd hardly call it a failure.

She has my number.

And my shirt.

I'll see her again ... soon.

"Hey, you doing all right?" One of my so-called friends, Trey, gives my shoulder a squeeze, pulling me out of my drunken trance. "Feel like I haven't seen you all night."

"Get these people out of here." My words are thick in my mouth. I need to down a glass of water, pop some Advil, and go to bed. "Party's over."

I push myself up and stumble toward the house, my

body numb. Though it's nothing new. I don't tend to feel much of anything—sober or not.

"But it's still early," Trey calls after me.

I wave my hand, trekking inside.

Trey's an old pro at this, clearing out crowds, knowing when I'm done.

By the time I get to my room, the music has been killed. The stadium-quality security lights have come on, and muffled voices grow more distant by the minute.

Wrestling my phone from my pocket, I toss it on the bed before peeling off my clothes and landing in a heap on top of the covers. With heavy eyes, I fight drowsiness and wake my screen. I tap in my code and pull up every last social media account I own, running up searches of my elusive Rose girl.

Much to my surprise, nothing is private ... though she's not exactly active. Only a handful of photos display across three apps, hardly any of them from the past year.

Sigh.

I drop my phone on the pillow beside me and close my eyes. If tonight was any indication of what I'm dealing with, I'm going to have my work cut out for me.

But God damn, will she be worth it.

A smirk claims my lips when I think about the look on my father's face if he were to know I'd had Rich's daughter on our property—and worse—in my room. I imagine him screaming, red-faced, about what a liability that would be for us. But this isn't about defying orders. This isn't some rebellious itch I need to scratch.

This is about making things fair.

Once upon a time, my beautiful mother was alive and well and my father was a model family man with a stellar reputation. Rich Rose took that from us. He destroyed the man my father should have been, and he robbed every last shred of happiness from our family the day he killed my mother.

Sheridan is nothing more than a pretty little pawn.

A means to an end.

A heart I intend to shatter into a million jagged pieces.

I won't hurt her physically. Frankly, that isn't my style.

But I will ruin her.

I'll ruin her for any other man.

And when she runs home to daddy to dry her tears, I'll have the satisfaction of knowing that this time, a Monreaux broke a Rose.

CHAPTER SIX

Sheridan

"WELL, THERE SHE IS!" My father calls from the kitchen Saturday morning when I get home from Adriana's. I thought I could sneak in through the back door—thought wrong. "Wondered if you were going to make it in time for breakfast. You hungry?"

The scent of his famous once-a-weekend fare—scrambled eggs, maple bacon, and cinnamon chip pancakes—fills the air.

"Sheridan?" Mom calls when I don't answer right away.

I was hoping to slip past them, sunglasses over my tired eyes, and duck into the shower to wash the scent of party and cigarette smoke from my hair, alas...

"Yeah, I'll be right there," I call back. Hurrying to my room, I change out of my clothes and spritz body spray through my messy locks before tying them in a high bun.

When I get to the kitchen a few minutes later, my mom

has already fixed my plate. They'll never view me as an adult. Forever their baby. Their *only* baby.

"You didn't have to do this ..." I tell her, especially because it takes all the energy she has just to make her own plate these days. She's already breathless. She should've known better. "But thank you."

"I won't get to do this much longer," she says, sipping her coffee with a shaky grip on her mug. "Let me enjoy these last few weekends we have like this."

"You act like I'm going away forever." I tease. "I'll literally be two hours away. I'll come home all the time, I promise."

"That's what you say now, kiddo." Dad winks from behind his wiry glasses, his gray-streaked hair still damp from his morning shower.

Kiddo.

I bury my reaction with a bite of eggs, pushing away thoughts of what it would do to them if they knew where I went last night, what I did, who I spent time with ...

"I thought maybe we could go shopping next weekend?" Mom says. "Your dad's been putting in so much overtime lately ... We should be able to get you some more things for your dorm room. A fridge? Extra linens? And you'll need slippers for the shower. You know how dirty those things can get ..."

I wince at the thought of bringing some strange disease or fungus home to Mama. Her immune system is going haywire this year, attacking itself and weakening her ability to fight off things like ordinary colds.

She sips her coffee, rattling away about all the college necessities we've yet to buy. Her medical expenses have grown lately, making our budget tighter than usual. At least that's what I've overheard them saying over the past few months. I picked up a few extra shifts at Priority Cellular for that reason—so I wouldn't be a burden on their wallet. Lord knows they could use one less thing to worry about.

"You don't have to do that. I still have all my graduation money." All three hundred dollars of it. "And I've been saving my checks."

I have a few grand in my bank account, enough to ration out over the school year since I won't be working. It should cover gas and groceries and a few necessities. It isn't much, but it's enough.

I get up to grab a glass of OJ. It's almost translucent when I pour it into the glass, as if someone diluted it to make it last longer.

"Oh, sweetheart. We insist. This is practically a rite of passage for parents." Mom tries to make light of it.

I shoot my father a look and he nods. Anything to keep the love of his life happy.

"Maybe we can make a whole day of it? And we can eat at that restaurant you like with the sweet butter rolls." Mom raises her brows and grins.

"Magnolia Lake?" I haven't been there in ages ...

"That's the one," she says, eyes lit.

We went there more often when I was younger. Junior high, to be specific. That was before Dad lost his assistant night manager job at the meat locker—and before Mom's condition took a turn for the worse.

"Are you off next Saturday?" Dad asks.

"No," I say. "But I'm pretty sure I can get Adriana to cover for me."

After all, she owes me ...

"Perfect." Dad reaches across the table, his hand covering Mom's.

I've been so wrapped up in my own world lately with

all the excitement on the horizon, that I haven't stopped to think about how much of their world will be flipped inside out once I leave. They'll do fine with me gone. But it'll be an adjustment.

I'm their whole world.

Always have been. I always will be.

When I was about eight or nine, I overheard Mama crying to someone on the phone one day after school. Being nosy, I pressed my ear up to the door and listened. I'm not sure who she was talking to, but I heard her saying something about "the baby had no heartbeat this time." And later that day, I remember seeing tears in my father's eyes after dinner. It took me years to put it all together—that they'd lost a baby. Though they never came clean about it to me. Guess it wasn't the kind of thing that came up in ordinary conversations.

I've always wondered if things would've been different had I not been an only child. And when I was a small child, I'd often ask for a baby brother or sister for Christmas. But they always told me I was enough, that I was everything they ever wanted and then some.

It's a lot of pressure to put on one person.

But I've never known any other way.

"So, kiddo," Dad says. "What's on the docket for today?"

I'm about to respond when my phone buzzes in my lap. Swirling a quick sip of watery juice, I steal a glance—and nearly choke.

ENEMY DEAREST—Morning, sunshine. Let me know when I can pick up my shirt.

"Sweetheart, are you okay?" Mom leans to pat my back.

How did he get my number? He programmed his info into my phone last night … but I never gave him mine.

"Yeah." I cough. "Just swallowed wrong."

They study me. I pray they buy it and let it go.

I take another sip. "I'm fine, I'm fine."

Their attention lingers for another endless minute until my father finally changes the subject to yard work and catching up on his To Do List. Finishing my breakfast in record time, I excuse myself to my room and read his text again.

I pace the small space beside my bed before mustering up the courage to respond.

ME — How'd you get my number?

ENEMY DEAREST—I have ways, Rose girl …

ME— Tbh, I'm a little creeped out right now.

ENEMY DEAREST—I appreciate your honesty.

ME—Anyway, I told you I'd get your shirt back to you as soon as I could. I haven't even been home for thirty minutes …

ENEMY DEAREST—Patience has never been my virtue.

ME—I'll text you when it's ready.

Three bubbles fill the screen before vanishing, only to be replaced by a new message two minutes later.

ENEMY DEAREST—What are you doing next weekend?

ME—Coming on a little strong, aren't we?

ENEMY DEAREST—As opposed to coming on weak?

ME—I'm busy.

ENEMY DEAREST—Liar.

ME—I don't lie.

ENEMY DEAREST—Safe to assume your parents know where you were last night then?

ME—Are you bored right now? Is that what this is? Because this doesn't feel like it's about a shirt to me anymore.

ENEMY DEAREST—I want to see you again.

A lump forms in my throat. I stop pacing.

ME—You've literally met me three times. Are you always this thirsty?

ENEMY DEAREST—Not thirsty, Rose girl. Curious. Big difference.

ME—Curious about what?

ENEMY DEAREST—Wonder if all the things I've heard about you are true.

Exhaling hard, I wrack my mind trying to think of the types of rumors that could possibly swirl around this town about me. I've always kept my head down. Walked the straightest of lines. I've held various part-time jobs since the day I turned fourteen, earned a full-scholarship to nursing school, and graduated top ten in my high school class. The number of "boyfriends" I've had, I can count on one hand. And the worst thing I've ever done is not hold the door open for someone behind me—which was an accident because I was texting on my phone and not paying attention.

I'm practically a modern-day saint by some people's standards. Virginity and all.

ME—You're bluffing. Nice try.

ENEMY DEAREST—You dated Brett Rathburn last year.

ME—Yeah, me and, like, half the school. Your point?

ENEMY DEAREST—I'm just saying, people talk.

ME—So?

ENEMY DEAREST—I want to know if what they say is true.

I tug out my hair tie, pace the room, and redo my bun before replying. This man has an agenda. I just don't know what it is it. He's trying to get me fired up, trying to keep me engaged in this bullshit conversation.

But for what?

I collapse on the foot of the bed and grab my phone again.

ME—I don't know what game you're trying to play, but I've never been the competitive type so I'm going to forfeit this one. I'll text you when your shirt is ready. Bye.

I wait until my message shows it's been delivered.

No dots or bubbles color the screen.

Instead of some smart-mouthed response, he's given me silence.

Interesting ...

I hit the shower and wash the events of the past twenty-four hours out of my hair—but the thoughts remain.

Two in particular.

Who is August Monreaux? I mean, who is he really?

And what does he want with me?

CHAPTER SEVEN

AUGUST

THE POOL AREA practically sparkles Saturday morning. Trent and his crew did their thing. Can't even tell there was a single stoned soul here last night. Not a wrinkled Solo cup. Not a smashed beer bottle. Not a single silk bra hanging off the back of a lounge chair.

Spotless.

Like it never happened.

Like it was all a dream.

Only it wasn't. Despite my drunken state, last night's memories come through with crystal clarity, from the second Sheridan Rose moseyed onto the premises, arm in arm with her spitfire best friend, to the moment she dashed out of my house like fucking Cinderella at the stroke of twelve.

I flick my shades down over my eyes and recline as the mid-morning sun beats down. Dad and his newest girlfriend *du jour* are out on yet another weekend adventure in the most expensive parts of BFE.

The image of my father in his midlife-crisis-red Ferrari with his twenty-two year old girlfriend on his arm makes the bile churn in my stomach. Vincent Monreaux, arguably one of the most powerful businessmen in Missouri and its surrounding states, is a walking, talking cliché.

I've never been one for daydreaming, but at times I've caught myself wondering what our family would've been like had my mom and sister survived. Would we be one of those wholesome kinds who actually eat dinner around a table and play Scrabble and have inside jokes and family portraits on the wall?

Or would my mother shop away her boredom every day while my dad drowns his in a fifth of imported liquor.

It's easy to idealize what might have been, what could have been.

Maybe we wouldn't have been happy or perfect, but we would've been something more than this dysfunctional excuse for a dynasty. All the money a man could need and then some—and all the misery that comes with it.

If people around here aren't afraid of us, they're cursing our name. My father quit donating millions to charities years ago because it was never enough to stop the rumors. Nothing he could do painted us in a different light, so he stopped giving a fuck.

My phone buzzes on the table beside me. I don't make a habit out of scrambling over a text, but today I'm making an exception.

I let out a sigh.

Not who I hoped it'd be.

SOREN—Got you those tix. How you been? Haven't heard from you in a while ...

My oldest brother—the shining perfect beacon of the family and my father's pride and joy—is a bona fide celebrity in the music world. I lost track years ago of how many platinum albums and number one singles he'd accumulated.

When the rest of the world looks at him, they see a rock God.

Me? I see the only older brother I can stand.

For a Monreaux, he's not that bad.

ME—Busy. The usual. Dad's got me "interning" again this summer.

For tax purposes, our father calls it an internship. But if the IRS ever knew I sat around in a spare corner office, watched cam girl porn, and fucked around all day, I don't think they'd be thrilled.

SOREN—You can always "intern" with the band ...

ME—Road life's not for me.

Not to mention I've never needed to score ass by riding his coattails, and I'm not about to start. Plus groupies are notoriously STD-ridden and someone always winds up fucking pregnant with a mystery baby daddy.

Not my scene.

SOREN—Glad you're finally coming to a show. Who you bringing?

ME—Not sure.

It'll be Sheridan. One hundred fucking percent. She's going even if she doesn't know it yet.

SOREN—Cool, cool. I'll have my manager shoot you the barcode for the tix. Will be good to see you, man.

I was in my middle school heyday when Soren got signed by some top tier label out of LA. He was in college, playing his guitar at open mic nights and coffee shops for nothing more than whatever a few broke college kids could toss into his tip jar. But the thing about Soren is, he was never looking for fame. And God knows he didn't need the fortune.

He was just pure fucking raw talent.

It's a shame he couldn't keep his name. Some middle-aged, balding big-wig at the head of the table came up with the phonetic MUNRO. All caps, to stand out even more because it would appeal to the Gen Z demographic. And that's all it took for Soren to sign on the dotted line.

I'm happy for him.

Even if he's half a stranger to me these days.

We're not close, then again, I'm not close to anyone.

I set my phone on the side table and stretch my arms behind my head, basking in the early heat. I'll give Sheridan a few more days. I came on pretty strong this morning, though I had no choice. Subtle isn't going to work on this girl. But come mid-week, I'll drop the invite in her lap. Front row center tickets to a sold-out show with a backstage pass ... there's no way she'll say no, even if she hates me.

But for now, I'll give her some time to miss me ... to wonder ... *what if?*

CHAPTER EIGHT

Sheridan

"IS it just me or does August Monreaux always look like he hates life?" Adriana shoves her phone into my hand Wednesday after we lock up the shop.

"Why are you looking up August Monreaux?"

"I'm not," she says. "I was trying to find that Isaac guy and happened to see him in his pics. They went to high school together."

We stroll to our cars, parked side by side in the back lot. "And why are you looking up Isaac? I thought he used you to make his girlfriend jealous or something?"

"He did. But I'm nosy. You know that. I just wanted to see what I was up against. I didn't get a good look at her at the party because he was sucking her freaking face off like a damn Hoover."

"Ew." I point my key fob at my car. "Tell me you're not going to DM him."

"God, no." She flicks to another picture. "Look, here he is again. He looks miserable."

"August?" I inspect this picture. A bunch of guys in football jerseys stand in a half circle, their beefy arms around one another.

Everyone is smiling—except him.

"He's definitely different," I say.

"You still have his shirt?"

"It's at the cleaner's." Surprisingly, the cost to dry clean a dress shirt isn't much different than the cost of a venti vanilla bean Frappuccino—which I could really use about now because I'm dragging. Our AC is still out so sleep has been a sweaty hit-or-miss mess. Dad claims he's going to fix the unit himself. Mom keeps claiming the heat wave is almost done, reminding me this isn't normal even by southern Missouri standards. I'm just waiting for the night when I can fall asleep without a rickety box fan blowing warm air on me. "Did I tell you he texted me last Saturday?"

We stand by the front of my car.

"Um, no!" Her jaw hangs. "What'd he want?"

"His shirt." I laugh and quote the air.

Adriana squints. "Ugh. Why do guys have to be so transparent? I can see through that a mile away. He just wants ass."

Lucky Adriana is blissfully unaware of our families' history. While she's a local, she's not a local-in-the-know. Some people around here fashion themselves official town historians. Her parents are Rhode Island transplants who moved here when Adri wasn't even a year old. There's a lot they don't know, a lot that they probably don't even care to know.

"So you going to do it?" she asks. "You going to hook up?"

"Of course not."

"Dang. I mean ... if you want me to take one for the team." She winks.

"If you want him, he's all yours." I lift my palms in surrender.

"Really?"

"Totally. He's not my type. At all. Not even close," I say. "I think it's the long hair."

And the tattoos. And the nose piercing. And the last name.

"Seriously? He's, like, every girl's wet dream." Her eyes widen and she studies me, as if I'm trying to punk her. "But if you like those clean cut good boys, you do you."

Yawning and eyes watering, I say, "I should get going."

"Yeah, yeah, yeah."

"You're still covering for me Saturday, right?" My parents would be heartbroken if we had to cancel our afternoon shopping plans.

"Eight to four. I'll be here. 'Night, babe." She struts to her driver's door and ducks inside. The engine of her little blue Dodge fires up with a purr, and she plugs her phone onto her charger before buzzing away.

I stop for a few gallons of gas on the way home. And when I pull into the driveway, I sit in my car, AC blasting, for a solid ten minutes. The second I get inside, I'm going to melt into a puddle. Last night the thermostat read eight-seven degrees at bedtime. I'm about ready to fix the dang unit myself.

"Hey, Mama," I call from the front door when I finally come inside. I kick off my shoes and head for the living room, where the TV flickers against her sallow complexion.

Credits roll on the screen. Another Lifetime movie. I swear she must have seen them all by now. "What'd you watch? Anything good?"

"Dancing with Danger," she says. Her eyes light the way they always do when she's no longer alone. "I'd give it an A minus."

I take a seat beside her and she spreads her throw blanket out until it covers both of our laps. Sometimes I get sad thinking about her like this—sitting here watching TV all day like a zombie, barely able to get around. Living for those moments when my father or I come home so she has company again. Then I think about all the loss and misfortune that's blanketed her life in her forty-odd years and how she still manages to smile through it, never once asking for pity or feeling sorry for herself.

I refuse to believe life's going to rain on her like this forever.

It has to get better.

"Mama, aren't you hot?" I ask, gently shoving it off my lap. "I've been inside less than a minute and I'm sweating already."

She frowns. "No, actually. I was feeling a little chilly."

"You're not getting sick again, are you?" I don't know how she could get sick—she never leaves the house. Daddy or I must've brought something back ...

"I'm fine. Maybe I'm just a little too acclimated to this heat." She sells me on a smile I desperately want to believe. But we both know this is exactly what happened last time she got sick. It started with chills and ended with her in the hospital with an immune system gone haywire.

Mama yawns, and I suggest she head to bed, but she flicks to the news instead. Lord help her if she doesn't watch the nine o'clock news every night.

We sit in silence, listening to the weather and some interview with a local kindergarten teacher who donated a hundred knitted scarves to a school in Alaska. Then there's the piece about the thirty-two car pile-up on the freeway at rush hour. No deaths, thank goodness. But it's the next segment that sends a chill to the humid air.

"Local Meredith Hills man, Vincent Monreaux of Monreaux Corporation, has recently acquired Starfire Granite and Quarry in Emmetville in a record deal—" the handsome news anchor reports.

Mom lifts the remote to change the channel as an image of Vincent Monreaux, a silver fox of a man with the same wicked gray glint as August, fills the screen. Her hand trembles and her breath heaves.

"Mama ..." I say, trying to calm her.

"Evil bastard," she speaks through gritted teeth. She's going to work herself into another episode if she isn't careful. Her vagus nerve is finicky. Sometimes it takes the littlest upset to make her black out for a few seconds. Some people react to stress with a surge of adrenaline, but Mama's brain has the power to make the whole operation shut down.

The segment ends almost as soon as it started. They're on to discussing an upcoming career fair at the local community college.

"Don't let him have this power over you." I place a hand over hers.

She draws in a jagged breath, eyes fixated on the screen as if she's watching but not paying attention. Lost in thought, maybe. It isn't often we get an opportunity to discuss the Monreaux family, but with all my August run-ins lately, I'd have to be remiss not to seize the moment.

"Why didn't you and Daddy leave Meredith Hills?" I ask. "After everything that happened?"

She doesn't answer immediately. Instead her gaze falls to her lap as she picks a thread in her blanket.

"Your father's too prideful to be run out of town with his tail between his legs," she says. "Plus, the public defender said running off would only make him look guilty. And we both know your father's as innocent as the day he was born. He'd never hurt a soul."

"Yeah, but don't you guys feel like you've been living in this heartbreaking shadow the past twenty years?"

Turning to me, her eyes are filled with a spark of clarity. "No. This is our home. We grew up here, your grandparents grew up here. We wanted to raise our family here, and that's exactly what we did. We live in no one's shadow."

I don't bring up my aunt. Breathing her name is a sure-fire way to bring tears to Mama's eyes, and she's already worked up enough.

"Have you taken your night meds yet, Mama?" I change the subject.

"Not yet."

I hop up and head to the kitchen, retrieving five pills from her organizer and a glass of tap water. A minute later, I'm helping her into bed.

"'Night, Mama." I kiss her forehead and pull her blankets up. Her skin is cool beneath my lips and she shivers. "Get some rest, okay? We've got big plans for Saturday."

She manages a smile before cupping my cheek. "Wouldn't miss it for the world, sweetheart."

Mama gets out of the house once, maybe twice a month. It's always an exhausting endeavor, but seeing the smile it puts on her face makes it all worth it. Even if only for a few hours, we get to pretend we're just a normal family doing the sorts of things most families take for granted.

I close her door behind me and head to my room, checking my phone as I stumble through the stuffy hall.

It's been four days since I've heard from August. He came on so strong and then ... crickets.

Maybe this is all a game to him.

Some guys get off on screwing with people's heads.

Or maybe he realized I wasn't going to be an easy lay and he found someone else to chase.

An hour later, I'm still wide awake, damp with a thin layer of sweat and staring at the ceiling. Vincent Monreaux's ice-white smile lingers in my head along with those familiar piercing gray eyes. And the way she reacted—with potent and virulent anxiety. It only created more questions—questions I couldn't ask her for fear of making things worse.

Much like the baby they lost all those years ago, I can't help but wonder what other things they've neglected to tell me over the years. What else has been glossed over and rewritten for the sake of leaving the painful past buried deep in the ground?

Sitting straight up, it hits me ... there's an album in the living room.

Mama calls it a memento mori—a reminder of death and mortality. A shrine, of sorts, to my aunt Cynthia. Though she's always asked me not to touch it. But that was before, though, when I was too young to understand.

Tiptoeing to the living room, I dig the faded peach photobook from the TV cabinet and flick on the lamp by the side table.

The number of times my parents have discussed Cynthia's death in front of me, I can count on one hand. At first, it was because I was too little to understand. Later, it was because it was too painful to unbox those memories. I never pried. I didn't once feel the need go digging. I knew what I needed to know—that Vincent Monreaux killed my aunt and the local authorities helped cover it up because his daddy paid them off.

I don't blame my parents for tabling that kind of talk. They'd already lived it once. They didn't need to go through it all over again for my sake. But there are gaps in what I know. In all my life, I've never been given the full picture.

Settling into the sofa, I flip open the album, immediately greeted with the soft, sweet image of Aunt Cynthia's school portrait. It's faded, and the colors are a little off, like someone put an Instagram filter over it, though it's nothing but age.

I stare at her features, memorizing them and trying to determine if we really do look alike. I've seen this picture before at my grandparents' house. Daddy says I'm her spitting image. Though I've always favored the Rose side. We share the same blonde waves. The same deep set ocean-blue eyes. The same pointy chin and slightly-upturned nose.

I wish I could've had the chance to meet her.

Mama said Aunt Cynthia had the kind of personality that entered the room before she did. And the most contagious belly laugh. Long legs too. She said all the boys wanted to date Cynthia, but she had her heart set on Vincent—her brother's best friend.

Inhaling, I turn the page, only to be met with a clipped newspaper obituary.

CYNTHIA GLADYS ROSE. AGE 17.

Cynthia Gladys Rose passed away unexpectedly Thursday, October 18th. A junior at Clark High School, Cynthia excelled in the dramatic arts, with a particular affinity for theater and debate club. Her favorite pastimes included summers at her grandparents' cottage in Vermont and annual family camping trips in the South Dakota badlands. Cynthia had recently toured Great Western State University, with future plans to apply to their pre-law program.

She leaves behind her parents, Lorelai and Conrad, her brother, Rich. Her paternal and maternal grandparents. Fifteen cousins, a host of close friends, and her beloved rescue terrier-mix, Winnie.

My eyes prick with tears that I swipe away the second they slide down my cheeks.

My poor sweet aunt. It isn't fair that she wasn't able to live long enough to see adulthood. Or that her life was summarized in two brief paragraphs.

My heart tightens and aches for my parents, for my grandparents, for Cynthia.

Drawing in a deeper breath, I page ahead to another clipped article. Brief and vague.

The body of a local female resident was discovered at the Monreaux Quarry late Saturday night. Police have determined her cause of death to be strangulation. An investigation is underway and no suspects have been officially named.

The next article is wrinkled and blotted in parts. Tears, maybe?

Police have identified the victim in last week's homicide as seventeen-year-old Cynthia Rose, a local junior at Clark High School. The county coroner has confirmed her cause of death as strangulation. Police Chief Rod Holbach states, "We have narrowed our list of suspects tremendously in the past week, and I'm confident that Cynthia's killer will soon be brought to justice."

My stomach drops when I get to the fourth page in the album—a mug shot of my father along with the headline:

LOCAL MAN ARRESTED IN MURDER OF MEREDITH HILLS TEEN.

Meredith Hills Police have made an arrest in the murder of seventeen year old Cynthia Rose. After a thorough investigation, they have determined Ms. Rose was lured to the quarry by her older brother, Rich, where a physical altercation ensued and she was then strangled. A witness confirmed the two had not been on speaking terms and had been disputing over ownership of a personal property item. Multiple witnesses also said the night of the homicide, Rich Rose had been using illegal substances at a local party. Surveillance footage from Monreaux Quarry shows the blue and white 1986 Ford pickup belonging to Rich Rose at the scene of the crime.

All these years, not once did my parents tell me my father was actually arrested for *Cynthia's* murder …

Knowing my father and the kind of man he is—and I have no doubts about how much he loved his little sister—there's no way he'd be capable of doing something like that.

I don't need to read another clipped article to know that my father is innocent, that he was set up.

Still, I'm ravenous for information. To piece together and make sense of all the things I never knew until now. But as I flip to the next page, my father's headlights fill the living room window.

He's home early.

My stomach flips, and I scramble out of my comfortable spot.

Closing the album, I return it to the TV cabinet, turn out the light, and head to my room.

It makes sense now—their over-protectiveness through the years. They must have been terrified of losing me the way they lost my aunt. And, knowing what the Monreauxs were capable of doing and the power they held over local law enforcement, I understand their intentions.

All of those exchanged glances that I could never quite interpret, finally make sense. Their hushed tones any time they vaguely discussed that dark period of their lives is now understandable. The reasons I was warned to stay away from that family at all costs...

My stomach in knots, I lie on top of my hot covers, warm air blowing in my face from the fan on my dresser.

I never should have snuck into his pool.

I never should have gone to that party.

And I sure as hell never should've given him my number.

My parents were right—Monreauxs are not to be trusted.

CHAPTER NINE

AUGUST

"MORNING, AUGUST," the white-haired receptionist in the front lobby greets me Thursday morning. She doesn't point out the fact that I'm ninety minutes late or that my father would shit a brick of he saw me with my shirt untucked. He loves to remind me I'm a "practicing professional," whatever the fuck that means.

"Morning, Rhonda." I head to the elevator, sunglasses still covering my eyes. I find it helps with avoiding eye contact and uncomfortable small talk.

I fucking loathe small talk.

I arrive at my corner office with the generic mahogany desk and the stiff leather chair and the company-issued iMac and tug the wooden blinds shut.

I'm not here by choice.

My father requires that I show my face a minimum of twenty hours a week so he can write off my "internship" on his corporate taxes, but on the plus side, I earn a handful of college credits for literally doing nothing, so it's not the worst thing in the world.

Double checking the lock on the door, I return to my assigned seat and pull up a private browser on my phone. I've been on the hunt this week for a Sheridan-looking cam girl, but every site I've found has been a dead-end.

I tap on the image of a full-lipped blonde with natural tear-drop tits when a message pops up on my screen.

ROSE GIRL—Your shirt is ready. It's at the Budget Cleaners on Broadway. I already paid. You can pick up whenever. Thanks again for letting me borrow it.

Whoa, whoa, whoa.

ME—I was hoping for an in-person delivery.

ROSE GIRL—Sorry to disappoint you. Been a busy week. Take care!

I chuff, rotating in my chair, knee bouncing as I ponder my next move. A rush of adrenaline passes through me, the way it used to when I'd storm out onto the football field before a big playoff game. Sheer determination. Plays mapping out in my head in real time.

ME—My brother's band is in town Saturday. I have an extra ticket.

ROSE GIRL—How fun for you!

ME—Come with me.

ROSE GIRL—I told you the other day, I have plans.

ME—And I told you I don't believe you. Be ready to go by 7. I'll pick you up.

ROSE GIRL—Not lying. I do have plans. Family outing.

I exhale through clenched teeth.

ME—Surely you can work it out so you're back in time for the show? I'd hate for you to miss out ...

ME— Show is sold out.

ME—People are scalping tix for $3000.

ME— Front. Center. Backstage.

It's not my style to shoot off this many texts in a row without getting a response, but this is for emphasis. I'll blow up her fucking phone if it means getting her to say yes. Besides, I don't know a single fucking soul who wouldn't suck a train of dicks for a MUNRO ticket. They're the hottest band in the world, their fans are insane, and their tours sell out within hours.

ROSE GIRL—Sounds amazing. But I told you, I can't. Thanks anyway.

ME—Can't or don't want to?

I wait.

And wait.

Five minutes turn into fifteen. Fifteen turn into twenty. Twenty turns into a fucking hour.

She did *not* just ghost me …

Ordinarily, I wouldn't do something this desperate, but I compose another text to her, this time taking a softer approach.

ME—I know I'm coming on strong. I've been called intense a time or two, and I'll fucking own that until my dying day. But I've been curious about you for as long as I can remember, and then you just walked into my life out of nowhere the other day … and now I can't get you out of my damn head.

ME—So yes, Sheridan. I'm curious about you. I want to get to know you.

ME—Seven o'clock Saturday. I can pick you up wherever you want. And I'll make sure you get home safely. Let's shed these heavy fucking last names for one night and just have fun. That's all I'm asking of you.

She leaves me on 'read.'

I'm a manipulative bastard, and I deserve it—just as my mother's memory deserves justice.

This isn't going to be easy, but it's going to be so fucking worth it in the end.

CHAPTER TEN

Sheridan

"I THINK we should keep her overnight for observation," Mama's doctor says Saturday night.

We'd just topped off an afternoon of school shopping with dinner at Magnolia Lake when she collapsed on our way back to the car. It happened so fast—the color drained from her face, her hands trembled, and her knees gave out and her lower body quit working. Another Guillain-Barre episode, they're thinking.

Luckily, my father caught her before she hit the concrete parking lot. It could've been much worse.

Things can always be much worse …

"We can run some more tests tomorrow," Dr. Smithson adds. "I suspect it's another flare, which we can treat with IVIG therapy while she's here, but until we get bloodwork back and run some scans, we won't know for sure."

"Thank you, Doctor." Dad shakes her hand, and I give my mom a jug of ice water from her bedside tray.

"Don't scare me like that, Mama." I brush a messy strand of silver-blonde hair from her forehead. "You said you weren't getting sick on us again …"

"I know, sweetheart. I'm sorry. Guess I was in denial." She exhales as she attempts to sit up, wires running beneath her gown and machines beeping. It's a familiar scene. One that always serves to shock the appreciation of life back into me just when I need it.

Into *all* of us …

It's so easy to take one another for granted, so forget how fragile we all truly are.

"Love you," I whisper, leaning close.

I wish I could've known her before she was sick. She was a cheerleader in high school, I've been told. Had the loudest voice on the team. And she ran track, holding the Missouri state record for the girls' 100 meter sprint until recently. Before her nerves started failing her, she'd take afternoon walks around the block, collecting pretty leaves and wildflowers and pressing them between the pages of her books. And when her short-term memory was still in working order before all the meds, she would crochet the most beautiful baby blankets with matching hats and donate them to the local NICU.

She's a beautiful soul and she doesn't deserve this.

"Love you too, baby girl," she whispers before turning to my father. "You two should go home, get some rest. Pretty sure visiting hours are almost over anyway."

Exhaustion colors my father's face with gray lines and deep shadows. We exchange looks. I lift my brows, leaving the decision to him. I'm too tired to decide.

"We'll be back first thing in the morning. Get some rest now." He bends over her and kisses her forehead. Then he turns to me. "Kiddo? You ready?"

We're halfway to the elevator when my phone buzzes in my purse. I haven't checked it in hours because I've been by Mama's side. I opt to wait until the car ride home to see who it is. It'll give me something to do besides stare at oncoming headlights for the next fifteen minutes.

When we leave the parking lot, Dad messes with the radio, tuning it to a classic country station. He always listens to country when he doesn't want to think because he can't help but hum along. *When you're too busy humming, you're too busy to worry*, he always says. And it reminds him of summers at his grandparents' farm as a kid. Happier times.

Dragging my phone from my bag, I pull up my messages ... and my stomach flips.

ENEMY DEAREST *has sent you a video.*

I mute the volume, dim the screen, and hit play.

It's a thirty-second clip from the MUNRO concert he invited me to.

ENEMY DEAREST—Wish you were here.

I darken my screen and power my phone down. I don't have the energy for this right now.

Dad mumbles along to an old Clint Black song. Whether or not he knows it, he's white-knuckling the steering wheel. I don't want to think about what would happen to him if he lost Mom. With me going off to college next month, he'd be truly alone.

"I was thinking ..." I say after clearing my throat. "Maybe I should wait another year?"

He dials the volume to nothing. "What are you talking about, Sheridan? School?"

"Yeah," I say. "I can put it off one more year. Stick around and take care of Mom."

He doesn't hesitate. "Absolutely not."

"Who's going to take care of her when I'm gone? You

have weird work hours. She sometimes gets spacey when she's on her meds. What if she forgets a dose? What if she has another spell and falls and no one's home to help her? What if she has one of those days when she needs help washing her hair? Making a bowl of soup?"

Reaching across the console, he gives my hand a squeeze. His fingers are ice-cold from the blasting AC. "We'll figure it out, kiddo."

"Will we?"

"No," he says. "Not *we*. Your *mother and I* will figure it out. That's what parents do. If you put your life on hold for our sake, we'll have failed you. All we want is for you to be happy, kiddo. To live the life you were intended. Nothing more, nothing less."

Resting my cheek against the cool glass of the passenger window, I close my eyes, take a deep breath, and tell myself everything will be okay ... even if I don't believe it.

My world is tilted, wobbling on its axis.

Funny how a person can be floating through life, thinking everything is always going to be a certain way, and then the bottom drops out.

We ride in silence, and I think of that *memento mori* album from the other night; specifically the articles and how my father was falsely implicated in Cynthia's murder. I need to talk to him about it, get some answers.

But not tonight.

The exhaustion weighing down the day is already too heavy, no sense in adding anything else to the pile.

The house is dark when we pull into the driveway. And our footsteps echo when we shuffle inside. This isn't the first time Mom's been hospitalized, but her absence is always a palpable, lingering silence in our home.

It's never something we get used to.

"Goodnight, Dad." I head to my room.

"'Night, kiddo."

I turn my phone on and place it on my nightstand before switching on my box fan. It's cooler tonight, but the stuffiness of the past two weeks loiters in the air.

I'm almost asleep when my phone screen lights the room.

ENEMY DEAREST—You awake, Rose girl?

ME—Leave me alone. Please!!!

Rolling to my side, I tuck my pillow in half and shove it under my head before wrestling with the sheets for the next several minutes.

Fidgety and hot with a mind that won't stop conjuring up worst case scenarios, I can't get comfortable.

I drag myself out of bed and trek to the kitchen for a glass of ice water. My parents' door is closed but my father is sawing logs so loud I'm sure the neighbors two houses down can hear.

I grab my favorite glass, an old Flintstones jelly jar, and drop three ice cubes in, one at a time, so as not to wake him. I'm halfway to the sink when his phone illuminates the dark space with a text.

Normally I wouldn't read my father's text messages, but with Mama being in the hospital and him out cold in the bedroom, the urge comes over me to make sure it's nothing. Just in case. His screen turns dark before I have a chance to read it, but it comes back to life as soon as I pluck it off the charger and give it a tap.

KT—Just checking on you ...

KT—Just remember, it'll all be over soon. Mary Beth isn't going to suffer forever. And neither are you. Soon this will all be in the past.

KT—Keep your head up and know that I'm here for you. It's going to get better. You're on the right track. Too late to give up now after everything we've worked so hard for. We're so close ...

I re-read the messages through squinting eyes.

What does this mean? My mother isn't going to suffer forever? It'll be in the past? Last I checked, the doctors said they could treat her Guillain-Barre, but that she'd have the nerve disorder and heart defect the rest of her life. She'll always be sick or suffering in some capacity.

My stomach drops.

Nausea steals my thirst, so I abandon my cup of ice by the sink.

With shaky hands, I plug the phone in, leaving it exactly where I found it, and return to my room. And for the rest of the night, I wrack my brain in an attempt to figure out who "KT" is or why my father would have someone's name stored in his phone as simply their initials or why they'd be talking about ending my mother's suffering.

For hours, my mind wanders down the darkest alleys and the most unspeakable paths.

What if the accusations against him are true? What if he did kill his sister? What if he did cause Mrs. Monreaux's death? What if the man who raised me and sacrificed for me and taught me *everything I believe to be true* ... is nothing more than a self-serving liar?

By morning, the sunrise paints my curtains shades of orange and pink. I still haven't slept—and I'm not going to sleep. I can't rest until I know what's going on.

I slip into a pair of jean shorts from the floor and dig a t-shirt from my dresser. After freshening up, I leave a note by the stove and head to the hospital—alone—before my father wakes.

I can't tell Mama what I saw because I've yet to make sense of it.

But I can't take another minute of being under the same roof as my father...not until I get some answers.

CHAPTER ELEVEN

AUGUST

"HEY, HEY. WHAT BRINGS YOU IN?" Adriana sidles up to me at the cell store the instant I walk in the door Sunday afternoon.

My head throbs from last night's concert, and I haven't slept a fucking ounce after partying all night on the tour bus just to make Soren feel like I give a shit about our "relationship." But I'm here on a mission. Unfortunately, a quick perusal of my surroundings tells me Sheridan isn't working today.

"Need a new charger," I say, handing her the broken one I brought in. Or rather the one I destroyed this morning with the help of a pair of pliers.

"Oh." She examines the frayed wires. "How'd this happen?"

"Does it matter?"

"Um, I mean. Yeah. Sort of. I can warranty-it-out for you if it's from the phone you just bought the other week?"

"It's not." I'm in an honest mood today.

"Okay. Do you want to go with a six foot cord or ten?" She leads me to a wall covered in an endless assortment of phone chargers. "Sometimes ten can be a little much. Six is standard."

"Whatever."

She clears her throat and plucks one off the hook. "I can check you out over there."

I follow her to the register, scanning the room once more in vain.

"Sheridan working today?" I ask.

Biting her lip, she winces. "No. Her mom's in the hospital."

Fuck.

No wonder she wasn't putting up with my shit last night.

"Sorry to hear that." I hand her my card. "Anything I can do?"

I don't know what I could possibly do in this situation, but it feels like the right thing to say in this moment. Plus, it wouldn't be the worst thing if Adriana relayed my sympathy to her friend.

She slides me a pen and the receipt to sign. "Um, I don't think so?"

Twirling a dark strand of hair between her fingers, she tucks it behind one ear.

"Can I say something?" she asks.

I lift a brow, sliding the receipt across the counter. "What?"

"It's probably not my place, but Sheridan ... she's not interested."

"Well aware." I smirk. "And you're right; it's not your place."

Her eyes widen and her cheeks tinge with cherry-pink heat. "I just mean ... I don't want you to get your hopes up with her or anything. She's not really the dating type."

"Neither am I."

"And she's really into the clean cut guys," Adriana adds, eyes trained on mine as if she's trying not to stare at my tattoos, piercings, or messy fuck-if-I-care hair. "I have this friend," she continues. "You're *so* her type."

Dragging in a deep breath, I check the parking lot out of boredom.

"I'm having this party on Friday. My parents are going to be out of town and my sister said she'd buy us a couple of kegs. Just a few people. Maybe, like, ten or fifteen at most. But you should come. If you want, I mean ..."

"Maybe."

Her eyes light, as if I've just handed her a giant Publisher's Clearinghouse check. "Really?"

"Yeah, sure. We'll see."

Grabbing a slip of paper, she scribbles her number in blue ink and hands it over. "Cool. Just text me so I have your number, and I'll send you the details on Friday."

I don't commit to anything, ever. It's against policy. But I'm happy to keep my options open, especially if there's a chance Sheridan will make an appearance.

CHAPTER TWELVE

Sheridan

"HEY, sweets. How's it going? How's your mom?" Adriana greets me Thursday afternoon at the cell store with a wilted hug and pouty face.

"She just got out yesterday. Finally." I hug her back, and then hide my purse in the employee office before signing in. "The spells stopped, but she's basically on bed rest for a few days, at least when she's home alone."

"That's good, right?"

I shrug. This is par for the course. "It is what it is."

"You look so sad, babe. I'm so sorry. I wish there was something I could do." Adriana examines me. The other night she offered to drop off a pizza for my father and me, which was sweet of her, but by that point, he was on his way to work, and I wasn't in the mood for company. "How often does this happen?"

"A few times a year lately," I say. "You think I'd be used to it by now."

"That's not something you get used to." She rubs my shoulder. "Don't be so hard on yourself. You have to think positive. My grandma had a stroke last year, and they told us she had a fifteen-percent chance of making it out of the hospital alive. It's been eight months, and it's like it didn't even happen. She made a full recovery. Doctors can be wrong sometimes."

I don't want to get my hopes up ...

"Yeah. Anyway." I force a small smile and head to the register to wait for a client. Thursday afternoons are notoriously slow.

"Keep that pretty little head up," she says, resting her chin on her hand after she follows me to the counter. "And know that I'm here for you, doll."

Her words are an off-kilter echo of the ones I read on my father's screen several nights ago, the ones I've now practically memorized.

My bottom lip trembles. My eyes well until my vision blurs. A wave of repressed, tamped-down anger floods my veins until my skin burns.

Those texts are all I've been thinking about all week.

I even see them when I close my eyes.

"Oh, my God, Sher." Adriana gasps as she lunges for me, her hand on my back. "What's wrong? Was it something I said?"

A dense tear coats my cheek. I swipe it away and draw in a jagged breath. I'm not a crier. I'm not dramatic or emotional. But for the past few days, I've almost been living outside of my body. At least, that's the only way I can describe it because nothing feels real anymore. I don't look at anything the same. Every family picture I pass in the hall. Every clever or sweet quip or dad joke that comes out of my father's mouth. Every endearing, lovesick gaze my mother gifts him when their attention intersects. It all feels … empty.

"You need to sit down." She guides me to a chair in the corner meant for guests. We're not supposed to sit on the job. Ever. But no one's here. "Okay, take a deep breath …"

I inhale so deeply it hurts, my lungs aching at capacity, and then I let it all out.

Everything.

Staring ahead, unfocused, I tell her everything.

"Last Saturday, we came back from the hospital," I say. "Dad went straight to bed, but he left his phone out on the charger. I was getting a glass of water when someone texted him. It must have been ten, maybe ten thirty? I checked it, you know, in case it was my mom." My lip quivers again. "But it wasn't."

"Oh, God." Her hand clamps over her mouth, as if she knows where this is headed.

"It was someone named 'KT' and they were telling him my mom's suffering would be over soon and it would all be worth it and all this other weird stuff …" I frown. "It was vague. But I couldn't stop thinking about it, what it could mean … why my father had their name as initials in his phone. None of it made sense. My father lives for my mom. He would be lost without her …" I switch gears because where I'm about to go with this conversation needs context. "I've never talked to you about this before, but my parents have a thing with the Monreauxs. A long-standing feud, I guess you could call it."

"Who doesn't? They piss off a lot of people in this town." She snaps her gum. "What'd they do to your parents?"

"It's bad." I bury my face in my hands. "Worse than bad."

Her eyes widen. She leans closer.

"Years ago—before I was born—my father's younger sister was killed. They found her body at the Monreaux quarry. She'd been dating August's dad, Vincent. My father, to this day, believes Vincent killed her. My mother thinks so too. That's what I've always been told, what I've always believed. I've never questioned it because ... why would I? But the other week, I found these articles they'd saved ... Adriana, my father was *arrested for my aunt's murder*. The papers even reported that *he* was the main suspect. My parents *never* told me that."

She stands in silence, studying me, digesting my words maybe. "Obviously he was never found guilty. Maybe he didn't feel the need to tell you?"

"Yeah, maybe? But then several years later, Vincent's pregnant wife was killed in a hit and run on *our* street," I say. "Vincent once again tried to say it was my father, but there were no eyewitnesses and my father had a solid alibi— my mother—so they couldn't arrest him."

"Okay, so he's innocent and Vincent clearly has it out for him. Makes sense why he'd hate the man so much. But what are you getting at with all of this? What's this have to do with those texts?"

I tuck my hair behind my ears and sit straighter. "This KT person said something about ending my mom's suffer- ing, how it'll all be over soon, how they've worked so hard for this to give up now ... is he planning on ...?"

I can't say the words out loud; my lips refuse even though they're on the tip of my tongue.

"What if he *did* do those things? What if he killed his sister and Vincent's wife and now he's planning on ..."

I still can't say it.

"Jesus, Sher. I don't know." She bites her lip, taking the

spot beside me and shaking her head. "I don't even know what to tell you."

"It gets worse."

Adriana rests her elbows on her knees, buries her face in her hands, and exhales. "Wow. Okay. What else?"

"So I've been following my dad this week ... he doesn't know."

"And?"

"I've caught him in a few lies ... like he'll say he's running to the hardware store or meeting a friend at a coffee shop, but when I follow him, he doesn't go to the hardware store or he goes to a different coffee shop than the one he told me," I say. "And then when he's there, he's always meeting up with this brunette lady."

"No fucking way."

"And she's gorgeous, Adri. From what I can tell, at least. I never get that close. I'm always in my car. But she drives this silver Mercedes coupe and wears these expensive shoes, and she's got this long, shiny hair that bounces when she walks. She's always in dark sunglasses. Always greets him with a hug and leans in for a kiss, though I can never tell if it's his mouth or his cheek. Then they disappear inside wherever they're meeting. Sometimes they're in there for twenty minutes, sometimes it's over an hour. They always come out smiling and he walks her to her car. I think that's her. I think that's KT."

"That's ... man ... I don't know ..."

She seems as speechless as I've been the last few days.

"None of it makes sense," I say. "And what do I do now? I can't tell my mom any of this. And even if I did, she won't believe me. My father is the love of her life. The man we know isn't capable of this."

"Then you should go straight to the source."

I exhale with an exhausted chuff. "You don't know my father. He's an expert at shutting down conversations that make him uncomfortable. And if I'm right about all of this, he'll never admit it in a million years. He works hard to be the perfect husband and father we've always known him to be."

"So what are you going to do?"

"I wish I knew." My head throbs with tension, my jaw clenching tight. I need a break from thinking about all of this, from piecing together this strange puzzle. Just one night to relax, to clear my head and examine my options, and then I'll go from there. "You want to hang out this weekend or something?"

My father works weekends—it's the only reason I feel comfortable leaving my mom alone at this point. Which is ironic, because before it had always been the other way around. And it was why he worked nights—so he could be there with her during the day while I was at work or school.

"Actually, it's funny you should ask because my parents are going out of town, and I'm having some people over Friday night. You in?" Adriana gives me a pleading smile. "We're just hanging out and listening to music and chilling. My sister's getting us a pony keg. You can stay the night and drive home in the morning. It'll be fun—"

"—sure," I interrupt. I don't need the sales pitch this time. "I'm in."

Adriana binds me in a hug so tight it forces the air from my lungs. "You have no idea how happy this makes me. You're going to have the time of your life. I promise."

CHAPTER THIRTEEN

I FIND her on the back of Adriana's patio Friday night, sitting next to some dipshit in a crew cut and starched button down. Corporate baby blue. My least favorite color. If I'm not her type, I hope to God he isn't either. I'm not easily insulted, but this would do it.

It'd be like preferring a rusted Honda over a rare French sports car.

Surely she knows she can do better than *this*.

"Have you ever tried to, like, count the stars? Just to see how high you can count?" he asks, slurring as he bumps his shoulder against hers.

Is he trying to impress her?

Trying to sound deep or metaphorical?

Going to have to try harder than that, idiot ...

I lean back, taking a sip of my beer and watching the shit show unfold as I wait for the perfect time to crash this little love nest.

"No," she says, staring up at the sky. "That sounds … honestly … pretty boring."

He laughs. "Yeah, I guess you're right."

She takes a sip, and he makes no effort to conceal the fact that he's checking her out with some shameless side eye. It's like a scene from a movie, where the guy is fidgety and nervous and the girl is oblivious and has no idea he's counting down the seconds until he tries to kiss her.

Not on my watch.

Honda guy leans in—just as she take another sip.

And they bump heads.

She laughs. He laughs.

"You all right?" Sheridan reaches for the side of his head, running her fingers through his short pricks of shit brown hair.

"Yeah." He cups his hand over hers and doesn't once ask if her fucking head is okay. "That was my fault."

"Damn right it was," I interject because I can't take this any longer.

They whip around in tandem and Sheridan gasps, hand over her chest.

"August, what the hell are you doing here?" She rises from the step she was occupying. Generic Honda guy follows suit, his watchful gaze darting between hers and mine. I know his type. I went to school with millions of crew cut ass wipes like him. If I wanted to, I could shoot him one look that'd make him shit his pants.

"Didn't Adriana tell you? She invited me." I hide a satisfied smirk behind a swig of beer. "Supposedly there's a friend she wants to hook me up with. Apparently I'm *just her type*."

Sheridan squints. Either she doesn't believe me or all of this is news to her.

But honestly, this worked out. Dad is spending a rare weekend at home, which means I wouldn't have been able to entertain the Rose girl at my place. And I would have. If Adriana wasn't throwing this little get together, I'd have organized another beer bash at my place solely as an excuse to get Sheridan on my territory again.

If I tried to sneak her in tonight, though, my father would lose his shit. And the last thing I need is him interfering in any of this and making it about him.

"So maybe you should go look for her friend?" Sheridan folds her arms, though it's an uncoordinated effort. Hard to know how many cheap beers she's downed, but I'd venture to guess it's enough for a solid buzz.

Honda guy is silent, and he might as well be invisible—which says a lot. But judging by the way he dresses, I'm sure he's used to it.

He's a nothing and a no one; a background guy.

I'm the main-fucking-character.

"Pretty sure I found her," I say. "In fact, I'm looking at her right now."

She wrestles a smile from her lips but it makes its way to her glimmering irises. "You knew I was going to be here, didn't you? She told you. I know she did. I'm going to kill her ..."

"Actually, I had no idea if you were coming."

I'd merely hoped.

I drove back and forth past the house tonight until I saw her car outside and then I waited to make my arrival. It's a stalker move, but it worked. Because here she is. And here I am. And everything is turning up fucking roses —literally.

I take a step toward her. Honda begins to say something, but I silence him with a murderous look. When the imbecile tries to speak again, I interrupt him before he can get the first word out.

"Do yourself a favor and get the hell out of here," I say. "Have some pride, man. Your game is weak."

"*August.*" Sheridan swats at me, though she's still too far away to touch. "Don't be mean. Garrett, I'm so sorry ..."

The guy heads inside without a word. I'm not sure how much time we have alone out here. That house is hardly big enough to hold a family of five and there are probably a couple of dozen people inside already and the night is young.

Before coming outside, I slipped a guy in a backwards trucker hat a fifty and told him to make sure no one sets foot on the patio of the night ... but the jackass seems to have left his post. I should've known better than to trust a drunk dressed like Ashton Kutcher circa 2008.

"On my life, I didn't know you were coming." I step toward her again, until her sweet perfume fills my lungs. And then I cross an X over my heart. "Swear."

She rolls her eyes. For whatever reason, she doesn't believe me. But that's okay. I'm not here to convince her of anything. I'm only here because she has the one thing I want—a piece of her.

"Heard you had a bad week." I change the subject. "Sorry about your mom. She good now?"

Sheridan takes a sip, staring at me—yet through me, like her mind is somewhere else. "She's at home now."

That doesn't answer my question ...

"Let me know if there's anything I can do for you. Anything to make things easier."

Without missing a beat, her eyes come back to life. "You can hire a home health aide for her. Someone to be there when I'm not. If you want to help out, do that."

"Done."

She shakes her head, laughing through her nose before she takes a sip from her Solo cup. "I wasn't serious."

"I am."

Our gazes intersect. "I would never expect you—or anyone—to do that."

"If it would make your life easier, I'm happy to do it."

Head tilted, her expression narrows. "That's an extremely generous offer, especially since you'd get nothing out of it. What's your angle?"

"Angle? There's no angle."

"Don't lie to me." Her fist clenches for a second. "Nothing worse in this whole world than a liar."

I'm not sure what a home health aide costs, but I'm pretty sure a day's worth of interest from my trust fund account could cover an entire month of care.

It's literally pocket change.

And if it means getting into her good graces—and getting what I want—it's more than worth it.

"What do you want?" she asks. "What's in this for you?"

"You. *You* are in this for me. Isn't it obvious?"

"Me?" She presses a finger against her chest, her full lower lip falling. "I don't understand. You can literally have anyone you want. You don't even know me."

"For starters, I don't want anyone else. And you're right, I don't know you. I only know that my entire life, my father has told me not to go within a damned mile of you."

"So this is a rebellious thing? An act of defiance?"

"Not at all." I've never been a rebel for rebel's sake.

"Then what is it?"

"Does it matter what this is? You told me not to lie and I just told you what I want out of this."

She crosses her arms and her beer sloshes over the side of her cup—she doesn't notice. "I'm just trying to understand what you're offering and why. So if I sleep with you, you'll pay for a home health aide for my mother? Because ... *reasons?*"

"Don't worry about my reasons. And don't think of it as a transaction. I'm not buying your services. I just want you to look at me and not see a monster. And if you decide to fuck me ... well, then it's a win-win for all, isn't it?"

She hesitates. "Can I think about this?"

"My offer expires at midnight." I check my watch. If there's anything I've learned from being the spawn of a ruthless businessman, it's that the man who sets the deadlines always gets what he wants. I have the upper hand here. And I've made her an offer she'd be stupid to refuse. "You have two hours."

A warm breeze tousles her wavy blonde hair across her face.

"I feel like I should tell you ... I'm not exactly ... I've never been with ...," she says. "I mean, I've done everything but ..."

Jesus H. Christ.

She's a virgin.

Even better.

I don't allow myself to react. I tamp down my excitement at the prospect of deflowering the Roses' only daughter. I'm a sick bastard, but this penance is long overdue.

"Good for you, Rose girl." My cock strains inside my jeans, pulsing, but it's too dark to notice.

"I need a refill." She waves her near-empty cup and cuts past me to head inside. She slides the door open with one hard push, leaking music and conversation outside before closing it and disappearing into the crowded house.

So much for Adriana's "small gathering."

I could have told her this was going to happen …

Amateur.

I take a seat on a rickety metal patio chair and check the time. It's been three minutes, almost four. It takes two more for her to return, and this time she's carrying two cups.

"Double fisting?" I ask.

She sits one in front of me. "Figured I'd grab you a refill while I was up."

This beer is weak. Piss water. But the gesture is sweet … and definitely a promising indication.

"You didn't have to do that. But thank you." I dump my warm, half-empty beer over the edge of the deck and stack the new cup inside the old.

"Don't go reading anything into it just yet. I still haven't decided."

"Of course."

She takes the chair beside me, the warm glow of the house lights bathing her in soft shadows.

"Did that hurt?" She points to my eyebrow. "The double piercing?"

"Like hell. But only for a few seconds. Then it was over." I can think of a million things that hurt worse than two barbells in the eyebrow.

"What about those?" She traces her fingertips down my sleeve of tattoos. It's been a work-in-process for the last year and a half, and I'm almost entirely filled now on that arm—much to my father's dismay. It's why he makes me wear long-sleeved shirts to my "internship," even when it's a hundred degrees out.

"Tolerable," I say. I don't tell her I'm one of those rare freaks who enjoys the pain. The relentless microscopic pokes. The sting. The burn. "The pain makes me feel alive, reminds me that I'm stronger than it. What about you? Anything hiding under those cute little sundresses?"

I'd eat my fucking fist if she said she had nipple piercings.

She laughs, shrugging. "Nothing. I'm pretty boring. Just singles on my ears."

"Maybe we should do something about that." I take a drink.

"I'll pass. I'm going to nursing school this fall and they're pretty strict about things like that. Fresh piercings and whatnot. They don't even want us to wear nail polish. It's a hygienic thing. And school policy."

"Where are you going for school?"

"Briardale Community College," she says. "A couple hours from here."

"I know where that is. I go to Bexler … about an hour south of there. Old man's making me study business. He's convinced I'll never amount to anything without a practical degree."

Little does he know, a significant portion of the monthly allowance he deposits into my account goes straight to the overachieving brainiacs who take most of my classes for me online. I can get a ten-page research paper for three hundred bucks with a forty-eight hour notice. It's amazing, really. And I don't feel bad for any of it. The idiots with the fancy degrees designed a flawed system. I'm doing what anyone with two brain cells and a fat bank account would do if they were forced to go some overpriced college in the middle of fucking nowhere.

"That's that old school mentality," Sheridan says. "They think a college degree is everything, but anyone can be successful without one. A lot of people sell our generation short, but we're still young. We still have time to prove them wrong."

"Says the girl taking the tried-and-true track to a career in nursing," I say.

"What's wrong with nursing?"

"Nothing. Nurses are fucking angels. I just mean, you're not exactly stepping outside the box here, so I find your advice ... interesting."

"You're right. But I want to save lives and make people feel better, and that's the way to do it. It doesn't disqualify me from having an opinion about our generation's career options."

I study her in the moonlight. She watches me in return, soaking me in as if she's studying every angle on my face.

"So what are you going to do when you're done with school?" she asks.

It's not a question I'm ever asked. At least not personally.

If you ask my father, he'd say I'm going to cut my hair, yank out my piercings, and come work for him. That's the expectation anyway. To be one of his loyal Monreaux soldiers. The Vice President to Gannon's President one of these days.

Years ago, Uncle Rod was Dad's right hand man. Then shit got ugly between them and Dad decided to replace him with Gannon, who was fresh out of college. Moldable and pliable and desperate for our father's approval. Still had that new-graduate smell.

Uncle Rod still isn't over the betrayal. Can't say that I blame him. Knowing how my father operates, I'm sure Rod's been fucked seven ways from Sunday more times than he can count.

I'd rather stab myself in the balls with a rusty butter knife than work a single day under Gannon.

"Still trying to figure that out," I tell her.

"I assumed your dad would have a job waiting for you the day you graduate."

I exhale. Take a swig of beer. "He does."

"But you don't want it?"

Before I have a chance to answer, her phone chimes.

"I'm sorry—it's my mom. Two seconds." Focused on her screen, she taps out a handful of quick messages before sinking back in her seat. "Okay, she's situated now. She forgot if she'd already taken her four o'clock meds."

"Must be hard for you."

"Excuse me?"

"Having to be the parent." I point to her phone. "Always being on alert. It must get exhausting. Adriana told me about your mom being hospitalized last weekend. I didn't realize she was sick."

She chews the inside of her lip, attention holding on her blackened phone screen.

"I'm serious about the hired help," I add.

Truly, I don't give to charities. My father said most of the time, ninety-two cents of every dollar you give goes straight into the untaxed pockets of those who run those operations. It's rare to find a legit organization.

At least in this case, I'd know where my money's going.

And I'm getting something better than a tax write-off in return ...

If my father knew I was offering to save the life of a Rose, he'd blow a gasket. He'd disown me, kick me out of his mansion, and revoke my trust fund so fast every head in a fifty mile radius would spin.

But if he knew what I'm really gaming for—if he let me explain—he'd be proud.

There's no one on this earth he hates more than Rich Rose. And there's no one in the world Rich Rose loves more than his precious, innocent, untouched daughter.

Oh, sweet Rose girl—the dirty things I'm going to do to you ...

CHAPTER FOURTEEN

Sheridan

"ADRIANA'S DAD has a fully restored '69 Cadillac DeVille in the garage. Chalice gold firemist ..." I tell him in an attempt to steer the conversation into a more neutral direction. Plus, my legs ache from sitting in these hard chairs. And I could use a change of scenery. "Maybe you've seen it in the annual Fourth of July parade? It's basically my dream car ..."

"I've never been to a parade in my life."

"Really?" It never occurred to me that people like that existed. I can't count the number of memories I have of my parents plopping lawn chairs by the curb and telling me to wave at the funny-looking floats that passed as they helped me gather the candy tossed in our direction. Such a simple, joyful childhood experience. I almost feel sorry for him. But I'm sure the other *joys* and privileges of his childhood more than made up for it.

"You want to go check it out?" I point to the garage. "I'm sure he wouldn't mind as long as we don't touch anything."

"You really have no qualms about trespassing, do you?"

"It's not trespassing." I swat his hand. "Plus, her dad loves me. I think he'd be thrilled that someone's showing off his car. He spent years sourcing original parts and rebuilding it. He's told me about it so many times, I could probably recite it for you, verbatim."

"Please don't."

"Come on." I wave for him to follow. I don't care if he is or isn't a car buff. I'm obsessed with this thing. I once teased Adriana's dad about adopting me so I could inherit it—a morbid request in retrospect.

August follows me down the deck stairs, toward the freestanding garage at the back of the house. The side door is unlocked, and I reach up and tug on the string, giving us just enough light to help us navigate around the single stall garage without bumping into the antique beauty.

"He named her Barbara-Ann." I chuckle, peeling back the canvas cover. "Don't ask me why."

"Probably after an ex-girlfriend."

"Don't tell Adri's mom that ..."

He makes his way to the trunk and drags his middle finger against the length of the rear fender, a move my body suddenly decides is oddly sexual. For whatever reason my brain fixates on his hands—his fingers inside me. And his lips...have they always appeared so pillow-soft? Not too full, not too narrow. For a moment, I imagine them pressed against mine, silky and burning hot, followed by the wet slip of his tongue piercing through.

Heat flushes my ears.

Maybe it's the beer.

Or the fact that we're truly alone right now.

Or that, for the first time all week, I'm able to relax.

Or the fact that I'm locked in a gaze with a man who wants to change my entire life (and my mother's) in exchange for one night with me.

If I sell him a little piece of my soul, I'll get priceless peace of mind in return.

That alone should be reason enough.

But I'm in no condition to make that kind of decision.

And it certainly isn't happening tonight.

I slip my hands into my back pockets and drag in a slow, cleansing breath. I'm getting ahead of myself. I need to slow down. If he wants this enough, he's not going anywhere.

"So, what do you think?" I teeter on the balls of my feet, definitely buzzing. "Of the car, I mean."

"It's gorgeous." He makes his way to the driver's side, pops the door open, and climbs inside. Adjusting the mirror with one hand, he runs his other palm along the skinny black steering wheel. "Look at this. Keys are in the ignition."

Adri's dad would *never*. But in any case, I lean over the passenger door to check.

"Liar."

"Get in," he says.

"What? Why?"

"Just humor me."

I prop the passenger door open and slide inside, scooting across the buttery leather Adri's dad has worked so hard to condition, and ensuring I don't track a single grass blade onto the floor mat.

"If you could be anywhere in the world, right now, where would you want to go?" he asks. "Anywhere at all."

"That's a hard question ..."

"Not at all."

"Maybe not for you. You have go-anywhere-in-the-world money ..."

"This isn't about money, Rose girl. Just tell me where you want to go."

"I don't know?" What is it about on-the-spot questions that turn your mind into a blank slate? "Portland, Maine. I've always wanted to go there. But in the fall. I guess maybe Charleston? Or Savannah? What about you?"

"Here," he says without hesitation. "I'm right where I want to be."

I roll my eyes and pretend to gag myself with my finger. "I knew you were extra, but I had no idea you were capable of being this cheesy."

"You asked, I answered. Just telling the truth." He watches me from his periphery. "You intrigue me."

I roll my eyes again. Harder this time. "Bull. August, let's be clear. Lines like this don't work on me. If you're trying to flatter me, it's having the opposite effect. I'm cring-ing. Like, head to toe."

"I mean it." He angles his body toward mine, his left arm resting on the driver's door. "My entire life you've been this enigma, this ... forbidden fruit, for lack of a better term. And honestly, I didn't give two shits about you until you walked into my life, and now you're all I can fucking think about."

My mouth runs dry because I don't know what to say. No one's ever been obsessed with me, nor has anyone told me I'm all they can think about.

He exhales, staring straight ahead. "It's fucked up, I know. This level of obsession."

Silence settles between us.

"Aren't you curious about me? Have you ever thought about me?" he asks. "Wondered about me?"

"There was never a reason to."

Reaching across the bench seat he brushes hair from my forehead and tucks it behind my ear. The sheer sensation of his fingertips against my face sends a spray of goosebumps down my arm.

"But what about now?" he moves a few inches closer. "Now that we've officially met, do you ever think about me? Do you ever wonder what it'd be like if I kissed you?"

A fluttery, arrhythmic sensation spreads across my chest as my breath hitches.

"You're scared. Is that it?" He leans away but only slightly. "Maybe I should describe it for you?"

I lick my lips, focusing on the Cadillac emblem protruding from the hood.

"Or better yet, I'd be happy to demonstrate." He comes in closer again. Cupping my jaw, he angles my face toward him until our eyes meet. His attention drops to my lips for a second before returning. "Maybe you're a hands-on learner."

I try to swallow but I can't.

I try to speak but the words are stuck.

"I'd take it slow." August leans in until the heat of his mouth almost grazes mine. We're not touching. Not yet. "Let the anticipation build. That's important."

The faint remnants of his expensive aftershave fill the air around us. Leather and darkness. The scent of a man much more experienced than he should be at nearly twenty. His nose rubs against mine, soft and teasing as his thumb runs along my jaw line and down the side of my neck.

Abandoning my mouth, he presses his lips into the soft spot below my ear next, peppering kisses lower, lower still, until he reaches the top of my shoulder, and then he pushes the fabric of my blouse aside to taste my skin.

My sex throbs and my stomach caves with each deep breath. He works his way to the other side of my neck and for a moment, I almost forget to breathe. When he's finished, he lifts my wrist to his mouth and kisses the tender underside, making my pulse quicken.

I've fooled around with guys before, but none of them took their time. None of them kissed me or touched me solely for my pleasure. The best they could do was a sloppy make out session with a side of fully clothed grinding.

"Curious yet?" He stops to glance up at me. "Want to experience the real thing?"

My jealous lips are on fire, aching from abandonment. I try to speak, but I'm quite certain whatever words come out of my mouth would be incoherent.

"Safe to say that's a yes?" His mouth closes in on mine in one slow and endless move. It isn't a frenzied crash, it's reckless euphoria.

I don't exist on this plane anymore.

In this oil-scented garage.

In this buzzing, live-wire body.

I'm somewhere else entirely.

I never thought being the object of someone else's fantasy would be a thing for me—but this is ... incinerating me from the inside out.

August's tongue parts my lips until it dances with mine, and in one slick move, he pulls me into his lap and takes my spot on the passenger side. Cupping my face in both hands, he guides my face away until our eyes hold and everything in this moment pauses, suspended in time.

"You're making the right decision." His eyes glint, silver with a side of wickedness. And he reaches down to lean the seat back.

His hardness presses between my legs as I straddle him,

and his grip moves to my hips, pressing me down so I can feel more of him. The want in his eyes is undeniable, like a wild animal seconds from his feast.

He begins to say something when I place my palms on his chest and sit up.

"I don't want to do it here, like this," I say. "Not in Adri's dad's car. Not in a garage. Not when I taste like beer and someone could walk in on us at any second."

This isn't remotely how I want my first time to be.

August exhales, angling his head. "So, you want ... what? A hotel room? Champagne? Flowers? Some fake romantic shit to make it special?"

"I don't want *fake romantic shit*. I just don't want to do it *here*."

I've successfully killed the mood—but I don't suppose it matters since this isn't happening tonight anyway. He can kiss his deadline goodbye. I need more time to decide if I'm going to do this anyway.

I climb off of him and into the driver's seat. He adjusts the bulge in his jeans.

"I'm sorry," I say.

"Of course you are." He's annoyed at me, and I get it. I got his hopes up. Any hot-blooded male would be disappointed right now.

I lean against the back of the seat, head resting on my hand. "Look. This past week has been one of the most emotionally draining weeks of my life. I've slept maybe a total of eleven hours, if that. And your offer is extremely generous. I'm tempted, yes. I just don't want to jump into anything crazy right now. I want to think about it a little more. I need more time."

He says nothing, simply stares at me with an expression I couldn't possibly try to read.

"I'm going to head in." I sit up and reach for the door handle, no longer willing to bask in the awkwardness of this moment.

"Wait."

I turn back to him. "Yeah?"

"You're staying here tonight, right?"

I nod.

"You're not going to get any sleep in there. It's too fucking loud." Slipping his hand softly around my wrist, he guides me closer, until I'm nestled under his arm, my cheek against his chest.

It's strange at first—falling asleep in someone's arms.

But then we settle into some kind of rhythm, our breaths syncing and our bodies giving off just enough warmth to keep us comfortable. Outside, the evening crickets chirp and faint pop music plays from the house, leaking through old windows and getting lost in the cooling night breeze.

Within seconds, my eyelids grow heavy and the night fades away as I drift off in the arms of my enemy dearest.

CHAPTER FIFTEEN

AUGUST

"YOU STAYED," she says the next morning with a sleepy smile. She sits up, stretching her arms overhead, and I move for the first time in fucking hours.

I watched her sleep—all night, studying the way her mouth twitched into half a smirk when she was dreaming, inhaling the sugar-sweet scent of her shampoo as it radiated off the top of her warm head. And as the sun came up and flooded the tiny garage with warm light, she looked like a goddamn Disney princess. If she wasn't a Rose, I might have allowed myself to feel some kind of way ...

I huff. "You think I'd leave you passed out in some garage?"

If she were anyone else, then yes. Yes, I would do that. One hundred fucking percent.

But I'm so fucking close to sealing this deal.

"How'd you sleep?" I ask. If I'm being honest with myself, there's something sexy about this undone version of her, with her hair in her face and her makeup rubbed off (on my shirt), all fresh-faced. I'm not used to seeing girls like this —sans perfection. It's refreshing.

"Like a million bucks actually. Best sleep I've had in forever ..."

Just imagine how she would've slept after the triple orgasm I was going to give her ... fingers, tongue, and cock—my personal forte.

Ah, well. Soon enough.

"Oh, geez." She yanks her phone from her back pocket. "Adri was texting me all night. I forgot to tell her we were out here." Climbing out of the car, she says, "I should head in and talk to her—assuming she's up."

"You have my number."

Fighting the tiniest flicker of a smile, she stops in her tracks by the door and says, "I do."

I re-cover the car, show myself out, and drive home.

Sheridan Rose is a sweet girl. Trusting. Naïve. And she doesn't deserve any of this. In fact, all of this would be a million times easier if she were some snooty little priss who needed the attitude fucked out of her. Instead, she's a walking, talking heart of gold with perfect C-tits and honest intentions.

Steeling myself, I roll down my window, crank my music, and drown out the conscientiousness who decided to make a surprise appearance out of fucking nowhere. I can't get soft about this. It's a once in a lifetime opportunity and I'm seizing the fuck out of it.

It's a shame she has to pay the price her father refused to pay.

My father always said everything in life trickles down. All the good, all the bad.

The key is controlling the way it falls.

I can't change the fact that my mother's no longer here, but I *can* even the score. Rich has caused us pain and suffering for the last twenty years.

I'm simply returning the favor.

I pull into my driveway ten minutes later and catch a whiff of Sheridan's subtle-sweet perfume on my shirt after rolling up the windows. I'll admit, there was something peaceful about holding her while she slept. Something serene about sitting with someone and doing nothing but breathing. The outside world didn't exist. I couldn't so much as move to grab my phone from my pocket to piss away some time. I simply held her—something I've never done with anyone before. The strangest part of it all, was that it wasn't torturous.

Dare I say I enjoyed it?

I even let my mind wander down a path or two—out of sheer boredom, of course. Imagining a future with her, a relationship, being one of *those* couples.

Regardless, it doesn't matter.

We don't have a future—we have a score to settle.

And then we're done.

CHAPTER SIXTEEN

Sheridan

"SHER, you mind doing the dishes this time?" Dad asks as we finish breakfast Saturday morning. Normally it's a team effort. He washes and I dry. But the bags under his eyes are heavier today, the circles a shade darker than usual. He worked last night, but this isn't the look of physical exhaustion. This is something else, I know it. "I'm going to see if I can't grab an extra hour of sleep before I go in again."

"Yeah, I've got it." I don't look him in the eye. I haven't been able to all week. Every time I try, I get nauseous. Or I end up biting my tongue to keep from vomiting words and accusations all over him. I'm not ready to confront him. I need more evidence or else he'll gaslight me with that fatherly smile of his as he pats me on the head and calls me "kiddo."

"How was the sleepover last night?" Mom asks as I fill the sink with soapy water. "What'd you girls do?"

"We watched a movie," I lie, wincing. "That new one

with Robert Pattinson. And we ordered pizza. Stalked her ex online. The usual."

I hate lying to her, I do. But in this case, telling the truth would do more harm than good. No point in upsetting her.

She chuckles. "Oh, you girls ..."

"So ..." I draw in a long breath as I rinse bits of scrambled eggs off a floral plate. "I know this is kind of random, but I was thinking ... and I leave for college in a few weeks."

"Yes, sweetheart. I'm well aware."

"Adriana said there's this charity in town, where you can apply for these grants or something for home health aides ..." I'm a terrible liar. "I don't know all the details. She said her grandma got into the program a couple years ago."

I'm going to hell with a one-way ticket.

"Oh? I've never heard of such a thing." Her voice inches up, as if her curiosity has been piqued. "You'd think the doctors would've said something about that years ago?"

I rinse the plate under a stream of cold water before placing it in the drying rack. "I think it's kind of a word of mouth, in the know kind of program? Private donors ... or something. Anyway, would you be okay with me putting your name in the hat?"

She's quiet. And after a few more seconds of silence, I turn to make sure she's still there. Only I find her staring out the window, lost in thought.

I twist the faucet handle to 'off' and take the seat beside her. "Mama, sometimes you forget your meds. And other times you get those spells. And there are times you—"

She swats her hand at me. "I know."

"In a few weeks, I won't be just a phone call away anymore. And Dad can't leave work on a whim if something happens." I wring my hands. "At least let me apply for this and see what happens. It's not like you have anything to lose."

Mama drags in a slow breath and lets it go, shoulders falling. "Yeah, I suppose you're right. Couldn't hurt. Just don't go getting all hopeful."

I finish the dishes and help her to the living room to get her situated for her mid-morning nap. And when I'm done, I hit the shower, squeezing my eyes tight and letting the water drip down my neck slow and teasing, just the way he kissed me last night ...

... just the way I'm going to let him kiss me again—soon.

A good time for a good cause.

How could it go wrong?

AUGUST

"AUG, CHECK OUT MY NEW DRIVER." Dad is polishing his golf clubs when I get home Saturday morning. "Top-of-the-line Hartford. Custom made. Look, they even engraved my monogram on the grips. Nice, eh?"

He attempts to hand it to me, but I ignore the gesture, making a beeline for the door.

There are few things on this Earth I hate more than golf.

My father must have paid for hundreds if not thousands of hours' worth of golf lessons over the course of my childhood, always desperate to be the best on the green. If only he'd put that kind of effort into parenting, maybe I'd have taken more interest in his hobbies.

Though I will give him credit—he allowed me to accompany him to his favorite course once. When I was ten. Though I could only watch. After four hours in, I was growing restless and thought it'd be funny to drive off in our cart. My juvenile brain was convinced he'd find it hilarious, that we'd be laughing by the end of it. Instead he had me escorted off the grounds like a fucking criminal and made me wait in the back of his SUV for two hours while he finished his eighteen. After that, he never invited me golfing again.

"What, can't say hi to your old man?" He chuffs, clearly insulted. Though he's never struck me as a person capable of feeling anything. "Where were you last night, anyway? Who's the lucky lady?"

"Oh, hey, August." My father's girlfriend, Cassandra, emerges from inside. "Haven't seen you in a while. How have you been?"

Cassandra's as fake as the double D tits hanging out of her unbuttoned, hot pink golf polo. That or she's literally an imbecile. They've been together nearly a year, and I've yet to decide if she sucks at making conversation or if she's just stupid.

Knowing my father, probably both.

God forbid he dates a woman smarter than him, or a woman my mother would've approved of. She was educated and eloquent. Fluent in three languages. An avid reader and a lover of the arts. At least from what I can glean from home videos and a handful of stories people used to throw around at the annual family reunions we used to host. She'd roll in her grave if she saw the kind of women keeping him company these days. Honestly, it's embarrassing.

"August, a little respect, please. Don't ignore Cassandra," my father says. "No need to go shitting on someone else's day just because you're in a pissy mood."

"Vince, it's okay." Cassandra's breathy voice reminds me of a cheap Marilyn Monroe impersonator. I'm convinced it's all some kind of act she uses to hook men. Like Hilaria Baldwin pretending to be Spanish when she was Boston born-and-raised. I suppose, if my father were with her because he found her interesting, it would matter. But she's quite literally a bed warmer, a social accessory, and a human pocket pussy all rolled into one—much like the woman before her and the one before that …

My father checks his glimmering Patek Philippe timepiece. "We should head out if we're going to make our tee time."

It's not like they'd turn him away if he showed up late. They'd rearrange everyone else's tee times before they did that.

"Oh, wait. Let me grab my visor, baby …" Cassandra disappears inside, and I cringe on the inside because a man of his age should never be referred to as *baby*. I don't care who you are.

"Any productive plans on the docket for this afternoon?" he asks while he waits. "Or are we planning to laze around the pool."

"It's a Saturday, so …" I shrug, smirk, and insert a sarcastic undertone to my words. "Definitely lazing."

He peers down his bumpy snout at me. Thank God I took after my mother in the looks department. "I'd expect nothing less."

"And I'm happy to meet those expectations." I head inside before he can get the last word—a dick move, but I am my father's son.

I finish the breakfast plate Clarice left for me in the fridge, hit the shower, and take care of the nasty case of blue balls I've come down with courtesy of the Rose girl. Only something's … off.

My usual mental rotation of bukkake fantasies, nine

person trains, and squirting pussies seems to be doing—quite literally—nothing for me.

I stroke myself faster, tighten my grip just a little more, pinch my eyes shut, and bite my lip, conjuring an image of my favorite cam girl. My cock throbs for a moment ... before deflating.

"God damn it," I mutter, rubbing faster.

Eyes shut tight once more, I visualize another tried and true classic—a farmer's daughter getting railed on the back of a tractor by the hired hand. (I never said I was creative). And still—nothing.

Unsatisfied, I let it go, pressing my forehead against the shower tile and take a break. I didn't sleep last night. Could be that. I stared at Sheridan for hours, my mind ruminating into the darkest corners, remembering things I'd once forgotten, fantasizing about things only a monster would be proud of.

But it's her bitten smile that comes to mind next. The way she acted annoyed with me last night yet only left my side once. And how she slept so soundly in my arms, like it was the safest place in the world for her.

Her tongue was sweet like cinnamon, and her lips were soft like clouds.

She was worried that she'd taste like beer. And she did. But it was mostly cinnamon. Hot and sweet. And her skin was fucking cashmere. I could've touched her all night had she not pulled the emergency brake.

For the hell of it, I stroke myself to the fantasy of what would have been—what *will* be. Only it's some kind of boring vanilla version. *Regular* sex. And just like that, my cock responds in record time.

Before long, I come so hard I have to sit down to catch my breath.

Stumbling out of the shower a minute later, I toss my damp, naked body on the bed and pass out for hours ... because I don't want to think about what this could possibly mean.

CHAPTER EIGHTEEN

Sheridan

I'M on my way home from work when I spot KT's silver Mercedes at a red light.

She's in the left turn lane on Rosemont, phone pressed against her ear, oblivious. Engaged in conversation with someone who's putting a big, old dopey grin on her face.

Without thinking twice, I hook a right into an empty battery store parking lot and come out the other side so I can catch the light going in her direction as soon as it turns green.

Only I get stuck behind a garbage truck and a Buick going negative five miles per hour.

When the traffic clears, her shiny little coupe is MIA ... until I spot it parked at a little hole-in-the-wall café off Market Street.

Rain drops pepper my windshield, clouding my view as KT makes a mad dash to get inside. Her tail lights blink as she locks it, trotting away in her sky-high heels.

The last several minutes are a blur. I'm pretty sure I cut off a minivan to make this turn. And someone honked, maybe even two someones, but, I was so hyper-focused, every noise had a faded, distorted edge to it, like it was coming from a tunnel a world away.

I park two rows away, waiting and watching like a stalker. Too curious to leave, too paralyzed to charge in and address the woman who promised my father she'd put Mama out of her suffering.

With a death grip on my steering wheel, and the radio playing some melancholy Adele song on low volume, I talk myself into taking the confrontation route because I didn't drive like a bat out of hell just to sit here like some pansy. I didn't do all of that just to slink of quietly into the night.

I kill my engine and shove my keys into my bag—just as my father pulls up and parks our family sedan in the empty spot beside her Mercedes. Thunder rolls; angry, booming and unapologetic. Rain pelts harder, bouncing off my roof like marbles on tin. Within seconds, Dad disappears into the cozy café with the beautiful woman.

I start my engine and the dash clock blinks to life—8:11 PM.

He should've been at work an hour ago.

I start my car, and as I peel out of the parking lot, my hands are locked so tight on the steering wheel that I can't feel my fingers. Thick tears blind my vision and leave itchy tracks down my cheeks, and I drive until I can't anymore.

And now here I am—in the library parking lot at eight o'clock on a Saturday night, bawling my eyes out. Alone. Lungs gasping for air. Weight of the world on my shoulders. My head pounds, fierce with pressure as I rest it against the steering wheel and wipe my tears on my sleeve.

I need to head home and check on Mama, but until

these tears stop falling, driving in this rainstorm would be a death wish.

I check the radar, the way my dad taught me. The storm should clear in about twenty minutes.

I mess with the radio for a bit, dry my tears on a wrinkly napkin from the console, and scroll through my phone to kill the time. I'd text Adriana, but we just worked an eight-hour shift together, and she's probably getting ready for her Bumble date anyway.

Scrolling through my contacts, I stop when I get to ENEMY DEAREST, and, for the hell of it, I read through our old texts. Every single one. By the time I'm done, I catch my reflection in the rearview mirror—my mouth is curled up at the sides. He's crazy. Hot, but crazy. And he's obsessed with me. Which is also hot. A weird kind of hot but still hot.

And his offer to help my mom is beyond generous—assuming his offer hasn't expired. Maybe it isn't from the kindness of his cold little heart because he's made it clear he wants one night with me. But still. It counts for something, and it was so kind of him to let me sleep in his arms last night.

He may have a façade of steel and a signature wicked glint and naughty intentions, but I don't think he's the monster everyone thinks he is. Misunderstood maybe. And a spoiled Monreaux with unlimited access to fuck-you money. But if those are the worst things about him, I'd hardly call him a monster.

He doesn't scare me.

He's intense, sure. But he owns it. That's more than most people can say.

The rain picks up, beading harder on my windshield as the worst of the storm makes its way through this side of town. I text Mama to let her know I'll be home soon, and then I tune to a local radio station—the one that doesn't fade in and out every three seconds.

A MUNRO song plays—A Thousand Words for Summer, and I hum along with August's brother. I've never been a big MUNRO fan. For whatever reason, their music never resonated with me. It always made me think of lying on my bed, crying into a pillow and missing someone I could never have.

Maybe that's a theme with them. Unrequited love. Missed chances. Too little, too late. Regrets.

But this song is catchy. It isn't as sad. It's about this girl and how there aren't enough words in the world to describe how much she means to him. With nothing else to do but wait for the rain to finish, I snap a picture of my radio and send it to August because I need something to take my mind off of what I just witnessed. Can't think of a bigger distraction than him ...

ME: Listening to your brother's new song. Is "Summer" a real person or a marketing ploy?

I add a winking emoji in case I come off the wrong way.

It takes a couple of minutes, but he replies.

ENEMY DEAREST: Not sure. I'll ask him.

ME: Appreciate it.

ME: What are you up to tonight?

ENEMY DEAREST: Literally sitting around waiting for you to text me.

ME: Whatever ... What are you really doing?

ENEMY DEAREST: Top secret project.

I laugh under my breath. Such a smart ass, this one. But, for all I know, he might not be joking. I heard a rumor once that the Monreauxs have a "blacklist" and if your name so much as touches that list, they'll destroy you from the inside out. A slow and painful reckoning. It's probably why my father has had so many jobs in the last twenty years. Every couple of years he gets a pink slip, and it's always for some asinine reason.

They went after a local guy a few years ago—Mark Greeley—who had some kind of road rage incident with Vincent. Thirty days later, the guy lost his job of fifteen years at the power company due to "gross misconduct." They said he sexually harassed one of the secretaries there. Never mind the two of them didn't so much as work in the same unit. Shortly after that, he spent six months on unemployment. And when his bills wouldn't stop piling up, that's when his marriage began to crumble. He'd gained weight. Lost his spark. And had all but given up. By the end of that year, his wife took the kids and filed for divorce.

I've seen him around town a handful of times over the years. He's put on at least fifty pounds, gone all gray, and wears a full beard to hide half of his face.

It's crazy how a single incident can have a ripple effect that spans the rest of your life.

I should count my lucky stars that our family didn't crumble like that. My father has spent his fair share of time standing in the unemployment line over the years, but we never went hungry and we never had our water shut off and he and Mama never once considered divorce.

Then again ... look where we are now.

I exhale, pressing my cheek against the cool glass as the rain drops diminish to almost nothing but a few tear shaped trickles.

I could go home now.

But I have a wild hair to ask a favor of August.

ME: Can I call you?

ENEMY DEAREST: ???

ME: Is that a yes or a no?

I nibble my thumbnail. Maybe he's one of those guys who hates phone calls. Who only text. Or maybe he's with someone?

ENEMY DEAREST: Yeah. Give me 2 secs. I'll call you.

Resting my phone in my lap, I make sure the ringer's on, and I wait. Only the ringtone is different, and it takes me a moment to realize he's Face Timing me.

Oh, god. I wasn't ready for this.

I flip my visor down to check the damage. Swollen eyes, pink nose, puffy lips, humidity-kissed hair.

Screw it. It's dark in here anyway.

I accept his call and manage a cool yet casual, "Hey."

"Hey, you." His voice is low, intimate almost. Judging by the motion behind him, it would appear he's walking down a dimly lit hallway. A second later, he closes a door behind him. "What's going on?"

"I just have a weird favor to ask, I guess."

"And you couldn't text it?" He runs his hands through his messy waves and his hair falls in a deep side part. "Wait. I can hardly see you. It's super dark. Where are you?"

"In my car."

"Just sitting in your car in the dark?" He climbs onto his bed and rests a tattooed arm behind his head. "Everything okay?"

"You have resources, right? Like you can find people?"

He sits up, almost choking on his words before chuckling. "Are you high right now? You're acting so fucking weird, Sher."

Sher. He's never called me that before.

It's always been Rose girl, which I've always attributed

to the fact that I'm some kind of fetish to him so it's some kind of turn on-slash-reminder.

"No, I'm not high. I just need to figure out who someone is. A name. I have initials. And I have a picture of her car," I say. "I figured you might have more connections or you might know people who know people. It's a stretch. But I wanted to ask."

He's sitting cross-legged now, one hand covering his mouth as he breathes over his fingers, examining me from his side of the screen.

"I think … I think my father's having an affair, and I just want to know who this woman is," I say. I don't love the idea of sharing this fact with August. After all, his father would probably go to town with this little detail. But for some insane reason … I trust him. "Her initials are KT. I've seen them together a handful of times, but I haven't gotten close. I just want to have all of my facts straight before I confront him so he can't brush me off."

"Jesus." He mumbles through his fingers. "Is that why you look like you've been crying?"

My cheeks burn in the dark. I didn't think he'd be able to notice.

"I had a moment, yes."

He leans against his headboard, shaking his head as he stares off. "I don't know much about your situation, but I do know that cheaters never come clean unless they're caught red-handed. Having a name isn't going to do you any good. He'll deny it. They avoid confrontation like the plague—it's partly why they cheat. They're allergic to the art of breaking up with people. Deep down, they're cowards."

A month ago, the word coward would have never sat beside my dad's name in a sentence.

"And you know this from experience?"

"Psh. I've witnessed it first-hand all of my life." He's talking about his father. I should've figured. "The man's got it down to a science."

That must be hard for August, having grown up with the revolving door of women his father whisks in and out of their lives, each a reminder of his irreplaceable mother.

"Do you think you can find her?" I ask.

"Send me the pic. I'll do my best."

It's getting late. "Hey, I have to go. My mom's waiting for me. Let me know if you find anything okay? Anything at all."

I swear a flash of disappointment registers on his face, but it's hard to tell for sure on a five-inch screen.

Maybe I'm imagining things ...

"Sheridan," he captures my name, my attention, and my breath with his booming voice.

"Yeah?"

"When can I see you again?"

"Soon, August." My mouth inches up on one side. I bite my lip to make it stop. "Soon."

"Good," he says. "And just so we're clear, my offer still stands."

CHAPTER NINETEEN

"KARA TINDALL," Uncle Rod says on the phone Tuesday night. "That KT person with the Mercedes. Name's Kara Tindall. She's twenty-eight. Local attorney here in town. That's about all I got for you."

Uncle Rod is my father's youngest brother—and the guy we call whenever there's trouble in paradise. He likes to refer to himself as an "old school fixer" though sometimes I think the man watches too much premium cable TV. Regardless, there's no denying he can find out anything about anyone. He can sniff out liars and cheats from a mile away, like a bloodhound, and everyone who's anyone in this town knows to give him a straight answer the first time he asks.

"Kara Tindall." I sit up and grab a scrap of paper and pen from my desk and scribble it down. "You sure?"

"The hell kind of question is that?" He blows a puff of air into the receiver. "Of course I'm sure. Anyway, what's your business with this lawyer lady? You in some kind of trouble?"

"Always."

"Don't be a dumbass." He chuckles. At least someone in this family appreciates my sense of humor. "Let me know if you need anything else. You've got my number."

"Will do." I end the call and text Sheridan.

ME: Got the name for you. But I'd like you to come get it in person …

I'm teasing. Sort of.

Sheridan leaves for college in a few weeks.

I need to get this shit show on the road, to do what needs to be done, and then slam that chapter shut, so I can finally get the Rose girl out of my system.

I thought of her again today in the shower, and then because apparently that wasn't enough, I thought of her three other times today. Every scenario was vanilla-sweet with a side of her cinnamon mouth. Not my regular fare.

ROSE GIRL: For real? You have the name?

ME: Yes. Come over. I'll wait for you by the gate in twenty.

With everything going on in her personal life, I don't know if she'll be in the mood to get fucked seven ways from Sunday the second I lock my bedroom door, but God help me, I'm going to try to get here there.

She doesn't respond for a solid four minutes.

I pace my room. Check the window. Sniff the sheets to ensure the new housekeeper changed them today like I asked.

ROSE GIRL: I can't come now. It'll have to be later. Ten?

ME: Perfect.

I toss my phone aside and collapse on my bed, hands tucked behind my neck as I stare at the ceiling. The security camera in the corner blinks red. It's on a closed, password protected circuit on our network. One that only *I* have access to.

I had it privately installed years ago when I discovered someone was habitually stealing cash from my dresser. Then a watch went missing. And handful of other pawnable items. Turned out it was one of Gannon's fair weather "friends" whose name now resides permanently on our family's infamous blacklist.

Whatever we do tonight in this room will be recorded in crisp black and white footage with an aerial view, which means I'll be able to relive this moment as many times as I want. If I were pure evil, I'd send the video to her father. I'd let him know his sweet baby girl was defiled by the son of his lifelong enemy. It's an idea I've entertained far too many times lately, envisioning the color draining from his face, tears filling his eyes. His clenched fists. A realization that what's done is done—forever and there's not a damned thing he can do about it.

I may be a sick bastard, but I'm not fucking abhorrent.

I won't send him the video.

I hit the shower and get ready.

Tonight's the night.

CHAPTER TWENTY

Sheridan

I UNZIP MY BLACK HOODIE, toss it on a chair, and sit at the edge of August's bed. It's late. And I'm exhausted. But I had to wait until Mama was sleeping and Dad had left for work before I could sneak out.

August retrieves a slip of paper from the top of his dresser. I run my damp palms along the tops of my thighs, holding my breath.

"Kara ... Tindall," he says, handing me the name. "Ring a bell?"

I jerk the slip from his fingers and read it myself.

Kara Tindall.

"Oh my god." I clamp my hand over my mouth. "No. She used to babysit me ..."

It had to have been ten years ago, maybe more.

"She's a lawyer here in town," he says. "That's about all I could get."

Sliding my phone out, I type her name into Google,

tapping on the first result: a website for Rowe, Harper, and Slattery PC. I click on her profile, which is listed under junior partners. She specializes in everything from family law and child custody to workplace litigation and medical malpractice.

"Is that her?" he asks.

I nod. "Yeah."

She was a high-schooler when she used to watch me. And while I was young, seven or eight at the time, I always thought it was strange how she wanted to hang around our family so much. Even when my parents would get home from wherever they'd gone off to, handed her a twenty, and told her goodnight ... she'd always linger.

Mama said she just liked our family, that her daddy wasn't around and her mom was less than nice. At one point, she joked to my parents about being an honorary Rose. I wasn't a jealous child, but it lit a spark of something in me that day. A sharp jab to the chest. I didn't want to share them, not with her. They were *my* parents.

After she went off to college, we never heard from her again, and my parents hired some other girl to watch me every once in a while. I never thought about Kara again, and as far as I knew, neither did my parents. Babysitters came and went. That's just how it was.

"That bastard." I grip the comforter in my fists. "Why would he do that?"

"I assume you're referring to your father?"

"How could he do that to my mother? She's sacrificed everything for him. And she's not well. Why would he run off with our old babysitter?" I rise and pace his expansive room. "I mean, how cliché does he have to be? And not only that, but what would she want with him? She's obviously doing very well for herself. My father can't even pay to have our AC fixed for fucks' sake."

I drag my fingers through my hair, tugging on fistfuls.

Tears cloud my vision and my chest tightens so hard I gasp for oxygen, but it's not enough.

Despite the enormity of his room, the walls close in around me. Making my way to his window, I switch the latch and shove it open until I'm met with a blast of tepid summer night air.

"He's a liar, August. He's such a fucking liar." I turn on my heels, pacing back to the bed to grab my phone again—only I run straight into him.

"Hey." He captures my wrists, gently lowering them to my sides yet not letting go. "It's okay. You're okay. Everything's going to be okay."

"She texted him," I say. "The last time Mom was in the hospital. Kara texted my father, something about how it'll all be over soon and the suffering will end. I don't know what that means, but ..."

I don't think it's worth stating what we both know—that my father has *twice* been accused of murder in his lifetime.

August leads me to the bed, takes a seat on the edge, and pulls me into his lap. Cupping my cheek, he angles my face until our eyes meet.

"Are you serious about your offer?" I ask. "About the home health aide?"

At this point, I need to do whatever it takes to keep Mama safe and healthy, especially if my father's about to jump ship ... or worse.

"I mean, technically it expired," he says with a satisfied smugness in his words. "But I'm willing to give you *one* extension ..."

I lift my hand to his face, brushing his messy hair from

his sun-kissed forehead before tracing the two metal barbells in his eyebrow. Everything about him is hard and soft at the same time. Warm skin, soft embrace, cold gaze. Trust fund baby who looks like he grew up on the wrong side of the tracks. A man with every ability to devour me, but who has been nothing but patient and gentle.

Even if his offer weren't on the table, I'd still go through with this because at the end of the day *I* want this.

My father would be destroyed if he knew what I was about to do, but August has only ever been off limits to me because of a past that has nothing to do with either of us. And I refuse to be held accountable for my father's actions from here on out.

I'm a Rose.

But I'm my own Rose.

And tonight, I'm taking back my power.

I don't care if this breaks my father because as far as I'm concerned ... he no longer deserves my unwavering trust and loyalty.

"You seem torn," he says.

I blow a strand of hair from my face. "What gives you that impression?"

"You're a good daughter," he says. "But your father's a dick. He doesn't deserve what he has. And deep down, he probably knows it."

I nod, swallowing the painful lump in my throat. August is right.

"Doing that to your mom ... while she's sick and help-less? What kind of piece of shit does that?" His face twists. "And everything you've sacrificed ... it's messed up, Rose girl."

I cup his cheek and bask in this unexpected sympathy. "You can call me Sheridan, you know."

I don't think he realized he called me "Sher" earlier.

"I like Rose girl," he says. "It suits you. Makes me think of roses ... beautiful from afar but covered in thorns, like some kind of warning to stay away."

"Clearly the thorns didn't deter you ..."

"They did for the longest time." He grazes my lower lip with his thumb, and my stomach somersaults. I wait for him to kiss me. He doesn't make a move. It's almost as if he wants to savor this moment, make it last forever because it'll never happen again.

"Have you ever gone by anything besides August?"

His mouth forms a hard line. "My mom called me AJ when I was a baby—short for August John. After she died, my father thought it was too cutesy or some shit. Made me go by August. It was his great grandfather's name and he thought we needed to honor him properly."

I can't picture him as an AJ. It's too sweet. Too relaxed. It isn't intense enough for a man like him.

"I like August. It's different. And it suits you." I smile, studying his angled features in the dark of his room. Moonlight from the open window trails in on a path that illuminates the floor by the bed. "Plus, August is the hottest month of the year. And I met you on the hottest night on Meredith Hills record. Also, you're pretty hot yourself. It all works."

I'm flirting—or trying to anyway. I don't know. I'm terrible at it and likely making a fool of myself, but I don't care. I'm comfortable and it's keeping me from fixating on sadder things right now.

His mouth lifts on one side. "You think I'm hot? Thought I wasn't your type."

"You're not. But it doesn't mean I can't be attracted to you."

His hands slide to my waist. "So you're attracted to me."

"Pretty sure the entire Meredith Hills female population is attracted to you ..."

He traces the side of my jaw before trailing down my neck, and without warning he leans in to press a kiss against my pulse point. He sucks the flesh, softly, and grazes his teeth against it. My eyes roll to the back of my head, and I lose my fingers in his hair as he moves to the spot beneath my ear.

He moans as he tastes my skin, his tongue dragging small circles against tender spots.

I'm going to be covered in marks tomorrow ...

"Your heart's beating a hundred miles an hour," he says. "Are you scared?"

"No." I breathe him in, his spice and leather scent intoxicating my senses. "I'm excited."

Bringing his mouth to mine, he crushes my lips with a kiss. "Good."

His fingers trail along the hem of my t-shirt, and he grazes them against my caved stomach, teasing before pulling it over my head. He moves for the satin straps of my lace bra next, sliding them down my shoulders before leaving a trail of kisses in their place.

Unfastening my bra with a single flick, he tosses it into the dark void behind him. A light chill blankets my bare flesh, along with a spray of goose bumps.

"God, you're so fucking beautiful." His words are hot against my flesh as he slides his palms down my sides and grasps my hips.

With one fluid move, he rolls me to my back and hovers above me. Slipping my breasts from their lacy cups, he tongues my nipples, sucking until they're painfully pert, before trailing down my stomach and stopping at the top of my jean shorts. One yank and the button gives. A single tug and the zipper is next. He slides them down my hips leaving my panties in place.

Separating my thighs, he lowers himself between them, sucking on my mound through my panties. My sex pulses, throbs. Aches for him. After a minute of teasing torture, he slides the gusset aside and runs the tip of his tongue down my seam before returning to circle my clit.

Everything tingles.

I don't want to come yet.

I clench my middle, fighting the wave my body so badly wants to surf.

He slips a finger inside me, and another, curling them just enough that I lose it. I freaking lose it. I can't fight this any longer. I grind against him as he sucks and thrusts his fingers in perfect rhythm, and within seconds my pussy spasms from the inside, like a deep kind of orgasm I never knew was possible.

Holy shit.

"And that, Rose girl, was your G-spot ..." A proud smirk shades his full wet mouth. But to be fair, he earned it.

He rises, leaving me to catch my breath. The clink of his belt buckle fills the dark room. That was an appetizer. A preview of what's to come. We're only getting started.

My clit aches, still longing for a piece of the action.

Gathering myself, I sit up as he approaches the bed in nothing but boxers, and I run my fingers down his chiseled abs, stopping to admire the V that points to his rising bulge. Tugging the fabric down, I free his cock and take it in my hand. His girth overflows in my palm, and I stroke his length with slow, gentle movements until bringing my mouth to the tip. Tasting the salty bead of pre-cum, I circle my tongue against his head. August moans, gripping a fistful of my hair in his hand as I swallow him inch by inch.

The harder he gets, the more my sex throbs in response.

Sliding from my mouth, he makes his way to his nightstand, returning with a shiny gold packet, which he tosses on the mattress beside me. Kneeling, he spreads my thighs before ripping my panties off.

I gasp.

"Sorry, Rose girl," he says with a smirk as he slips his tongue into my wet folds again. My clit swells, tingling back to life, and I hook my thighs over his shoulders until his face is buried.

August devours me, unrelenting, not so much as coming up for a breath. With fierce and deliberate possession, he drinks my arousal until my body quivers with the threat of euphoria all over again.

"Don't fight it, Rose girl," he whispers against my sex. "Let go ..."

Sinking into the mattress, I take a deep breath and release the tension in my body until I'm warm and pliable, dissolving into a sweet surrender.

Licking, sucking, and lapping, he coaxes me to another climax so powerful it should be labeled a narcotic. Molten waves of pleasure undulate through my body as it writhes and rocks. August doesn't stop. He continues until he's pulled every last ounce of pent-up orgasm from me.

My clit is swollen and pleasurably sore when he's done. Our eyes catch in the dark, and his glint with satisfaction.

"Think you can keep going?" he teases.

He crawls next to me, propped on his elbow as his gaze scans my naked length. Tracing the outline of my breasts with a single fingertip, he draws an invisible line down the center of my stomach, through the middle of my left thigh, then along my damp slit before finishing at my mouth.

"Have you ever tasted yourself?" he asks.

"Never …"

Just when I think he's about to slip his finger between my lips, he brings them to his own and tastes my arousal. "You're really fucking sweet. In case you want to know."

Before I can respond, his mouth fuses to mine, and suddenly I'm pinned beneath him, tasting my sweetness. It's a power move. His tongue finds mine, turning our kiss into a molten liquid that drips straight through my center like warm honey.

Positioning himself on his knees, he spreads my thighs wider, taking in the view, before reaching for the foil packet and ripping it between his teeth.

My heart stops. I hold my breath. Squeeze my eyes.

"Look at me, Rose girl," he says under his breath. When I open my eyes, he's rolling the rubber over his veined erection. Leaning over me, he sweeps my hair from my face, deposits a hard kiss, and studies my face for a single endless moment. "This is going to hurt … but then it'll feel good for you. I promise. So fucking good."

Biting my swollen lip, I nod.

Positioning his cock at my entrance, he slides in the tip. It burns for a flash of a second, but I breathe through it.

"Oh, god …" He sighs, breathless, as he struggles to plunge his thickness into me.

I wriggle beneath him, a wordless urge for him to keep going, but he inserts another teasing inch, then another. And then, with one unexpected thrust, he's deep inside of me. I bury my face in his shoulder, bearing the shooting pain in silence as his girth stretches me.

I feel him.

I feel him *all*.

Running my palms along his lower back, his taut steel muscles undulate beneath me as he drives himself into me harder, faster.

The initial shock of pain is long gone, replaced with slick heat and fiery ache that can only be extinguished by one thing ...

In this cocoon beneath him, I gaze up at him, cupping his face as my hips answer his, thrust by thrust. It's like we fit together perfectly. The way our bodies match up. And perhaps I'm getting ahead of myself, but maybe this doesn't have to be a one-time thing?

I lift my lips closer to his, a silent plea for a kiss, but he turns his face.

Weird ...

He fucks me deeper, harder. His skin slapping against mine. I give him the benefit of the doubt. He's a guy. This was a fantasy of his. He's just really into it ...

His long hair hangs in his face, partially obscuring his expression. I brush it aside and find his eyes closed tight. Cupping his cheek, I try to angle his face towards mine again, but instead he pulls out of me completely and flips me to my stomach.

Lifting my hips until I'm on all fours, he spreads my thighs and plunges into me from behind. Leaning over me, he grips a handful of hair and presses the side of my face into the pillow as he fucks me like a dog. Cold, mechanical, animalistic.

For whatever reason, the tenderness is gone.

The euphoric magic has faded into nothingness—as if someone snapped their fingers and made it disappear without any warning.

I remind myself this was never about tenderness in the first place—it was, is, and has only ever been about sex.

Hooking a hand around the front of my thighs, he rubs my clit while he continues to take me from behind. My body responds, growing hotter by the second, the tension building all over again. I'm getting close—and judging by the restrained grunts coming from behind me, so is he.

Little tremors turn into euphoric waves as he fucks me through my next orgasm, and the second I'm finished, he pulls out of me, snaps the rubber off, and cums all over the small of my back. Long, hot spurts.

When he's finished, I lie on my stomach in this strange, euphoric aftermath, and he disappears into his *en suite* bathroom to clean up. When he returns, he says nothing. He simply changes into clean boxers and collapses on his bed, his forearm hooked over his eyes.

I slip into his bathroom to clean up, washing his drying, sticky seed off my back with a warm washcloth.

The tiniest trickle of blood slides down my inner thigh —my innocence leaving my body forever.

I clean that too.

When I emerge, he's out cold.

I find my clothes and get dressed quietly so as not to wake him. Before I leave, I scribble a note on a slip of paper and leave it on the pillow beside him as I fight a threat of tears and the cruel words circling my mind, mocking me for thinking for a split second we had something real, that he was different.

He's not worth the anguish.

He got what he wanted, now so will I.

CHAPTER TWENTY-ONE

THE OTHER SIDE of the bed is cold when I wake. There's no indentation in the pillow indicating she stayed the night—only a slip of paper with something scribbled on the front.

CENTURION NURSING AND HOME HEALTH SERVICES 555-3389

I crumple the paper and toss it aside. I hadn't had a chance to tell her yet, but I'd already aligned a home health worker through the same agency, which is supposedly the best in town. I requested their top nurse. And even threw in a bonus if they could start first thing Monday.

It was going to be a surprise, a show of good faith since our little arrangement was taking so long. I thought it'd help things along. But last night when she came over, we went from talking about her father's alleged affair with her childhood babysitter to fucking and there wasn't much time for anything else.

Either way, it's done.

I will forever own the priceless honor of having tainted and deflowered Rich Rose's precious daughter, and she can run off to college not having to worry about her mom.

Shuffling to the bathroom, I splash cold water on my face and brush up. The man staring back at me from the mirror doesn't wear the smug satisfaction I thought he would after completing this mission.

I took things slow with Sheridan last night—for her sake. At least in the beginning. I didn't want to scare her away with any ridiculous porn star positions, nor did I want to fuck her like some dead fish sex doll. That wouldn't have been enjoyable for either of us.

Her body was warm and pliable in my hands, willing to do anything I wanted, eager to please and be pleased. But somewhere along the line, I realized I was enjoying it ... in a different way. It's like someone flipped a switch, and I was no longer fantasizing about avenging our family's legacy—I was picturing the two of us *together*.

And not just fucking.

In my head, we were going to the movies, ambling around the mall hand in hand, taking weekend getaways ... normal couple shit.

So I fucked her harder, as if each time I filled her to the hilt it would jostle one of those ridiculous thoughts from my head. But it didn't work. All I could focus on was how natural it felt to be with her and how soon I'd be able to see her again. Bullshit lovesick nonsense.

None of it made sense—and the obsessive fantasizing refused to stop.

So when she lifted a tender palm to my face and tried to kiss me like that moment meant something, I lost it.

That's when I flipped her to her stomach and took her

from behind, pressing her face against the pillow so I didn't have to look at those radiant, hopeful, innocent blue eyes. Eyes that should belong to a white-collar nobody with aspirations of buying a cookie cutter house in the suburbs and starting a family with her so they can line their walls with perfect portraits of their two-point-five kids—not a spoiled rich kid with a heart of coal..

In a flash of a moment, I imagine Sheridan as a wife and mother. Doting. Kindhearted. Loving and loyal. I picture her mending scraped knees, reading bedtime stories, checking for fevers, and wiping tears.

My chest burns, swelling with ancient emotions that I force into the depths of my soul where they belong. And the voice that reminds me no one has ever shed a tear over me or worried about me or given two shits about me—I tell it to shut the fuck up.

Even if we weren't who we are, even if we didn't share tangled pasts, even if the universe hadn't conspired to keep us apart our entire lives—I'd still be the wrong guy for her.

At the end of the day, she deserves a man who can love her. And because you can't give something you've never received ... that man will never be me.

CHAPTER TWENTY-TWO

Sheridan

"DO you remember that babysitter we had way back when? Kara something?" I ask Dad over dinner the next day.

He doesn't flinch. Doesn't blink. Doesn't react.

"Ah, yes. Kara Tindall," Mom says. She perks up in her chair. "I remember her well. Very sweet girl. A little misdirected, I think. But very kind."

"Wonder what she's up to these days?" I ask.

Dad takes a drink of ice water before forking a chunk of pot roast. "Last I heard, she was practicing law downtown."

"Oh, you're kidding me." Mom sounds a little too delighted, which breaks my heart. "Good for her. You know, I was worried about her for a while. She always seemed so lost. She wanted to be a part of our family so badly. Her home life wasn't the greatest."

My father nods. "The odds were definitely stacked against her."

"We should reach out to her," I say. "Maybe have her over for dinner sometime? Catch up a bit?"

Dad shoots me a curious look. "Where's this coming from, kiddo? You haven't mentioned her name in a decade and now you want to have her over for dinner?"

He chuckles, shaking his head like he finds this amusing.

I lift a shoulder. "Guess I just ... randomly started thinking about her the other day."

I'm lying to a liar. Oh, the irony. At least this time I don't feel bad about it.

The tension between us is ripe.

Mom doesn't notice.

"Is that so?" He's playing dumb.

"Maybe I saw her face on a billboard or something." I keep my attention trained on him, searching for a nuanced expression or twitch of his brow, something to show he's uncomfortable.

But I get nothing.

Is this a skill he's honed over the years? Is this not the first time he's lived some sort of double life?

I shove my food around my plate, willing myself to take a bite. But I can't. My stomach is rock hard and my appetite is gone.

"Thanks for dinner, Mama." I rise and kiss her forehead before taking my plate to the sink. She doesn't often cook. Usually it's frozen pizza or something easy enough to throw together without much effort, but once a week she scrounges up enough stamina to prepare a Crock Pot meal. I hate that I couldn't finish it.

I hole up in my room and check my phone to find a handful of miscellaneous texts from Adriana ... and one from August.

It's been a couple of days since we had sex. And while I left that slip of paper by his pillow, I haven't had the nerve to reach out to him first to follow up. I needed to put some space between us. Take some time to breathe, to process what happened.

It was all so ... perfect.

And then, for some unknown reason, he went cold.

Dragging in a breath, I tap on his message.

ENEMY DEAREST – Mona Gillespie is your home nurse. I'll forward you her contact info. She starts Monday.

I rub my eyes and read it again.

He did it.

After I didn't hear from him right away, part of me didn't think he would follow through with his promise ... part of me was convinced I'd been played.

ME: Thank you.

He follows up with a screenshot of Mona's phone number, and I stare at my screen a little longer, waiting for him to say something else.

Something more.

Then again, what is there to say?

I place my phone aside and grab a nearby magazine from a stack that Adriana gave me. Her dad works in sales for some publisher, so she gets just about every magazine she could ever want for free.

Flicking through the neon pink copy of Cosmo from three months back, I skip the articles about "How to Get Your Biggest O" and "How to Give Him a Night He'll Never Forget" and go straight for the quiz in the back titled "Is He Into You?"

Does he text you out of the blue?

Does he call you by any nicknames?

Has he tried to make a move?

Does he ask your friends about you?

Has he tried to get you alone?

Does he flirt with you?

Ten yes-or-no questions later I score a solid eight (because he's never sent me flowers or written me poetry). And according to the test writer, that's a solid, "He's definitely into you, so make your move, girlfriend. What are you waiting for?"

I sniff and toss the magazine aside.

This is a waste of time.

I don't want nor do I need him to like me.

It shouldn't matter.

And I shouldn't care.

Digging my headphones out of my nightstand, I plug them into my phone and pull up my favorite melancholy playlist because apparently I'm in a mood. It's halfway into the third song when the chime of a new text comes through.

ENEMY DEAREST: Want to come over?

CHAPTER TWENTY-THREE

AUGUST

I THOUGHT it'd be a harder sell. I really did. I'm honestly shocked she's here, which makes this moment as surreal as it is satisfying.

Pacing my room, finger combing her hair into a messy ponytail, she vents about her dad, how much she hates being lied to, and how she can't understand how he could be so two-faced to his own family.

I let her ramble on, let her get it all out so we can get on with this. My advice would do no good here anyway. I learned long ago not to go around placing expectations on people. It only sets you up for disappointment. This is the sort of lesson a person has to learn on their own.

Plus, I could've told her what a sorry excuse for a human her dad was anyway.

I've known that my entire life.

It's a shame it's taken her nearly two decades to uncover the awful truth about his sorry ass.

Without saying a word, I dip into my hidden liquor cabinet, grabbing two shot glasses and a half-empty bottle of cinnamon whiskey because I love when her mouth is both hot and sweet and this woman needs to relax if she plans to enjoy herself.

"Here," I hand her a shot. "You need this."

She hesitates before accepting it.

"Trust me. It'll take the edge off." I toss mine down. It burns, but it's a burn I've gotten used to over past couple of summers.

She coughs. Typical newbie. But she hands me the shot glass. "One more."

"You sure?" I lift a brow.

Sheridan nods toward the bottle, hands on her hips. She didn't just come here to get fucked, she came here to get fucked up—and I'm here for it.

"I've never seen you so worked up before." I pass her the new shot. "It's pretty hot ..."

She rolls her eyes, shoots the whiskey, and yanks her t-shirt over her head.

"Oh, so we're doing this?" I tease. "This girl doesn't want to mess around."

"So we're clear," she says. "I think you're an asshole. But you're really good in bed and that's the *only* reason I'm here."

"You don't have to explain yourself." I already know ...

Moving in, she grabs me by the waist of my jeans and pulls me close before undoing the fly and shoving them down. A second later, she's on her knees, my cock growing inside her mouth as she swallows my length.

"Good god, woman." I moan as she sucks harder. "I don't know what I did to deserve this, but I'll fucking take it."

I let her take me to the edge before pulling out, and then I lead her to my bed. "As hot as that was, I very much prefer to be in control. Take off the rest of your clothes."

Eyes locked on mine, she slides off her lace bra before shoving her leggings and panties down her long legs. Tossing them aside, she moves to the center of my king-sized bed and waits.

Yanking off my t-shirt and dropping it to the floor, I grab a rubber from my nightstand.

"Spread your legs," I say.

She leans back, exposing herself, but it's not enough.

"More." I rip the foil packet with my teeth. "Show me how much you want this."

The soft-sweet scent of her arousal fills the air, mixing with a hint of her perfume. Positioning myself between her thighs, I run the tip of my tongue down her seam before kissing her clit.

"My god, you're so wet," I whisper, blowing a warm breath on her pussy before giving it another lick. "You want me to fuck you?"

She squirms, biting her lower lip, and nodding.

Sliding the rubber down my shaft, I tease her pussy with my tip, pressing against her just enough to leave her in aching anticipation.

Sheridan moans, and I silence her with a kiss. "You have to keep it down."

We don't have the house to ourselves tonight. It's late, and while the odds are my father is passed out cold from his nightly Scotch, I don't want to risk any unnecessary interruptions.

Shoving my cock inside her, I fill her to the hilt. She exhales, her entire body releasing one concerted shiver. Plunging inside her again and again, I tease her mouth with mine. With her head buried against my shoulder, she stifles a moan as I drive harder, deeper into her.

"Don't stop," she whispers.

So I don't.

I fuck her until we both come, her hips writhing desperately beneath me as my balls tighten and empty.

When it's over, we lie tangled in the sticky, sweaty mess we've created, breathless and speechless.

She gets up first, ducking into my bathroom to clean up. And when she emerges, she wastes no time getting dressed.

I don't think I've ever felt used in my entire life —until now.

"You don't have to leave yet." I mourn her curves as they disappear behind her t-shirt and leggings.

"I have to get home before my parents notice I'm gone." She steps into her sandals.

"You're an adult, what are they going to do?"

"They will literally send out a search party if they can't find me." She rolls her eyes. "And if they see my car here, trust me, it won't be good ..."

Yeah. It won't be good for *them*.

My father is untouchable. No one's ever successfully retaliated against him in any way. The Roses have nothing on him.

"You can park in one of our garage stalls," I say. We have eight and one just so happens to be empty as my father is having his Rolls serviced.

"Ha. Then what? We throw on a movie and pop some popcorn and hang for the night? Let's not pretend this is something it isn't. You called. I *came*. We both got what we wanted."

"Did you? Did you get what you wanted?"

Her gaze snaps toward the bed. "Yep."

"Are you still upset about your dad?"

She slinks her purse over her shoulder, head tilted as an incredulous half-smile paints her lips. "You don't have to do this."

"Do what?"

"Pretend you care." Folding her arms, she adds, "You made it perfectly clearly the other night that you don't. And not that I expect you to. But at least do me the courtesy of not pretending."

God damn it.

She's right.

If she only knew how fucked up my thoughts were. How they can turn on a dime. How easily I can talk myself out of things. How badly I need to resist whatever the hell is brewing between us.

This was never meant to be anything—but there's something stirring deep inside me. A sensation in the center of my chest every time she walks in the room. It's equally exhilarating and terrifying, and that's saying a lot because there isn't much that scares me.

"I'm sorry."

Her brows lift. "For what?"

"For kissing you like you meant something to me," I say. "And for fucking you like you didn't."

Her jaw hangs. Think it's safe to say she wasn't expecting me to be so blunt.

"It was definitely a dick move," she finally speaks. "But I'm over it. Maybe if I liked you, I'd be more upset."

Burn.

"But why did you do that anyway?" Her gaze tightens. "It was weird. You were so sweet and then ..."

The truth is between me, myself, and I.

And that's how it's going to stay.

"I could give you a million excuses," I say. "But at the end of the day, I'm just as fucked up as everyone. Nobody's perfect. Not me. Not your dad. Not even your mom. You've got to stop idealizing everyone. That's how you get hurt."

"You're side-stepping my question."

"I was caught up in the moment," I say, which isn't a complete lie. "You have to admit, it was really fucking hot."

Clearing her throat, she straightens her shoulders and fights a grin. "Yeah. It was all right."

I deserve that.

"You should stay though," I say. "You had a couple shots of Fireball. I don't think you should drive home yet. Give it a little more time to wear off."

Her shoulders fall and her attention moves to the floor. A moment later, she lets her bag slide down her arm and takes a seat at the foot of my bed.

"Just for a little while," she says, spoken like a true good girl.

"Now don't go thinking that I care about you all of a sudden," I tease, nudging her with my foot. "I'd just hate for you to get hurt on the way home. It'd ignite our family feud all over again."

She turns back to me, smirking. "Was it ever extinguished?"

"Probably not." I climb off the bed and slip into my boxers and jeans, and then I grab a couple of waters from the mini fridge. "What all do you know, anyway? About what happened? What kinds of things have your parents said about my family over the years?"

"You really want to know?"

I hand her a bottle and uncap mine. "I wouldn't ask if I didn't."

"Most of what I know comes from the articles printed in the paper," she says. "Everything else … was kept pretty quiet. My parents never talked about the past much. They only ever said enough to make it clear that I was to stay away from your family at all costs."

I sniff. "You make us sound like the mafia."

"That's basically what you are in this town," she says. "Your family has connections everywhere you turn. And everyone's afraid of your dad. There are rumors. I'm sure you've heard them all."

I nod. "Every last one."

And I never bothered to set a single record straight, though most of them were true.

It's probably why no one so much as dared to fuck with me in high school. They were scared shitless, and their parents were scared shitless. Anyone in this town would be a damned fool to try to cross my father.

How Rich Rose got away with it not once, but twice, is a real life miracle.

I'd never tell Sheridan this, but as long as my dad has a fighting breath in him, her father's living on borrowed time. I'm convinced he hasn't offed him yet because he gets off on torturing him from afar. Making sure he can't hold down a job. Tarnishing his name all over town. Sometimes it's the little things that make the biggest impact, he always tells me.

"Why's your room so generic?" She changes the subject. "You don't have any pictures, any ribbons or trophies."

"I don't need reminders of things that have already happened." They live in my head enough as it is … "And I don't really get attached to things."

Or people.

Especially not people.

"Let me guess, your room is filled with mementos. On your bed is the quilt your grandmother made. And you've got a small desk with a bulletin board covered with participation ribbons and awards that will be meaningless to you in five years. Maybe a handful of photographs in mismatched frames ..."

"Geez. It's like you've been in my room or something."

"Really?"

Sheridan shakes her head and takes a sip of water. "I have a bedspread, not a quilt. Bought from a thrift shop. And I don't have a desk because there's not enough space to fit a bed and a dresser in my room. I do have a lot of pictures, but not as many as you probably think. And all of my meaningless awards are kept in a plastic box on the top shelf of my closet."

"Close enough."

She shrugs, and then she places her water on the floor, fixes her ponytail, and checks the time. I can't let her leave yet. It isn't safe.

"Out of all the pools that night, why'd you pick mine?" I ask to stall her. Plus, I'm curious. "There must be hundreds of pools in this town."

"Easy," she says. "Yours is placed farther away from the house. Everyone else's pools are basically right off their back patios. I guess I thought no one would see me if I took a swim in yours ..."

Smart.

"Why'd you break that beer bottle?" she asks, her turn.

"I was angry."

"Because I snuck in?"

"Because you ran from me when I was talking to you," I say. "I knew exactly who you were the second I saw your face. And when you took off, you were just another Rose who disrespected a Monreaux and had the audacity to avoid the consequences."

My jaw sets the way it did that night.

But I don't want to be angry. I'm too fucking spent.

Rising, she gathers her things and saunters my way. "Pretty sure I've paid my penance now though. Don't you think?"

Her sweet scent invades my lungs, and her mouth is so close I could kiss her.

"We should do this more often," I say. "Maybe make it a regular thing ..."

Her glassy eyes search mine. "I leave for school at the end of the month."

"Same."

We remain motionless in a thick silence, the space between us heavy with things neither of us are saying.

"As long as we're on the same page," she says after a minute of quiet contemplation. "It's just hooking up."

"I wouldn't dream of anything more." My chest tightens because I'm a lying bastard. I dreamt of her last night, and the night before. And there are daydreams too. I'll be going about my day and suddenly catch myself thinking about the way she tastes, the way her body fits perfectly with mine, the sweet scent of her hair, or that coy face she makes when she's trying not to smile at something I said.

Fuck.

Fuck, fuck, fuck.

"Rose girl," I say.

"Yeah?"

I hook my hands around the small of her waist and pull her against me. "I don't think you should leave yet."

She frowns. "I can't stay all night ..."

"You shouldn't drive yet. It hasn't been long enough."

She begins to protest, but I crush her petal-soft lips with mine. "Get back in bed. I'll make it worth your while."

CHAPTER TWENTY-FOUR

Sheridan

"YOU KNOW it's the strangest thing, I got up in the middle of the night last night to use the bathroom and the back door was wide open," Mom says the next morning. "Then I checked on you and you were sound asleep. About scared me to death."

Shit. I must have not latched it when I came home. The lock is loud, and I didn't want to make too much noise. I thought I got it, but apparently not. I'll have to be more careful next time—and there *will* be a next time because August and I are ... hooking up now.

The sweet ache between my legs pulses, but I tamp down my ill-timed excitement.

Mom sips her coffee and cinches her terrycloth robe, gazing out the window above the kitchen sink like she might spot some kind of evidence in the back yard.

"So guess what?" I change the topic. "I just found out you were selected for that home nurse program."

She turns to me, eyes wide with a grin so big it nearly stretches to her ears. "What?! Sweetheart, that's amazing." But in a flash, her expression darkens. "Are you sure it's not some kind of scam? Why would they pick *me*?"

"I don't know. Maybe they liked the essay I wrote?" I die a little on the inside every time I lie to her. But this is for a good cause. "Anyway, your nurse is Mona and she starts Monday. I'll train her and everything the first few days. And by the time I'm off at school, she should have everything down."

"Does your father know?"

"Not yet." I didn't want to say anything in case my arrangement didn't pan out.

Her mouth twists at one side. "You know how he is about being left out of big decisions like that ..."

"How could he say no to this? It's going to make his life easier. And yours. And mine."

"This is true ..." She lifts her mug to her lips but doesn't take a drink. "It's going to be an adjustment for all of us."

"But it's for the best," I remind her.

"Absolutely."

"By the way, I'm staying at Adri's this Friday night." I have no idea if or when I'll see August again, but I figure I should plant the seed now so she knows I might be gone.

"What are you girls going to do without each other in a couple of weeks?"

My mind wanders to August before it goes to Adriana.

"We're just taking things one day at a time."

"Will she come visit you at school?" Mama asks.

August's sexy smirk fills my head.

"I don't expect that, no." My answer applies to both of them. Adri might come up and convince me to find some frat party to crash, but she's got her own life back here. I don't expect her to drive two hours to see me on a regular basis. That's what FaceTime is for.

"Well then you'll see each other on breaks," Mama says.

"Yeah ... I'm sure we will."

"I can just tell she's going to be one of those lifelong friends, you know? The ones who are there for you through it all. You're getting your color back, you know. You're sleeping better these days. And your eyes sparkle again. If I didn't know any better, I'd think you were falling in love with someone." Mama chuckles.

Oh, god.

There's no way ...

I'm not falling in love with August—I barely know him.

My stomach somersaults in protest.

It's lust. Hardcore lust. We have insane physical chemistry and he's a distraction and release for me—that's all.

"Speaking of Adriana, I should get ready for work." I kiss Mama's cheek and trek to my room. Plucking my phone off the charger, I find a text waiting for me.

ENEMY DEAREST—Tonight?

ME—I can't. How about Friday?

ENEMY DEAREST—I don't know if I can wait that long ...

ME—You're going to have to. I can't keep sneaking out like this.

ENEMY DEAREST—Then I'll come to you.

ME—You're insane. I'll see you Friday.

I catch my reflection in my dresser mirror—big, old, dopey grin and eyes lit like fireworks.

This isn't love. Not even close. But I *kind of* worry that it *might* be something ...

I just don't know what that something is yet—or if I can

tamp it down before it turns into something bigger than the two of us.

CHAPTER TWENTY-FIVE

AUGUST

IT'S HALF-PAST midnight when I park a block away from Sheridan's house. Jogging up the sidewalk, I shoot her a message.

ME—Which window is yours?

ROSE GIRL—What?

ME—I'm outside your house. I told you I was coming over tonight.

ROSE GIRL—Omfg. You're lying.

Her little blue Nissan is parked in front of her family's bungalow.

She's home.

ME—Is it the one with the flower curtains? And the lamp light on?

ROSE GIRL—My parents are home ...

ME—Are they sleeping?

ROSE GIRL—Yes, but that's not the point. You literally. Can. Not. Be. Here.

I rap on her window, light but audible enough. A second later the curtains fly open and she slides the lower portion up.

"What the hell are you doing here?" she yell-whispers.

"I told you—I can't wait until Friday."

"You have to go home." She keeps her voice low, turning back to check the door.

"Help me up." I climb up the siding. To my surprise, she pops out the torn screen, grabs onto my arms, and pulls me into her room, which is exactly the way she described it last night, only she neglected to mention the unicorn snow globe on her nightstand.

"You're truly insane. You know that, right? One hundred percent. Certifiable." She crosses her arms. "I cannot believe you're here right now."

I silence her with a kiss.

"Shh," I remind her. Capturing her wrist, I lead her to the bed, but she resists.

"No," she says, "it's too loud."

Fine. Floor sex it is.

I crush her lips with mine and part them with my tongue, tasting her spearmint toothpaste and soaking in the heat from her body. A minute later we're on the floor, Sheridan grinding on my lap as I slide her pajama bottoms aside and she impales herself onto me. With every slow, intentional roll of her hips, she brings us closer to the edge. And when she's almost there, she buries her face in my shoulder and rocks against me so hard the lamp on her nightstand shakes.

Quick and dirty, we finish in record time—for me personally—and she walks me to the window.

Her cheeks are flushed orgasm pink. For a second, the image of some drunk college douche trying to jam his pencil dick into her comes to mind, and a flash of heat crawls up my neck. In a couple of weeks, she'll be free game. A pretty little freshman like her, with those perfect tits and those baby blue eyes would be ripe for the picking. She wouldn't last two seconds at Bexler. The assholes I know would be stag-fighting for first dibs.

She deserves better than that.

She doesn't deserve to be objectified—which is also why I've recently deleted the security videos from our trysts in my bedroom. And from here on out, I'll disable the cam when she's over. What happens between us, stays between us.

"August, you have to go." She nods toward the window. "Seriously, don't do this again, okay?"

Yeah, it was a crazy move—but I couldn't get her out of my head all day, waiting until the weekend was out of the question, and there was nothing else to do.

I hoist myself out the window and land on my feet. Sheridan leans her head out, her messy hair falling down her shoulders and spilling into her cleavage.

"Friday," she says. "Your place."

I scoff. As if I need the reminder.

A minute later, I drive to my side of town, drowning out my cacophony of obsessive thoughts with some random MUNRO album I have on my phone. I crank the volume until the music echoes inside me, through me, and all over me—like I'm made of hollow glass.

Halfway into the next song, I slam on the brakes—this isn't a hollowness I'm feeling ... it's a *fullness*.

I don't know what that means, but it isn't anything I've ever felt before with anyone else ... and it can't be good.

CHAPTER TWENTY-SIX

Sheridan

I ROLL to the empty side of the bed Friday night, fresh off of orgasm number three. He promised me no less than five, but we've been going at this since I stepped foot inside his bedroom, and I'm honestly exhausted.

"You want to take a break?" he asks, grabbing some waters.

I steal a glimpse of his naked backside when he isn't looking. He's got a body built for pleasure and sin, but I've never really taken the time to fully appreciate his chiseled abs or the way his muscles dip in the small of his back just above his perfect ass.

"Yes," I say.

Grabbing a remote, he points to a painting on the wall— which I'm now realizing was a TV all this time—and powers on Netflix. Sliding into bed next to me, he props a pillow behind his back and tells me to pick something.

It's strange how comfortable this is, how natural it feels to be with him.

Inside these walls, we're not a Rose and a Monreaux. We're two adults who happen to enjoy one another's company for reasons even we can't explain. Although I hardly know him, when we're together, I'm as comfortable with him as I am someone I've known my entire life. It's strange. And makes zero sense. But I can't deny it. And believe me, I've tried.

I force the thoughts away and focus on the menu.

No point in entertaining what could have been ... what will never be.

We're only hooking up. We both leave for college in a couple of weeks. Being together openly would have a myriad of consequences for both of us. His dad would disown him. My mother would be heartbroken. My father would be devastated—though he's honestly the least of my concerns right now.

I choose a featured documentary about an octopus and hit 'play.'

Nudging closer, August rests his hand on my bare thigh, his fingertips tracing the inside of my leg. The show is a little less than exciting, but I was trying to choose something neutral, something we could both enjoy.

"Trying to warm me up for round four?" I ask as he cups my cheek and steals a kiss.

It's three AM. We haven't slept a wink. At this rate, we won't be sleeping at all. And I'm supposed to be at work in nine hours ...

"Just getting as much of you as possible, while I can." He takes me by the wrist and guides me into his lap. His palms skim my thighs before he grabs my ass. His hardness grows between my thighs, his hot flesh against mine. One careless move and he'd be inside me sans condom, and we're not *there* yet.

I'm not trying to have a Monreaux baby ...

"You'd think the world was ending, the way we're going at it ..." I brush a messy wave from his perfect face. Our eyes rest in some intimate, otherworldly place, but I convince myself I'm reading into nothing, and I break the gaze.

I force myself to imagine him at Bexler this fall, which I hear is basically an all-you-can-eat buffet of beautiful co-eds. It's said that "all the pretty girls go to Bexler." I overheard someone in my French class saying that Bexler is the school where most women leave with a degree they'll never use and a guaranteed future as a trophy wife.

That'll be August someday. He'll marry a beautiful woman, provide her with endless orgasms and a lifetime of security—and I'm okay with that. Because I have to be.

Even if it breaks my heart a little ...

August leans close, kissing my collarbone before working his way down my shoulder—until my stomach rumbles.

He stops. "Are you hungry?"

"Yeah, a little." I'm *starving*.

A second later he digs in a dresser drawer. "Here, wear this."

He hands me a t-shirt, which I tug over my head. And he changes into a pair of silk pajama bottoms.

The hallway is pitch black, nothing but dimmed sconces on the walls every few feet. When we get to the top of the stairs, he takes my hand, and my heart does the tiniest flip.

A minute later we're in the kitchen.

"Have a seat." He points me to a bar stool as he rummages through the fridge.

A turkey sandwich, some fresh pineapple, and a few Red Vines later, my stomach no longer rumbles. As we head back to his room, I taste remnants of licorice in my teeth, savoring the remaining sweetness. From this day forward, I'll probably always associate red licorice with August.

"August."

We're halfway to the second level when a male voice cuts through the quiet darkness.

I suck in a breath, clutching my chest.

Standing at the base of the stairs is a man who resembles a slightly older, cleaner-cut, darker-haired, darker-eyed version of August. It definitely isn't Soren. I've seen his image on enough billboards and watched him perform on enough late night talk shows to have it memorized.

"I thought you were in Philly for work?" August says.

"Who the hell is this?" The man ignores August's comment, drinking me in from head to toe in a way that makes me squirm. Squinting, he studies my face, like he's trying to place me. "You realize the minute you're gone, there'll be ten more in your place. Just like you."

"The fuck is wrong with you?" August takes a step toward him, wedging between the two of us.

"Just in case she was feeling special for a second," the man says to him. "Didn't want to get her hopes up. You have a habit of doing that to people. Making promises you can't keep."

"You really need to shut the fuck up right now." August grinds his words between his teeth and takes another step closer to the man, but I hook my hand into his elbow and keep him from doing something crazy.

"It's okay," I whisper.

The two of them stay in a stare off for what feels like forever, before August turns and leads me upstairs, his hand clenching mine though I don't think he realizes it.

"He's not fucking worth it," he says under his breath. I don't know if he's speaking to me—or to himself.

"Who was that?" I ask.

"Gannon."

"And does he always talk to you that way?" We're seated on his bed now.

"Our relationship has always been ... *special*." His shoulders rise and fall, muscles flexing with each breath. "But trust me, I give it to him twice as good."

Sitting on the bed behind him, I rub his shoulders. "He seems like a prick."

August chuffs. "Just forget what he said, all right? He was just making shit up to make you feel bad and to get to me. That's what he does. The bastard gets off on that shit."

"I mean ... it's not like we're dating. You're allowed to be with other people. I don't have any kind of claim to you ..."

He exhales. "Yeah."

We sit in profuse silence for a moment, an almost painful sort of quiet. For all I know he's conjuring up all sorts of uncomfortable memories in that mysterious head of his. Recollections he keeps bottled inside because he's got nowhere else to put them. I press my cheek against his back to let him know he's not alone.

The powerful strum of his heartbeat plays in my ear as I inhale his familiar scent.

I'm going to miss this.

"Have you ever pictured me with someone else?" he asks.

I sit up. He turns, angling his body toward mine.

"What do you mean?"

His mouth presses flat. "If you imagine me with another woman, how does it make you feel?"

Sinking back, I envision him with some pretty brunette with aspirations of nailing him down for life, and it doesn't feel *pleasant*. But I can't tell him that.

What would be the point? To torture ourselves?

We can't be together.

"When I think of you with another man," he says, "it feels like a sucker punch. That's the only way I can describe it. It knocks the wind out of me. I literally can't breathe."

I digest his words for a second. This is happening so fast —and his confession is beyond unexpected. I'd entertained these thoughts on my own countless times, only to pass them off as reckless daydreams and nothing more.

"What are you saying?"

He drags in a long breath, rakes his messy hair back and exhales. "I don't know. I don't know what any of this shit means. I just ... I just know it's different. Being with you. And I can't deny it. I don't know what to do with it, so I'm putting it out there."

He's rambling. And August *never* rambles.

"I know this is sudden," he continues. "But it's the realest—"

Lifting a finger to his lips, I quiet him.

"I know what you're trying to say," I tell him. "And I know what you're afraid to say—because I feel it too." I study his features in the dark, though even if my eyes were closed I'd still know them by heart. "So what do we do now? What the hell do we do?"

He answers me with a kiss, frenzied and wild, his

fingers in my hair, but I suppose it's because there is no other answer.

Our futures were written for us long before the day we met.

All we have is this moment.

CHAPTER TWENTY-SEVEN

I HAVE the unfortunate luck of running into Gannon Saturday morning after showing Sheridan out.

"Mind telling me what the fuck you were doing with Rich Rose's daughter last night?" he asks.

"Who?" I grab an orange juice carton from the fridge and drink straight from the bottle, purely because I know it pisses him off.

"Don't insult my intelligence. I saw her car. Had someone run the plates. It's registered to Rich and Mary Beth Rose."

"No shit? That girl was a Rose?" I play dumb as I take another swig. "Guess she left that out when I was asking her fifty million questions about her background before I fucked her."

"Does Dad know you're fucking Rich's daughter?"

"He doesn't. Would you mind filling him in next time you're up his ass?"

Gannon scoffs, hands on his khaki-covered hips. Who the fuck wears khakis on a Saturday morning anyway?

"What, you think he'd be proud? Rich Rose is a liability. What if he tries to have his daughter say you raped her or something?" He shakes his head. "Sometimes I really think you have shit for brains."

"Yeah, probably why I didn't get into Vanderbilt." He and I both know I never got in because I never applied. With my perfect SAT score and myriad of recommendation letters and high school accolades, I'd have been a shoo-in.

"I'm warning you, August. Stop messing around with that girl." Gannon's face is cherry-red, a surefire sign his gasket's about to blow.

Perhaps it was naïve of me to not consider the ways our little arrangement could get twisted by the wrong person. But Sheridan would never do that. She's above that shit.

"Or what? You'll *tattle on me?*" I return the tainted OJ to the fridge, and when I close the door, I'm met with Gannon's face in mine. "The fuck—"

"Good morning, boys." Clarice shuffles into the kitchen, broom in hand, impeccable timing as always.

When we were younger and Clarice was here full-time, she was constantly breaking up fights. Only one time it got physical and she wound up in the middle of it with a broken nose.

We vowed never to fight around her again—the only thing we ever agreed on.

"Morning, Clarice." I head for the stairs, only to be followed by the dipshit.

"I'm serious. Stay away from that family," Gannon says under his breath as he trails behind me.

I stop, turning back. "For once in your life, do yourself a favor and mind your own damned business."

"Her dad's a *murderer*."

"We don't know that for sure. He was exonerated," I say. I can't believe I'm defending Rich right now, but if it gets Gannon off my nut sac I'll do it.

"Oh now that you're fucking that bastard's daughter, you're willing to look the other way?"

"Hardly."

"Does Rich Rose know about you two?" He squints, his mouth formed into a devilish kink.

I can't tell him yes or no. I can't give him ammunition. While my original plan was to defile Sheridan out of spite, I actually give a shit about her now. I couldn't live with myself if I made things worse for her at home—or if Gannon stirs shit up just to get his own rocks off.

"It's really none of your business," I warn him. "And if you've got an ounce of intelligence, you'll leave it the fuck alone."

"Or what?" He laughs.

"I'll Dad you're fucking Cassandra," I say without missing a beat.

It's amazing how quickly the smugness evaporates from his face. I'm bluffing. I don't know that they're fucking, but I've seen them flirt when our father isn't looking and it always does a number on my gag reflex. But the expression on his face is enough to make me think that perhaps there's some truth to my little accusation. Or at the very least, wishful thinking.

Gross.

"You're a diabolical prick," he says.

I shrug. "Takes one to know one."

I wave Gannon off. And the asshole leaves, but not without shooting me a death look first. One that suggests he isn't through with me.

But he doesn't scare me.

The thought of losing Sheridan though? Downright fucking terrifying.

CHAPTER TWENTY-EIGHT

Sheridan

"HI, MONA, COME ON IN." I greet our new nurse Monday morning. "I'm Sheridan."

Mona wears pale yellow scrubs and carries an olive green duffel bag with a medical cross on one side and the nursing company's logo on the other. A stack of booklets and paperwork rests under one arm.

"Lovely to meet you, Sheridan." Mona offers a handshake, which is warm and soft, and she scrunches her shoulders when she smiles. Her chestnut hair is streaked with silver and she smells faintly of fabric softener and brown sugar.

I love her already.

"Mama's in the living room," I say.

She steps out of her blue Crocs and follows me to the living room, where Mama is set up in the easy chair. "You can have a seat anywhere you'd like."

Not that we've got many options. We have a sofa and a chair. And the chair's already taken.

For the hour that follows, I tell her all about Mama's needs. How they fluctuate depending on the day. Some days she doesn't need nor want help with anything, other days she can hardly get out of bed on her own. When we're done, I give her a quick tour of the house, finishing in the kitchen by the medicine cabinet.

"This is Mama's medicine schedule." I point to the list on the fridge. "I gave it to the person at your agency when we spoke on the phone the other day, but it's always here for easy reference."

"Wonderful," she says, rifling through the paperwork in her arms. "I actually have a few things for you as well. This is a magnet with our on-call and emergency information. Here's my card and a few spares in case you want to give them to friends, neighbors, or family members. Oh, and I have some paperwork that needs to be signed."

"I thought I already signed everything? A couple days ago? With the administrator?"

"Oh, this is for billing. Apparently the guarantor is a non-family member, so they wanted to have this special form on file. It's a formality." She places the sheet on the counter and hands me a pen, and I pray that Mama heard none of what she just said.

I go over the paperwork, signing on the lines and verifying that August Monreaux is responsible for any and all payments but that my family has authorized services. But when I get to the bottom, the date next to his name seems ... off.

Some quick mental math, and I realize the date shown would've been two days before we first had sex.

"What does this date mean?" I point to the bottom of the paper.

She turns it toward herself. "Oh. That's the date the contract was initiated."

"Is this correct?"

Mona's lips spread into a tender smile. "I'm quite certain, but I'm happy to double check for you."

I'm about to tell her it isn't necessary when I'm distracted by the other date—the end-of-services date.

"Does that ... does that say four years from now?" I ask.

"It sure does. It looks like your guarantor has pre-paid for forty-eight months of services."

I take a seat at the table, attempting to wrap my head around this. Forty-eight months would cover all of Mama's needs until I'm able to graduate with my bachelor's in nursing.

Not to mention he dropped well over a hundred grand on this—before I'd even slept with him.

Why didn't he tell me this?

Warmth and fullness floods my chest, filling it to an invisible brim—only to be replaced with a dark, sinking sensation that anchors me into place and steals all the beauty from this moment.

He was falling for me long before I realized it.

Maybe even before he realized it, too.

"Everything okay?" Mona places her hand over mine. "You seem a bit dazed. I know this can be a little over-whelming at first. It's a big change."

"Yeah, sorry." I force a smile. "I was just lost in thought."

"If you want to look everything over, I'll go check on your mother. If you have any questions, you just let me know, okay?"

"Perfect. And if you don't mind, please don't mention any billing matters to Mama. It wouldn't do any good for her to worry about it."

"Not a problem."

Mona heads to the living room, and a second later, their voices trail into the kitchen as they make small talk. Sliding my phone from my pocket, I snap a picture of the contract and text it to August.

ME: You're truly amazing. Just thought you should know that.

ENEMY DEAREST: So before I was crazy and insane ... but now I'm amazing? Which is it, Rose girl?

ME: You're kind of ... everything ... all rolled into one.

ENEMY DEAREST: A good thing, I hope.

If only it *weren't*—it would make it a million times easier to walk away before this explodes in our faces ... because it's only a matter of time.

Good things never last, especially when they weren't supposed to happen in the first place.

CHAPTER TWENTY-NINE

———————

AUGUST

SHERIDAN NUDGES my shoulder with hers as we walk to my car. "This feels so risky ... being out in public together."

We're in the next suburb over, a touristy antique town called Springdale. No one our age ever sets foot here and most Meredith Hills locals prefer shiny new shopping malls to mom-and-pop vintage fronts, so it seemed like the safest choice for a day together.

We found a seafood restaurant and walked around Main Street window shopping like an old married couple, something I'd never have been caught dead doing before I met this woman. We took pictures by a mermaid fountain—pictures that will never see the light of day outside of our phones—and she danced for me outside a little café that was piping Frank Sinatra from an outdoor speaker. I couldn't begin to remember what song it was either. I was too absorbed by her lightness, her contagious smile, and how the rest of the world melts away whenever we're together.

Pinning my gorgeous girl against the passenger door, I cradle her sweet face and replace the smile on her lips with a kiss.

I'm officially *that* guy.

The lust-struck asshole with the girlfriend he can't get enough of—only she's not my girlfriend. Technically, this isn't even a date. Despite establishing that we're both catching feelings, we've yet to tack on labels or make promises we can't keep.

Sheridan rises on her toes as she kisses me back, slipping her arms over my shoulders.

I don't make habits out of wishing for things I can't have, but what I wouldn't give to live in this moment, with her, forever.

An endless loop.

Until she came into my life, I never thought twice about the future. Never worried about the kind of man I wanted to be someday. Certainly never cared about giving back or making a difference in anyone else's life besides my own. But Sheridan makes me think about the future, where I'm headed and where I want to go. She's given me something to look forward to when before I had nothing—and no one. This woman is pure love and hope and radiance—outshining the darkness that has haunted me my entire life.

I can't go back to that.

I'll fucking die.

I'll waste away on a pathetic vine of hundred dollar bills and sports cars and meaningless sex with strangers and for the first time in my life, that sounds like some kind of fresh hell.

I want meaning and substance. I want her.

"Where you want to go now?" I unlock the car and get the door for her.

She checks her watch and winces. "I actually need to get home. Mom's having a friend over later and Dad's doing yard work ... I thought I'd corner him outside and confront him about those texts."

"I'm surprised you haven't by now."

We've talked about it here and there, and every time she either changes the subject or vomits out a lame excuse as to why she can't or why it wasn't the perfect time. I'm sure she's just scared.

Reality is fucking terrifying—especially when the truth has life-altering consequences.

"Me too." She sighs. "I just ...what if I'm wrong?"

"Right or wrong, you deserve an explanation for those texts."

"True."

She climbs in, and I close the door behind her.

A minute later we're heading home, back to our respective realities. She hums along to a Led Zeppelin song on the radio, something about a girl with love in her eyes and flowers in her hair. I silently memorize the lyrics so I can look up the song later and listen to it whenever I want to re-live this moment.

Reaching across the console, I take her hand and lift it to my lips. "I'm here for you, Rose girl. Anything you need."

It's not quite "I love you" but it's the closest thing I've ever said to it.

She rests her head on my shoulder as we drive, and, self-ishly, I take the long way home just to have an extra four minutes with Sheridan by my side.

The clock is ticking, the days are fleeting faster than they should, and if there's anything I've learned in my life so far, it's that all good things eventually come to an end. And in my experience, the best things tend to go down in flames.

CHAPTER THIRTY

Sheridan

"HEY, kiddo. Please tell me you came out here to shell some peas." Dad sits in a lawn chair by the little raised garden by the garage, two bowls in his lap. "There's a million of these little suckers."

My father and his wholesome hobbies—a stark contrast to his alter ego ...

Mom and her childhood best friend are in the kitchen, catching up over oolong tea and store bought coffee cake. If there were ever a time to confront my dad about those texts, it's now, while she's occupied and distracted.

"Actually, I wanted to talk to you about something." I slide my hands into my back pockets and plant my bare feet in the grass. Heat creeps up my neck, likely painting it in little pink blotches, but I clear my throat and swallow my doubts. August reminded me that I deserve to know the truth about those texts. And he's right.

Dad stops shelling the peas and adjusts his sunglasses. "Sure. What's up?"

"I saw some text messages on your phone ... from someone named KT," I say.

He's silent, stone faced.

"And I saw you with Kara Tindall," I add. "I've actually seen the two of you together several times."

Dad places the bowls on the wooden ledge of the raised garden, sits back in his chair, and crosses his legs. "Let me be very clear with you, Sheridan. You have it all wrong. I would be very careful not to jump to conclusions if I were you."

"Why'd you act so strange when I brought up inviting her to dinner the other night?" I ask.

He sniffs. "Because it was completely out of the blue. I didn't even think you remembered her name. It'd been so long."

"And the texts, I saw ... something about ending Mama's suffering?" I fold my arms. "What are you planning? Just tell me."

"This is an extremely personal and deeply complicated matter," he says, hand splayed out like he's going into defense mode.

"*Oh, my god.*" I clamp my hand over my mouth. "So you *are* having an affair."

My father flies out of his chair. "God, no. I would *never* do that to your mother."

"Then tell me what's going on." My jaw is clenched, and my shoulders burn, taut with fiery tension.

"I'd advise you to keep your voice down." The calmness in his tone digs under my skin, intensifying the maelstrom already happening inside.

I hadn't realized I was yelling ...

I glance back toward the house to make sure Mama and Laurie are still inside. God forbid they hear any of this commotion and come out to investigate.

"Why?" I ask. "Because you don't want people to know you're a murderer?"

With vanquished confidence, he removes his sunglasses, revealing a rare, tear-filled gaze. The number of times I've seen my father cry, I can count on one hand.

"Please stop asking questions." A quaver resides in his quieted voice. "And don't you *ever* call me that word again."

Just as I expected, he's not going to answer my questions.

"So that's it?"

"Yes, Sheridan. That's it."

"You're not going to answer *anything*?"

His lips press flat, and he returns his sunglasses to their rightful position before taking a seat in his chair and reaching for the peas.

The conversation is over.

Heading inside, I grab my purse and keys and dash out the front door. Mama calls my name, but I keep going. I don't want to cause a scene in front of a friend she only sees once a year nor do I want to have to answer if she asks what's wrong.

I'm half a block away when I call August.

"I just confronted him about the texts," I say when he answers.

"What'd you find out?"

"Nothing. He got all teary-eyed and told me it was complicated," I say. "And he warned me to keep my voice down and not make any assumptions. Then just like that, the conversation was over."

August sighs into the receiver. "Sounds about right."

"I know I just saw you an hour ago, but can I come over?" I ask. The hope in my tone is obvious, the desperation raw. I don't care.

He doesn't answer with an immediate yes, and my stomach turns. I crawl to a stop at the light ahead and hold my breath.

"My dad and Cassandra are home right now," he says. "But I'll meet you somewhere. You can get in my car and we can just drive. We'll go anywhere you want. And if we get tired ... we'll just get a room somewhere."

Tears blur my vision as the light turns green, and I nod despite the fact that he can't see me. "Yeah, okay. Where do I meet you?"

"How about the back parking lot of the library? Twenty minutes?" Rustling and shuffling fills his background, like he's getting ready. Keys jangle, followed by footsteps.

He's dropping everything—for me.

No questions asked.

No hesitation.

It's as if I'm his first priority and nothing else matters— and in this moment, the feeling is mutual.

CHAPTER THIRTY-ONE

AUGUST

"I'M SO sorry to drag you into this," she says when she climbs into my car.

Her eyes are red and her cheeks are swollen ... yet she's still the most beautiful thing I've seen in my fucking life.

I lean across the console and crush her pink lips with a kiss.

"I'm here because I want to be," I say. "No one drags me into anything."

For the next forty-five minutes we drive west, with no destination in mind. Hand in hand. Radio playing. Windows down and sunroof open.

The sun is setting and we're approaching the state line, but until she tells me to stop, I've no intentions of slowing down. I'll go anywhere with her.

"Should we stop?" She points to a billboard claiming the "world-famous" Luna Vista Overlook is three miles ahead. "Might be good to get some air."

"Of course." I kiss her hand and take the next exit. Signs lead us through a treed valley, over a mile-long bridge, and down a winding road, where we end up at a sparsely populated parking lot. Another sign directs us to a set of rickety wooden stairs. By the time we make it to the actual overlook, the sky has darkened and the stars are coming out of hiding.

In a way, it's perfect timing.

I wrap my arms around her from behind as the late summer heat of the day fades.

"It's beautiful up here," she says. "I don't ever want to leave."

To the left, a small town twinkles in the distance. But to the right—nothing. A dark void of dense trees, maybe. Not a hint of light to illuminate their shapes. It's as if there are two paths, one of them crystal clear, the other vast and mysterious. Perhaps much of life is like that. We can go with the familiar and the recognizable, the sure bet ... or we can jump into the unknown and hope it's worth it in the end.

"I wish I could've met you sooner," I say.

She hums. "I don't think it would've mattered. Fate screwed us both before we were ever born."

"Run away with me." The words leave my lips before I give them an ounce of consideration, and my chest tightens to the point of near suffocation, but the thought of living this bullshit life without this woman by my side is more painful than any emotional asphyxiation I can imagine.

She peers up at me through a fringe of dark lashes, laughing through her nose. "Another one of your insane ideas."

"I'm serious. We could start fresh somewhere. Give ourselves new names. Be whoever we want to be ... together."

"I couldn't do that to Mama. I can't break her heart like that."

"Then we'll take her with us."

"She'd never leave Meredith Hills. Or my Dad. They're her home. And if I ever made her get in a vehicle with you, she'd have a heart attack, and I'm being completely serious. She's got a weak heart. The thing's a ticking time bomb and seeing you would set it off, I know it."

I wouldn't know the first thing about fragility or weakness, only enough to know her mom's in a perpetual delicate state, and what affects Sheridan ultimately affects me.

"Okay, so what's your solution to all of this?"

She inhales, turning toward the view again. "If we stay together, we're going to hurt a lot of people in the process. And your dad ... who knows what kind of repercussions there will be for you? I don't know that there's going to be a happy ending for us."

I spin her toward me and tip her chin until our mouths align, brushing my lips against hers.

"You've changed my life from the second you walked into it, Rose girl," I say. "This can't be the end for us. Now that I've met you, I don't want anyone else."

"You're caught up, that's all." Her fading tone is less persuasive than her words, like maybe she's trying to convince herself as well. "We've been having fun."

"I've had plenty of *fun* with other women ... and none of them made me feel an ounce of how I feel when I'm with you."

She buries her cheek against my chest, wraps her arms around me, and closes her eyes. That warm fullness floods my veins again, but the thought of taking her home, of saying goodbye to her next week, turns it into an unbearable tightness.

"It's strange, feeling like I've known you my entire life." Her voice is barely a whisper. "And I've only just met you."

"I don't pretend to understand it."

Gazing up at me, she bites her lip, eyes searching mine. "I don't know what happened back then, between our families. I mean, I know what the newspapers say and what my parents have told me. But neither of us knows what really happened. August, if my father was responsible for what happened to your mom ... I'll never forgive him. And I know that doesn't change anything. It can't bring her back, but I mean it. And I'm so sorry for your loss. It makes my heart hurt just thinking about what that must have been like for you, growing up without her."

A million people have spouted off their condolences over the years, but not once has it ever felt like more than a greeting card line.

Someday I'll tell her about my childhood.

About my verbally abusive father, psychotic brother, absentee *other* brother, and the string of coke-addicted nannies who raised me. I'll tell her how we rarely had a Christmas tree. How my father always took vacations without us because he couldn't enjoy anything if we were around. None of us ever got along. Holes were punched in hundred-year-old walls more times than I can remember.

But I don't want to stain this moment.

"Let's get that hotel," she says. "Screw it. I'll tell my Mom I'm staying with Adri tonight. She saw me run out upset earlier. She knows I got into a fight with my dad, and I'm sure he gave her some vague excuse. It'll be fine. Let's do it."

"Yeah?"

She nods. "Yeah."

We drive toward the lights in the distant town and stop

at the first hotel we see—some three-star chain with a sign that boasts about a recent remodel, not that it matters. I'd spend the night in a junkyard Airstream if it meant having more time with her. She texts her mom while I get us a corner room on the top floor for privacy.

The skeletal, middle-aged clerk slides us a single room key, and I pretend not to notice when he gives us a once over. It's obvious we don't have luggage and we're here for a good time. As soon as he takes a call, we all but sprint toward the elevator, and the second the doors close behind us, I pin her to the wall and taste her lips. Her mouth curls against mine as she runs her fingers through my hair. A moment later we're deposited on our floor.

"Race you," she teases.

"You don't even know our room number," I scoop her into my arms, grabbing a handful of her perfect ass in the process.

I don't know what town we're in. I hardly remember the name of this hotel. But I'll remember this moment for the rest of my life.

We reach our room and let the door slam behind us. And despite the fact that the AC is blasting at sixty-five degrees, we waste no time stripping down. Tonight, we're fucking like the world is ending—because in a way, it is.

Sheridan perches on the edge of an oak writing desk. I shove the rolling swivel chair aside and fall to my knees, spreading her thighs and stroking her wetness with the tip of my tongue. Grabbing a fistful of my hair, she releases a soft moan—just as her phone begins to ring.

"Ignore it," I tell her, my breath warm against her slit.

She bites her lip, nodding, hips rocking in sync with my prodding tongue.

A minute later, the phone rings again.

"Keep going." She tightens her grip on me. "I'm so close …"

But it's the third time in a row that steals the moment from us.

She groans, sliding off the table, leaving her taste to linger on my lips.

"I'm sorry. Let me just see who's blowing up my phone …" Sheridan locates her bag in the dark, then her phone. The screen glows bright against her face, illuminating a concerned expression that wasn't there before. "It's Mama. Hold on. She left a voicemail."

She presses play and holds the phone to her ear, and while it's not on speaker, her mother is so frantic and loud, I can hear every single word.

"Sheridan, you need to come home immediately," she says. If I didn't know better, I'd say she almost sounds tearful. "I don't know where you are, but I know you're not at Adriana's because I just called her. Come home. *Now*. It's an emergency."

Her wide, shiny eyes lock with mine from across the room. She doesn't have to say anything. We throw our clothes on and skip the check-out desk on our way out— room's already paid for.

I get us back to Meredith Hills in a fraction of the time it took to leave, and I drop her off at the library parking lot, next to her car. She hasn't said a word since we left the hotel, and I can only assume she's thinking the worst.

"It's going to be okay," I tell her, but I don't know that. No one ever does.

Leaning over the console, she presses her cheek against mine, her lashes fluttering. "I love you, August. The words have been on the tip of my tongue all day, and I never found the right time to tell you that. But in case I don't see you again after this ... I wanted you to know that."

Her words breathe me to life—and shatter me at the same time.

"I love you too," I tell her. "And you'll see me again."

It's yet another thing I don't know to be true. Not because I wouldn't move heaven and earth to see her again, but because her mother is her entire world, and Sheridan would sacrifice her own happiness if it meant keeping her mom safe.

She climbs out of my car and into hers.

Within seconds, she becomes nothing but a pair of red taillights fading into the dark. I hold my breath, letting it burn. Paralyzed by the heaviness of this moment, I sit in my idling car for what feels like a lifetime, replaying our day together a hundred times before I have the energy to drive away.

If I never see her again, it's going to be me who dies of a broken heart.

CHAPTER THIRTY-TWO

Sheridan

I FIND Mama at the kitchen table beside a pile of mail. There's no ambulance in the driveway. My father's car is gone. None of this is screams urgent crisis.

"I don't understand," I say. "You said there was an emergency?"

She's breathless. An anxious kind of breathless. And her eyes are bloodshot and swollen. She's been crying.

"Take a seat, Sheridan," she says, voice raspy. I take the chair beside her, hands trembling because I've never seen her so calm yet so upset at the same time. And the fact that it didn't work her into a spell is a straight-up miracle. "We received a bill in the mail from Centurion." She slides it toward me. "Which I thought was odd because you'd said we were recipients of some kind of grant. I'll admit, it seemed too good to be true, but I trusted you. I believed you. Anyway, it was nothing but a standard invoice showing this month's fees have been paid ... but I was about to toss it in the trash when I saw this." She points to the name at the bottom. "Sheridan, why does it list August Monreaux as our payor?"

I suck in a hard breath, but before I have a chance to utter some bullshit excuse, the back door swings open, and Dad walks in with an armful of groceries. His gaze passes between us and he lingers in the doorway, as if he's afraid of stepping into a minefield.

"What's ... going on?" he asks.

"Apparently a *Monreaux* is paying for my nursing services," Mama says to him, though her attention is very much on me.

Dad places the groceries on the counter, abandoning them to come examine the evidence himself.

"I couldn't get a hold of Adriana earlier," Mama says. "So I called her mother. She said you weren't there, that they were in Chicago for a bridal shower this weekend. In fact, she told me she hadn't seen you in weeks."

"Sheridan, is this true?" Dad asks, as if he has any room to call me out for my web of lies.

My stomach clenches. For the first time in my life, two disappointed gazes anchor me to the ground. I'm no longer the apple of their eyes, I'm a rainstorm ruining their beautiful picnic.

"I knew it," Mama says. "The way you walk around here with stars in your eyes, putting on that extra coat of lip gloss, curling your hair. I figured you were crushing on some boy—but never in a million years did I ever think it'd be a *Monreaux*."

Disgust colors her tone.

Dad examines the statement again, his hand clamped over his mouth. "Sheridan, *what* did you *do*? Why is he paying for this? What kind of mess have you gotten us into with them? Is he blackmailing you? Does he have something he's—"

"—no," I say.

"Then explain it," Mama rises from her chair—only to collapse back into it.

"You're going to get yourself worked up," Dad says to her. "Please, try to stay calm. Sheridan's going to tell us everything, and then we're going to figure this out."

I grab Mama a glass of water and one of her "calming" pills and place them in front of her. If she reacts this way now, what's going to happen when she finds out the truth? That I love him? That I want to be with him?

"I'm calling Dr. Smithson," Dad says. "I think she's having another spell. You stay here with her."

I place a hand on her shoulder. "It's not as bad as you think, Mama. I promise."

Her eyes turn hazy, growing unfocused.

"She wants her to come in," Dad says when he returns from the next room. "Immediately."

We help her to the car and ride in silence, not a single utterance the entire trip. Knowing my father, he's preparing his lecture in his head, saving it for when we're alone and out of Mama's earshot. We can't risk upsetting her even more.

My father might be disappointed in me, but my mother could die of a broken heart.

I have to end it with August.

I have to accept once and for all that I can love him, but I can never be with him.

CHAPTER THIRTY-THREE

AUGUST

"MAYBE IT WAS SHOCK," I say over the phone after Sheridan fills me in later that night.

I'm sitting by the pool, in the very same chair she tossed her clothes onto the night she snuck in. The grotto is lit. The moon is full. And the crickets are in full effect. But on the other side of my phone, the situation is dire.

I can hardly hear her. Between the hum of the hospital vending machines she's standing next to and the hushed tone of her voice, as if she's afraid she'll get caught talking to me.

"That's my point," she says. "It *was* shock. She was devastated at the mere fact that you're paying for her nurse, that I'm associating with you—and she doesn't know the half of what we've been up to."

"Maybe when she calms down, you can talk to her about us? Maybe it won't be as big of a shock next time? Since she's already got some idea?"

"I don't want to test that theory."

I don't blame her. I'd feel the same if it were my mother.

"I meant what I said earlier," she says. "I love you. But I can never be yours, okay? Not in this life." Her voice breaks. "Maybe we can try again in the next one. Maybe then we won't be enemies?"

She chuckles, as if she knows how ridiculous she sounds, as if it could possibly soften the words that crush my soul.

But I'd live a thousand lifetimes if it meant I could spend just one of them with her.

"I need to go." Her words are fractured. And so is my world. "Goodbye, August."

I refuse to say goodbye.

"Goodbye, August," she says again, slightly louder as if she thinks I didn't hear her the first time.

But I can't. I can't repeat it. This isn't goodbye. I won't allow it.

"Please don't do this. Don't make this harder than it already is." Her voice is a whisper a million miles away. She inhales. Mutters a fraction of a word, as if she's going to say something more.

But then line goes dead.

Maybe she thought I'd argue or say something that would only make it worse.

"August." My father's voice steals my moment—and steels my façade. "Who was that you were just talking to?"

"No one," I say.

"It wasn't, by chance, Rich Rose's daughter, was it?" He takes the chair next to mine and reclines. "You can tell me. I know all about it anyway. Gannon let the cat out of the bag."

Fucking *Gannon*.

He called my bluff. He knew the Cassandra threat was bullshit. Though if it were true and I had proof, I'd throw his traitorous ass under the bus so fucking fast …

My fists clench until my knuckles turn white, and my blood flashes ice cold.

"Was actually hoping I'd get a chance to meet her one of these days." He slides his hands behind his thick neck. "So … what are your intentions with her anyway?"

I rise. I don't have the energy for his information fishing.

"All right, fine. Don't answer me," he says. "But just know that you don't have to hold back on my accord. If you like the girl, that is."

I rest my hands on my hips, studying him. I learned long ago that any conversation with my father requires you to stay one step ahead of him at all times, which can quickly become exhausting if you're not careful.

"I thought you hated the Roses," I say.

He laughs, readjusting his lounge chair. "Once upon a time, I hated the ground they walked on and the air they breathed. But honestly, August, who has time for all of that? The past is in the past. What good would it do any of us to stay angry about something we can't change?"

"I've just never heard you talk like this before. For years, all you did was talk about ruining Rich for what he did …"

"People are allowed to change." He puffs his chest, as if I should know better than to question him. "It isn't healthy to hold onto grudges. Maybe this would be a good way to bury the hatchet? And heck, if you marry the girl someday, it'd make for some powerful PR, that's for sure."

I roll my eyes. Inevitably his train of thought always circles back to the business and how he can benefit from something in the end.

"So you forgive Rich for what he did?"

He sucks in a humid breath. "When tragedy strikes, August, the first thing people do is point fingers. We want to make sense of it all. And at the time, Rich made the most sense, given our past and a few specifics surrounding what happened. But at the end of the day, he was never charged because there wasn't enough evidence. No one could prove it."

I hold my breath as disbelief washes over me, searing hot.

"I guess what I'm getting at here," he continues with a half-shrug, "is maybe I was wrong."

I've never heard my father admit he was wrong about anything ... ever.

"So you're saying if I date her, you're not going to disinherit me or punish me or anything like that ..."

My father chuckles, his middle-aged belly bouncing and his pristine white teeth almost glowing in the dark. "What do you take me for? A monster? Come on, you're my *son*. All a father ever wants is for his kid to be happy. If she makes you happy, son, then by all means, don't let me stand in the way of that."

"Okay, baby, I'm ready," Cassandra calls from behind us. "Oh! Didn't realize we weren't alone."

In my peripheral, she grabs a towel from the cabana and wraps it around her lithe, Malibu-bronzed body.

I don't even want to know ...

Heading in, I let my father's words play on a loop in my head all night, examining them from every angle.

It's possible for people to change—I'm living proof of that.

But this is a complete one-eighty.

Still, it's a step in the right direction. If my father is open to moving forward, maybe the Roses would consider doing the same, too. If I could just have a minute of their time, they'd see I'm my father's son, but I'm not my father.

Lying in bed, I re-read old texts from Sheridan. And before I crash for the night, I send her a message.

ME—Sher, call me when you wake up. I have big news.

The message delivers, but it's never read. I'm sure she's sleeping. It's been a fucking day.

I shove my phone under my pillow and close my eyes, drifting off with something I didn't have an hour ago ... hope —and relentless determination to bury the past so that Sheridan Rose can be my future.

CHAPTER THIRTY-FOUR

Sheridan

I'M LEAVING TOMORROW.

I fold the last of my clothes and seal the plastic tote. I've managed to squeeze all of my things into five containers, which doesn't include the box fan and random items already packed into my car.

Dad knocks on the door. He still hasn't answered my questions from the other day and we're not exactly on good terms, but we're trying to keep it cordial for Mama's sake.

"Your mom's resting," he says. "Mona's on her way."

I swear she comes home from the hospital more exhausted than when she went in.

"Okay." I don't meet his gaze. I still can't look at him.

"Sure you don't want me to follow you up there tomor-row?" he asks. "Kind of sad that I don't get to help my daughter move to college."

"It'd be a waste of gas for you to drive all that way to help me move five boxes ..."

"I don't look at it that way." He takes a seat at the foot of my bed, shoulders sloped, bonier than usual. I didn't realize he'd been losing weight. Guess I didn't notice a lot of things about him lately …

He watches me stack the boxes in the corner. I have nothing to say to him.

"Is this … about him?" he asks a moment later.

"You can say his name."

He hesitates. "I know you don't understand. And I can't blame you, Sheridan. We kept a lot from you. We sheltered you from a lot. We thought we were doing the right thing, and we didn't want to burden you with our family tragedies. I realize now, that we made a mistake. We should've told you what we went through so you'd understand exactly why we stay away from the Monreauxs."

"I read the articles in Mama's album." I keep my back to him, hands pressed against the top of a tote as I stare out my window—the very window August climbed through not long ago. "I know everything."

"You don't know the half of it," he says. "The way that man drug my name through the mud after what he did to my sister. Had his minions slash my tires and harass your mother. For years, I couldn't drive home from the grocery store without a police offer tailing me. And every year, on the anniversaries of Cynthia's death and Elisabeth Monreaux's death, we'd get a mailbox full of hate letters. And those are just the little things. Don't even get me started on the job sabotaging. He once tried to pay someone to falsify a drug test I'd taken for that position at the meat-packing plant. Monreauxs are pure evil."

"August is nothing like that."

"And you know this how? Because you spent half a summer with him?" Dad scoffs. "Vincent was my best friend, Sheridan. Since I was eight years old. *And he murdered my sister and pinned it on me out of spite.* Forgive me, but I find it difficult to believe he's capable of raising an upstanding young man worthy of being with my daughter."

I don't know what I could say in this moment to convince my father that I know August's heart, that he isn't his father.

"You know, Sher. You can always talk to me about anything. I know it's been a rough summer with your mother, but if you ever want to talk about anything, I'm here. You don't need to go running off—"

"—I tried to talk to you a few days ago."

"I mean, you can come to me with whatever's bothering you."

"The texts I saw certainly bothered me." I don't have the energy to play 'nice' with him, to beat around the bush or guilt him into confessing. Especially when he's being so dismissive.

He forces a hard breath through his nostrils, hunching and resting his elbows on his knees.

"I've already told two people about them," I add. "So if anything happens to Mama, you'll be the first person they look at. You and Kara."

"Jesus, Sheridan." He buries his face in his hands. "You really think I'd hurt your mother?"

"I don't know what to think ... you won't tell me anything except that it's personal and private. Sounds an awful lot like an affair to me."

"You have it all wrong." He glances at the door, as if he expect Mama to walk in at any second, and then he shakes his head. "Look. A few months ago, I lost my job. I didn't tell anyone, not even your mother. I didn't want to cause her any unnecessary stress. It was a bullshit reason, one I'm sure Vincent Monreaux had a hand in."

For as long as I can remember, my father would start a new job, work his way up after a couple years, only to be let go for some asinine reason. He always suspected Vincent was behind it, given their history and his penchant for causing chaos, but Dad never could prove it.

"Anyway, Kara is an attorney who specializes in employment law. She's been putting together a wrongful termination case for me. At least she's been trying. Sounds like they might settle out of court, maybe in the six-figure range. It'd be life-changing for us. We could pay off both mortgages, drive a reliable car for the first time in our married life, pay off all of your mother's medical bills, cover your tuition, and sock the rest away for retirement."

"I'm sorry, but how can you afford a lawyer if you're not working?"

"She's doing it pro bono—as a favor to us. You were probably too young to remember, but Kara was quite the fixture around here back in the day. She sort of looked up to us as the parents she never had. I'm the one who encouraged her to pursue a law degree. Guess she felt she wanted to pay it back, bring it full circle, what have you."

"Okay ..." I wrap my head around that. "So if you've been off work the last couple of months, where have you been going in the middle of the night?"

"Out to the cabin," he says, referring to a family friend's one-room fishing cabin on Lake Graystone. They've always given Dad free reign to use it, and it's about thirty minutes outside of town, so it's plausible.

"So you just ... go hang out at the cabin all night? Five nights a week?"

"I stay busy," he says. "Sometimes I do some midnight

catch and release. Other times I read a book. Take a nap. Watch an old movie on VHS. The time passes quickly enough."

"And Mom has no idea?"

"None."

"Why haven't you told her?"

"Isn't it obvious? She can't handle even the slightest stressful event. Can you imagine how she'd handle a lawsuit rollercoaster? That and I didn't want to get her hopes up in case it didn't pan out. She's had enough disappointment in her lifetime."

"So why couldn't you tell me?"

"You've had enough on your plate for one year. I didn't want you to worry. You were already entertaining the idea of putting off college. If you knew I wasn't working, there's no way I'd have gotten you to leave."

He's right. I'd have stayed, taken on full-time hours at the cell store, and insisted I contributed to our family's bottom line.

"I want to believe you," I say, after absorbing everything for a moment.

"Well, you should. It's the truth."

"Why didn't you ever tell me you were accused of killing your sister? That you were arrested for it?"

He folds his hands, clasping them until his knuckles turn white. "Because that was one of the darkest moments of my entire life. And I was worried you'd never look at me the same."

"I'd rather have heard it from you than read it in a faded newspaper article."

His jaw sets. "I would've told you eventually."

Guess we'll never know.

"Now that I've told you everything you need to know,

Sheridan, you need to tell me what really happened with Vince's son. Tell me why he's paying for your mother's nurse."

I can't tell him everything.

I just can't.

But I *can* tell him the abbreviated version.

"We met this summer." I pick at a loose thread in the carpet. "And we hit it off. I mentioned I was worried about Mama, that she might need some help while I'm gone ... he offered."

Dad runs his palms along his thighs, unsettled, unable to look in my direction. He isn't stupid. I'm sure he sees through my story. Nothing in this life ever comes for free.

"We really like each other," I add, keeping my head held high and my voice crystal clear. "He's a good person. He's not like his father. Maybe if you met him, you—"

He cuts me off with a wave of his hand as he rises. "I've heard enough."

"What?"

"I will never meet him and you're never to associate with him," he speaks through clenched teeth. "Do you understand?"

I want to tell him it isn't right that they're still using Mona. That he doesn't get to hate August and take advantage of him at the same time. But I'm sure he'd refuse to hear me out. And in the end, Mama would suffer the most.

I rise as well. "No, Dad. I don't understand you. If you could just—"

"—this isn't up for debate." He walks to my door. "We don't associate with Monreauxs. That's just how it is. How it'll always be." He pauses. "The worst thing you could do is accept money from one. Once they have you in their pocket, you'll owe them for life."

I fold my arms. "It's not like that with August."

"That's what you think now." He heads to the door. "End it. Immediately. And never speak of him again. Do you understand?"

His words slice through the room with an icy chill, and the man speaking them resembles nothing of the father who raised me.

My mouth runs dry, and I force a swallow, keeping my head held high. "Already did."

"Good. Now if you'll excuse me, it's been a long couple of days. I'm going to go check on your mother. And you should get some rest. You've got a drive in the morning."

He closes the door, and I collapse on my bed, lying on my stomach and burying my cheek against my flat pillow as I stare at the wall.

My phone dings from my nightstand, I stretch to reach it.

ENEMY DEAREST: Please call me, Sher. I leave tomorrow. I need to see you.

August's been texting for days, saying he has to tell me something big and he wants to tell me in person, but I've been ignoring him because I know how it'll go. He'll reel me back in and it'll make everything ten times harder than it already is. I've already told him what I needed to tell him. And I've already said goodbye. The sooner he accepts our fate, the sooner we can both try to move on—whatever that'll look like.

ENEMY DEAREST: I miss you.

With tears in my eyes, I write him back.

This will be the last time.

ME: I miss you too. But I can't.

____

CHAPTER THIRTY-FIVE

AUGUST

CLASS STARTS IN FOUR MINUTES.

I take a seat in the back corner of the lecture hall that smells like white board markers and overzealous body spray and crack my laptop open. It's strange, actually attending class. Taking notes. Doing real homework. But it's a much-needed distraction because if I don't busy myself with school, I obsess over Sheridan.

It's been two weeks since I saw her ... kissed her ... told her I loved her.

Two weeks since she said goodbye.

Every night, I check her social media accounts in hopes she posts something, anything. But it's still the same old pictures from last year. It kills me not knowing what she's up to. How she's adjusting to dorm life. If she's gone to any parties ... or if she's talking to any guys.

I wish I could tell her that I changed my major—from

business to software architecture—because of her. For the first time in my life, I actually want to do something worth a damn. I don't want to learn how to make rich corporations richer—I want to make a difference in people's lives. I've got an idea for a software program that would make running safer for runners, specifically an app that senses if the user has been hit or taken a fall. It'd immediately send out a call to 9-1-1 as well as ping their exact location.

I thought about telling her via text anyway, in an attempt to get the conversation going. But the last thing she sent me was, "I miss you too. But I can't."

Every text I've sent to her since has gone unanswered.

My professor takes the podium below, connecting his laptop to the giant screen. A girl with wavy blonde hair and full lips slips through the door just as the lights go out. My stomach flips for a second ... but it isn't her.

It wouldn't be.

Couldn't be.

My mind has always played cruel tricks, but lately it's been fucking brutal.

The girl finds the last empty seat next to me, and within seconds I'm engulfed in a cloud of raspberry body spray.

Digging around in her bag, she accidentally elbows me.

"Oh my god, I'm so sorry," she leans in, whispering. "I can't find a freaking pen."

Reaching down, I grab a spare out of my bag and hand it to her, keeping my attention focused on the lecture. Forty minutes later, the lights come on and everyone's packing up.

"Here you go." The blonde hands me my pen back— along with a slip of paper.

I unfold the note—her name and number.

When I look up, she's already gone.

Heading out, I crumple the sheet and toss it in the trash.

Not interested.

I'm not the man I used to be, not even close.

All I am ... is *hers*.

CHAPTER THIRTY-SIX

Sheridan

"I'M SO SORRY—I can't go tonight." I wipe the cherry-red lipstick from my face and sweep my hair into a low ponytail, staring at my reflection in the mirror, only to find the saddest girl in the world staring back.

"What? How come?" My friend, Stacia, says from the other end of my phone. "I'm literally on my way to pick you up right now."

I don't know what I was thinking when I said I'd go with her to a party at Bexler.

Actually, I'm lying. I know exactly what I was thinking: that somewhere on a campus, amongst fifteen thousand students, I might catch a glimpse of August. The scenario I'd imagined went something like this ... I'd spot him from across the streety maybe. He wouldn't notice me because he wouldn't looking for me. Maybe he'd be on his phone, making plans for the weekend. Or maybe he'd be sitting on a bus stop bench, finishing a quick homework assignment, lost in his own world.

I only wanted to see that he was okay. That he was moving on. Doing well for himself.

But as I started getting ready tonight, I thought about a different scenario: bumping into him at a party with another girl. The two of us locking eyes from across the room as he kisses some beautiful brunette in a Bexler sweatshirt.

I want August to be happy. He deserves that much.

But I won't be able to stomach the sight of it. Not yet. Not while everything's still raw. Not while I still miss him so much it physically hurts in the form of stomachaches, dreams so intense I wake up crying, and a heaviness in my chest that steals my breath when I least expect it.

For three weeks after I told him goodbye, he texted me every day.

I miss you ...

I need to talk to you ...

When can I see you again?

I love you, Rose girl ...

Then one day the messages just ... stopped. And I knew they would. He had to have been tired of beating his head against the wall and getting nowhere.

Or maybe he met someone ...

Time and time again, I caught myself typing something, only to delete it all and power off my phone to avoid further temptation. Engaging with him is playing with fire, a guaranteed way to get burned, and I'm still healing from the last time.

"Sher, please?" Stacia puts me on speaker, and a couple other girls chime in. We're all in the same basic anatomy class on Tuesdays and Thursdays, all of us from different parts of Missouri, and we've all become close. "Please, please, please?"

I've never been a clique sort of person, but these girls have been my saving grace so far this semester. I'm never without plans on the weekends, and a good distraction is only a phone call or text away any time I need it.

I want to go.

But it's a bad idea.

No good can come of it.

Only a hangover and heartbreak.

"I'm not really feeling well, guys." It's true. My stomach has worked itself into knots all night at the mere thought of running into August. Add some cheap beer into that equation and I'll be sicker than a dog all night.

"I told you not to eat food service sushi," Stacia says. "Should've listened."

I laugh. "Yeah. It must've been the sushi ..."

"Are you sure you can't come with?" She tries one last time.

"I'll let you ride shotgun and pick all the songs," Hadley chimes in.

"Tempting, but I'm still going to pass." I pluck a makeup wipe from its container. "You guys have fun without me, okay?"

I'm met with a symphony of groans and whining, and Stacia promises to call me tomorrow and tell me all about it.

For a split second, I contemplate changing my mind, because what are the odds I'll run into him? One in fifteen thousand?

I end the call, peel out of my jeans and tank top, and change into pajamas—pajamas that happen to be the very ones I wore the night August snuck into my room.

Plopping on my dorm bed, I grab my laptop and pull up

my Netflix. Clicking on the octopus documentary, I settle against my pillow ... and grab a Red Vine from the bag in my nightstand drawer.

Maybe I'm just as crazy as he is.

It's a tragedy, how perfect we were for each other.

And it's heartbreaking that all that's left are memories of a star-crossed summer and Red Vines.

CHAPTER THIRTY-SEVEN

AUGUST

I SHOVE my hands in my jacket and barrel down the campus town sidewalks until I spot my car in the overflow parking lot.

I have to get out of here.

I need air. I need a change of scenery. If I stay in this fucking Sheridan-less bubble another minute, I'll die.

Ten minutes later, I'm taking the exit toward Briardale Community College. It's an hour drive from Bexler, and I have no intentions of seeking her out. I just want to be in the same stratosphere as her, breathing the same oxygen, taking in the same views ... anything to feel closer to her.

Led Zeppelin plays from my speakers—the same song she sang along to months ago, in the very seat that sits empty beside me. I crank the volume, settling in for the drive, knuckles white against the steering wheel.

This hopeless, helpless sensation is foreign to me, and

I've never been one to feel sorry for myself, but I don't know how much more of this I can take.

My life—without Sheridan—is an endless void.

A hamster wheel of college classes, beer binges, and meaningless monotony.

Resting my head back, I conjure up a mental conversation with her, imagining what we'd be talking about in this moment. School maybe. Weekend plans. How much we miss one another. It helps, sometimes, to pretend we never went our separate ways. And maybe in some parallel universe, we're still together. We made it work. Growing deeper and harder in love with each passing day.

I'm diving headfirst into another fantasy conversation when the radio cuts out and Soren's name flashes across the display. I clear my throat, sit up straight, and tap the green button.

"Hey," I say.

"Happy birthday …" It's loud where he is. I can barely hear him over all the commotion in the background. Someone's yelling.

Exhaling, I manage a quick, "Thanks."

I completely forgot today was my birthday.

"You out celebrating?" he asks, yelling over the noise.

I scan the empty highway and chuff. "In my own way."

"I'll do a shot in your honor tonight," he says with a chuckle. We don't have traditions, but if we did, this might be the closest thing to it. "One of these days I'll be there in person and we can do one together."

"Don't sweat it."

He covers the phone, his voice muffled for a second as he speaks to someone else.

"Sorry about that." He's back. "Was going to see if you had any plans for Thanksgiving. We're doing our eastern leg of the tour that week ... playing Madison Square Garden and working our way down. I could fly you out if you want to hang with us for the week?"

I've toured with his band once a couple of years ago, and honestly, once was enough. Their parties make mine look like a kiddie parade with clowns and balloon animals. It took me two solid weeks just to recover. And I'll be damned if I go within a football field's distance of Everclear ever again.

"Thanks but I'm good," I say.

He's wordless for a second. "You okay, man?"

"Yeah? Why wouldn't I be?"

"You just seem ... I don't know ... sad or something," he says. "It's, what, nine o'clock where you are? On a Friday? And you're alone? I call bullshit. It's some chick, isn't it?"

Sheridan is hardly *some chick*.

But Soren wouldn't understand.

And I don't have the energy to explain any of it.

"Just tired," I say. And it's not a complete lie. I am tired. Tired of merely existing while everyone around me moves on with their life and I'm treading water. If I could snap my fingers and get myself out of this trance-like state of despair, I would.

But I can't—I'm stuck on her.

"What's her name?" he asks, seeing through me. "This chick."

"It's no one you'd know."

"Obviously," he says. "Is this the same one you were going to bring to my show last summer?"

I told him she was sick. A lame, uncreative excuse in retrospect.

Sighing, I say, "Yeah. Same girl."

"Well, shit," Soren says with an exhale. "I have to get

out there for soundcheck, but my offer still stands. Come hang out with us if you want to get away for a bit. And if not, I mean, I understand. I get it. I've been there. I still think of mine sometimes. And hell, every song on my last three albums was about her in one way or another. Biggest fear is I'll marry someone else but see her face on my wedding day. They stick with you, man. Those first loves. It's heaven and it's hell."

A sign ahead tells me Briardale's exit is seventeen miles away.

"Thanks for the pep talk," I say, half-chuckling. Awkwardness of this "bonding" moment aside, it's good to know I'm not alone.

"All right, well, I have to go. You take care. Have a drink or something tonight, okay? Take the edge off. And I'm always here if you need me," he says. "And August? I hope you get the girl. Honestly, knowing you ... you will."

CHAPTER THIRTY-EIGHT

Sheridan

"*STACIA.*" I grip her arm under the table at a local sushi place. "You didn't tell me this was a *double date.*"

"Obvi." She smirks as her boyfriend and his friend make their way from the front door to our booth. "Or you wouldn't have come ..."

"So messed up."

She climbs out of her seat and wraps her arms around her boyfriend, Bryan. They've been dating a few weeks now and they're already exclusive, inseparable, and in love. I'm thrilled for her, truly, but every time I see them together, my heart breaks a little.

It could've been us ...

"Sheridan, this is my roommate, Dillon," Bryan says.

Dillon extends his hand, and flashes a megawatt smile accented with two perfect dimples. His hair is freshly cut, slicked back with brilliantine, and he's dressed like he's going to a job interview.

A lifetime ago, he would've been my type ... clean cut, preppy.

Stacia and the guys slide into the booth, and I brace myself for a night of small talk and awkward conversation.

"So you're a nursing major?" Dillon asks. "Like Stacia?"

I nod, sipping my ice water. "That's how we met."

"Awesome," he says with a little too much enthusiasm. "I'm studying accounting. Hope to be a corporate accountant someday. Got my sights set on a Fortune 500 company."

I stifle a yawn.

I should've stayed in my pajamas and called it an early night, but Stacia spent an hour blowing up my phone and begging me to get sushi. We were halfway here when she told me Bryan was joining us, which would've been fine had they not been setting me up for a surprise, blind double date ...

And I get it.

It's fun when friends date their boyfriend's friends.

And Dillon is cute—but he's no August.

"You have any brothers or sisters?" Dillon asks. I cringe on the inside.

"Only child." I flip open my menu. "You?"

"Five sisters," he answers with a wide grin.

"Sorry, man. Sounds awful." Bryan elbows him, teasing. "And I thought having one sister was bad enough."

"You're from Meredith Hills, right?" Dillon asks.

It's almost as if he googled me and stalked my social media on the way here ...

"I am. Ever heard of it?" I flip the menu over and flick my attention to him, trying to appear interested out of sheer politeness.

This is brutal.

"My grandparents used to live in Springdale," he says, referring to the little antique town August and I spent a single, beautiful day together once. "I'm familiar with the area."

Our server interrupts this painful conversation with immaculate timing, and I use the break in conversation to excuse myself to the ladies' room.

"I'll go with you," Stacia says. She trots after me, and once we're behind a closed door she tugs my arm. "So? What do you think so far?"

I take the last stall on the left. "I feel like he's interviewing me for a position as his girlfriend."

"I think he likes you," she says, ignoring me. "I can tell. The way he looks at you ... he hasn't taken his eyes off you once. Did you notice, he ordered the same thing as you?"

"I don't think that means anything ... everyone likes California rolls ..." I finish up and meet her by the sink. "

"But do you like him so far? Like, do you think there's potential?" Her mascara-coated lashes flutter with hope. "You guys would look so cute together."

I lather my hands and meet her gaze in the reflection. "He's nice."

But he's a little too ... uncomplicated. August had depth and layers. He was a thousand-piece jig saw of a man. Dillon is dead behind the eyes—nice to look at but there's nothing else there.

"You don't seem excited about him ..." Stacia bites her lower lip and tucks her dark hair behind her ears. "I'm sorry."

"No, no." I give her a hug. "It's fine. You meant well. He's just ... not for me."

"Are you still hung up on that one guy?" she asks.

I've told her and the girls about August briefly, giving

them an extremely abbreviated version of events. We had a fling. We ended it before leaving for college. Haven't spoken since. But she doesn't know the half of what went down. It never seemed like a relevant topic of conversation, and the idea of revisiting the past events of the summer felt akin to poking a raw nerve with a scalpel.

"What was his name again?" Her brows meet. "Atticus? Atlas?"

"August," I say his name out loud for the first time in months ... and it hurts. It physically throbs—as if someone took a dull knife to my soul and serrated it straight down the center. Changing the subject before it leads me down an emotional path, I say, "We should get back out there ..."

The last thing I want is for Dillon to think I'm in here talking about him, analyzing everything, getting my hopes up. Wouldn't want to give him the wrong impression.

He's a perfectly nice guy—so far.

But he's no August.

CHAPTER THIRTY-NINE

FOR THE FIRST time in years, I come home for Thanksgiving break. But I'm not here to partake in family traditions, seeing as we have none. And Dad and Cassandra are off somewhere tropical—Tahiti or Fiji or something.

The house is dark and empty, the way it was the day I left.

I toss my duffel on the bed, in the same place Sheridan surrendered herself to me months ago. Then I grab my keys and head back to my car. Fifteen minutes later, I'm on Sheridan's street.

When in Rome ...

Her little blue Nissan is glaringly absent from the street or the driveway.

From there, I head for the cell store, on the off chance she's home for the week and decided to pick up a shift. Parking out front, I kill my engine and head inside because regardless, I need a spare charger as I left mine back at Bexler.

"Oh, hey, stranger." Adriana approaches me the instant I set foot in the doorway. I'm sure she saw me coming. "It's been a while."

I scan the store in search of the charger section. "Need a charger."

"Sure thing." She points me toward the far wall. "I'll meet you at the checkout when you're ready."

A minute later, I pull my wallet from my pocket at the register.

"It's quiet here today," I say as she rings me up.

"Yeah. Things are kind of dead until Black Friday. Everyone waits until the big sale. Good thing you came in today and not after Thanksgiving. We'll have a line out the door." She raps her long nails on the counter. "Twenty-five fifty-six is your total."

I hand her my card. "You talk to Sheridan still?"

Her brows lift but she doesn't seem surprised. In fact, she almost smirks, as if she was waiting for that question.

"We talk sometimes, yeah," she says.

"How's she doing?"

She slides my card into the reader. "Great. She seems happy."

My chest burns. "Good. Good for her. Maybe tell her 'hey' for me next time you talk to her."

Adriana slides me a receipt and pen. "Or maybe you can tell her yourself? She'll be home next month for Christmas. I think she has three or four weeks off, I can't remember. She was going to come home this week, but her parents decided to go up there for a couple of days instead."

Good to know.

"Yeah, well, I don't think she wants to see me." I slide

the charger off the counter and tuck it into my coat pocket.

"August." She laughs through her nose, head tilted and hand on her hip. "When has that ever stopped you before?"

I sniff. She's got a point. But it's different now. I didn't care about her before. All that mattered was what *I* wanted. Any pain or confusion I inflicted on her was collateral damage and not my concern.

But she's made herself clear these last few months.

I may not agree with it, but I have to respect that—because I love her.

"Listen." Adriana leans in, voice low despite the fact that we're the only two here. "I shouldn't tell you this. But she asks about you every time we talk."

"What?"

"Yeah. She asks if I've seen you around town, if I've heard what you're up to," she says. "She misses you. And honestly, the way she talks, I think she still loves you—she's just afraid to admit it, you know? Because of everything."

"I'll be right back."

A second later, I'm sitting in my front seat, scratching out a note on a piece of notebook paper.

I fold it in half twice and run it back inside.

"I need you to give this to her next time you see her," I tell Adriana. "Can you do that for me?"

Her dark gaze drops to the letter. "Yeah. I can do that."

She slips it into her back pocket.

"August?" I'm halfway to the door when she calls my name.

I stop. "Yeah?"

"I hope it works out for you two."

Placing my hand on the door, I nod. "It will."

Because I'm not giving up on her.

Not yet. Not now. Not ever.

CHAPTER FORTY

Sheridan

MY PARENTS' house smells like a winter wonderland. The second I walk through the door, I'm met with a nasal cocktail of gingerbread, cinnamon, pumpkin and sugar cookies. Dad is apparently baking up a storm ...

"Hey," I give him a wave as I place my bag by the door.

I haven't been home all semester. I told my parents I was busy with classes and clinicals, but that wasn't entirely true. While I've lived my entire life in Meredith Hills, all it reminds me of now is that single, heartbreaking summer.

And *him*.

I wasn't ready to come back.

But I couldn't get out of winter break.

"Hey, kiddo." He slides off his oven mitts and places them by the stove before giving me a hug. "Mama's in the living room. She can't wait to see you."

I head to the next room, stopping in my tracks when I'm

met with a voluminous tree that takes up a third of our tiny living room and blocks the entire front window.

"Wow," I tell Mama as she moves and maneuvers Christmas ornaments, dispersing them ever so perfectly. She's having a good day. Dad said she's having a lot of those lately. And the doctors think her bout with Guillain-Barre is on the mend as she hasn't had an episode or showed any nerve weakness in months. "This is different ... why does it look so different? It's fuller than I remember."

She smiles, giving me a side hug. "That's because this one isn't from the early nineties."

"Aw, you got rid of the old one?"

"That thing was falling apart and you know it." She chuckles, though I kind of feel bad for the old tree. We'd had it since I was a baby and the thing was older than me. My parents got it for ten bucks at Goodwill one year. Never really could afford to replace it—until now.

My father won his settlement last month. It wasn't as much as they were hoping for, but it's enough to make a difference in their lives. It certainly seems to be making a difference in her health these days, that's for sure. And that alone is compensation enough in my eyes.

"Did your father tell you he's taking me on a little weekend getaway for New Year's?" she asks. "He hasn't told me where we're going yet. It's a surprise."

I'm happy that they're able to take a trip, even if it's only for a couple of days, but they've only had this money a month now and it's already burning cigarette-sized holes in their pockets. It's all going to add up if they're not careful.

"I was thinking, Mama ..." I say. "Now that you and Dad have a little extra money, maybe you should take over the home nurse payments? Get August his money back?"

She pauses, mid-reach, for a Santa ornament.

"It's the right thing to do," I say. "He only did that because he wanted to be with me—and you won't allow that. It's just kind of unfair now, don't you think?"

Her lips flatten. "After everything that family has done to ours, I think it's more than fair."

"But he had nothing to do with any of that."

"Trust me, the Monreauxs aren't missing a dime of that money. I doubt Vincent even knows it's gone."

"Still doesn't make it right."

"That family has caused a mountain of heartbreak for ours over the years. They've attacked our names, our reputations, our livelihood ..."

"Maybe just think about it?"

She fidgets with another ornament, moving it over and down a couple of branches.

"He's a good person, Mama," I add. "He's kind. And he's got a good heart. I'm sorry you'll never get a chance to see that."

Her lips press flat, like she's stifling what she really wants to say. And then she takes a step back from the tree to examine her work.

"There's something on your dresser." Her voice is so low, I almost don't hear her.

"What?"

"In your room. On your dresser. There's a note for you." She avoids eye contact.

I dash to my room, heart pounding in my ears, and find a slip of folded notebook paper sitting between my vanilla jar candle and a half empty bottle of a perfume I received two birthdays ago.

Unfolding it, I'm met with blue ink and a handful of words from the man I love.

Rose girl—

The night I first saw you, I was coming to save you. Believe it or not, I thought you were drowning. Never could I have imagined it would've been you saving me in the end.

Thank you for showing me what love is for the first time in my life.

Thank you for saving me from the monster I was destined to become.

I love you now. I'll love you always. And if you ever change your mind, I'll be waiting.

—Enemy Dearest

"How long have you had this?" I ask Mama when I find her standing in my doorway. "And how'd you get it?"

"Adriana dropped it off the week of Thanksgiving," she says.

It makes sense now, why my parents were so intent on coming to see me for Thanksgiving instead of having me home. They probably figured August would be back, and keeping me close and out of town would keep a safe wedge between us.

Adri texted me a few weeks ago saying she dropped a letter off at the house for me—I assumed she meant it was a piece of mail, like an old pay stub or tax document from work. It didn't occur to me that she meant a literal letter ... nobody writes letters anymore.

"I was only trying to protect you," Mama says, sighing. "I don't like that he's a Monreaux. And I will *never* forgive his father for what he's put our family through. But I'm willing to admit that maybe, *maybe* I was wrong about him."

"There's no maybe about it, Mama."

Grabbing my keys and bag and coat, I hurry to the door.

"Where are you going?" she calls after me.

"To *him*." I skip down snow-shoveled steps and cracked sidewalk and climb inside my still-warm car.

Two months ago, I deleted his number.

I'd gone out with my friends, enjoyed way too many rum and Cokes, and convinced myself I was doing the right thing. That if I no longer had his number, it would be easier because the temptation to text him or call him would be gone.

When I woke the next morning, it took me a second to remember what I'd done.

But instead of feeling empowered, I was nauseous with rum and regret.

Fifteen minutes later, I'm at the wrought iron gate to the Monreaux mansion, frantically hitting the buzzer.

"Monreaux residence, how may I help you?" An older man's voice greets me through the speaker.

"Hi, I'm here to see August. Is he home?"

"One moment, please." The speaker goes silent for a minute, then another. I'm about to hit the buzzer again when the iron gates part, and up ahead a man walks toward me in a hunter green parka, his hair blowing in the December wind.

I fly out of my car so fast I leave the driver's door open, and I sprint to him.

He catches me in his arms, squeezes me until my feet leave the ground, and swings me in a circle.

"Mama gave me your letter," I say.

His smile fades and his brows narrow. "How did your mom get the letter?"

"Adriana dropped it off at my house ... and I guess Mama took it upon herself to read it."

Maybe that was Adri's entire point—maybe she knew Mama had read it and hope it would help her see him in a different light? It's not like the letter was sealed. I'm sure she read it before she even handed it off.

His lips flatten. "And?"

"She said maybe she's wrong about you." Lifting on my toes, I kiss his spearmint-flavored lips. "Now we just need to work on your father ..."

"Done," he says.

She scrunches her face. "What?"

"Apparently hell has frozen over because he randomly gave me his blessing. He says he's forgiven your family, wants to bury the hatchet."

I study him. This all feels too good to be true. "Was he drunk or anything?"

"Fair question," he says. "But no, he was not. He was crystal clear and coherent."

"That's ... wow. I guess it's all coming together perfectly." I shrug.

The universe works in strange ways, I know. And generally when something sounds too good to be true, it is. But in this case, I don't want to question it. If Mama's open to this and his father has given us his blessing, I only want to move forward.

"I love you," he says into my ear, wrapping me tight in his arms and burying his head into my hair.

"I love you too."

"Come inside with me."

I nod toward my car, the engine idling and the door wide open.

"I'll have someone move it," he says before scooping me into his arms and carrying me inside.

He locks the door when we get to his room, and I perch on the side of his bed, running my hand along the cashmere-soft bedding.

"I've missed this," I say. "Being here with you. It's like the outside world stopped existing the second I was within these four walls."

August climbs in beside me, his body flush against mine, and he pulls my thigh over top of his hip.

"I've lived twenty years without you," he says, "but I don't know if I can do it another day."

"I'm not going anywhere this time."

"Marry me, Sheridan." His gray eyes flash with intensity.

"You haven't seen me in four months and the first thing you do is propose?" I chuckle, swatting his shoulder.

He isn't grinning though. There's no tease in his tone.

He's for real ...

"Why the rush?" I ask. "Told you I'm not going anywhere."

"Because I fully intend to make you my wife someday, and I'm terribly impatient." His full mouth curls up at one side.

"To say the least."

"So what do you say?" he asks. "Will you marry me?"

He rolls me over top of him, and I sit up, my hands flat against his chest. His heart gallops beneath my palms.

"It doesn't have to be today or tomorrow. Or even next year. And I'll get you a ring—in fact, my grandmother's ring is in the safe upstairs. If you like it, it's yours. Or if you want something else—"

"—it's not about the ring," I say, biting a half smile. "I just ... I just think you're insane."

He laughs. "Which we both know is what you love most about me."

"One of the many things ..."

"So is that a yes?" he asks.

Without a doubt, this is the craziest thing I've ever done, but the sense of peace that fills my soul when I look into his eyes tells me it would also be the wisest.

In many ways, I hardly know him.

But in stranger ways, my soul knows his. How else can you describe that feeling you get when you're with someone and they feel like home?

"Yes," I say. "I'll marry you, August."

We should wait before we spring this on my parents ... give them time to warm up to the fact that we're officially together again. But I'm certain once they spend more time with him, they'll adore him as much as I do. And of course, there's no need to rush the wedding. We can take our time, enjoy the butterflies and date nights and insatiableness that comes with the early parts of relationships.

Sitting up, he cups my cheek, laces his fingers in the hair at the nape of my neck, and crushes my lips with a claiming kiss.

"I'm yours," I tell him. "Always. Ring or no ring."

"I'll hold you to that, Rose girl."

I inhale him one last time tonight, bracing myself for the drive home—when a metallic clamoring steals our moment.

"What was that?" I ask.

August slides his phone off his nightstand, taps on an app, and pulls up a grid of camera images. Zooming in on the one in the middle, his lips press flat.

"My uncle's here," he says, monotoned. "And from the looks of it, he's hammered. I need to go deal with him. I'll take you out the side door."

I begin to protest. If we're getting married and this is his family, why the need to sneak me out? But before I utter a word, August slips his hand in mine, as if he picks up on my reluctance.

"He's not your problem, Rose girl," he says. His uncle's voice trails from down the hall, though I can't make out a single angry slurred word. "And you shouldn't have to meet him like this." His lips are warm against my forehead a second later, and he leads me across the hallway, down the stairs, and out a door I've never seen before. "Goodnight, Sher."

I rise on my toes to kiss him goodnight.

I need a nickname for him too, something more fitting than *Enemy Dearest*.

Because he never should have been my enemy—and he never will be again.

CHAPTER FORTY-ONE

AUGUST

"YOUR DAD HOME?" Uncle Rod slams kitchen cabinet after cabinet.

"No," I say, keeping a careful distance. "He's gone until tomorrow. What are you looking for?"

He takes a seat at the island, slaps a short stack of paperwork onto the counter, and exhales. Stale liquor invades the air between us.

A drunk *and* angry Rod Monreaux is never a good thing.

"I knew he'd do this," he says, his words slurring into one another as he ransacks the drunk drawer. "I knew he'd try to fuck me over with this handover deal. Your father's word is shit, August. *Pure fucking shit.* And a man's only as good as his word, which means your father's a sorry excuse for a man. But you already knew that, didn't you?"

"No idea what you're talking about. He doesn't tell me anything."

"The handover deal." His words blend again, though I can still make them out. "He was going to pay me with this grain operating outfit out of Milford. Worth seven figures. And at the last minute, he sold it out—and for less than half of what he said it was worth. The fucking bastard. I'm going to kill him. That was going to be my retirement income."

I'd say he's a Monreaux, and we're all pretty set for life, but I've seen what Uncle Rod does with his money. High-roller tables during his bi-weekly trips to Vegas. Escorts on the regular. Fast cars. I'm sure he *was* counting on that deal for income.

"I'm sure he had a good reason."

"His reason can kiss my ass," Rod says, spitting his words literally and figuratively. "He's a liar. A dirty fucking liar. Always has been, always will be."

I uncap my water, nodding. You don't become a multimillionaire business mogul overnight by being an Honest Abe and doing everything by the book.

"If you only knew half of what your dad's done to people over the years," he waxes on. "Just constantly screwing people over. It's game to him, to see what he can get away with, who he can pay off. And we're all pawns. He's sick, August. He's sick in the head. And I hope to God you don't turn out like him."

"Same."

"You know that girlfriend of his? Cynthia? Back in the day? The one they found strangled in the quarry?"

"Cynthia ... Rose?"

He thumbs the side of his nose. "Yeah, that one."

"What about her?"

"Your dad's the one who did it." Uncle Rod shrugs, like it's no big deal. "He set up his best friend too. Tried to make him take the fall. Used his truck and everything. It was all over some chick, too."

"What do you mean?"

"Your dad liked this girl—uh, Mary Beth, I think? But Mary Beth liked Rich Rose. Would have nothing to do with Vincent no matter what he tried. So Vincent started dating Rich's kid sister. Started out as a way to get under Rich's skin a little. Or maybe he thought Rich would dump Mary Beth and then Vince could have her. Anyway, nothing was going your dad's way and Rich still wouldn't end it with Mary Beth, so your dad killed Rich's sister and framed Rich for it. Wanted to teach him a lesson."

I shove my plate aside.

I've lost my appetite.

"Same thing with your mom." He points at me. "He wanted to teach her a lesson too."

"What the fuck are you talking about?"

"She was going to leave him. And she was going to get half the estate because the dumb ass didn't sign a prenup," he says. "Your mom was a smart woman. And she was tired of your father's games. She'd served him divorce papers the day before she went out for that run ... but the reporters didn't cover that little detail, did they? Nope. Your father made damn certain of that."

"So he tried to pin her death on Rich?"

"Yes, because he was pissed he didn't pull it off the first time. And he was still bitter. Rich and Mary Beth were married by then. It killed him that she went for some 'poor nobody' when she could've been the queen of this fucking castle."

Sheridan's mom.

"Anyway, he's had it out for her ever since," he continues. "Every couple of years, he gets the poor bastard fired from whatever job he's holding down at the time."

I bury my face in my hands, breathing hard through my fingers.

Now it makes sense.

Now I know why my dad was so keen to bless our relationship and act like it was a good thing, a peace pipe of sorts. It's nothing more than a revenge fantasy for him ... which means being together puts her in danger.

Uncle Rod says a lot of crazy shit sometimes—but he's also one of the most in-the-know guys this city has seen. For the longest time, he was my father's number one, his right-hand man. He did a lot of Dad's bidding until things cooled off between them.

"Do you have proof of this?" I ask.

He scoffs. "You think I'm an idiot, August? I've got proof of everything. I've got so much fucking proof your father would shit his pants if he knew."

Until I deal with my father, I'm going to have to keep Sheridan safe, which means keeping her as far away from me, this house, and my father as possible.

"I'm going to need to see those files," I tell him. "Immediately."

"Be my fucking guest." He shoves the bar stool aside and ambles down the hallway toward my father's study. A second later, he's browsing his priceless collection of antique books until he plucks a random one off the shelf and cracks it open. A small silver key lands on the polished wood with a clink. "This key opens the top left drawer of his desk."

"What is this?"

"It's his blackmail drawer," he says, as if it's the kind of thing everyone has in their home office. "Every time he has someone do his dirty work he records it. And if he's got any dirt on them, he keeps it in there. Like an insurance policy type thing. In case they try to double cross him, he knows exactly how to make their life a living hell."

"How's this going to prove that he killed Cynthia and Mom?"

"Because this town is full of people who know the truth," he presses his finger into the top of my father's mahogany desk top. "And they're all in there."

I swipe the key off the floor and pop the lock. Sure enough, the drawer is full of color-coded files labeled with vaguely familiar names, filled with papers and thumb drives and Polaroid images.

By the time I glance away from this shit show, my uncle is halfway to the door.

"Tell your father I'll deal with him accordingly," he says before disappearing down the hall. "You tell me the minute he's back in town and not a second later, you understand?"

Pulling out my phone, I snap image after image of everything. And for the hours that follow, I read every last document, make duplicates of every last thumb drive, and pore over every photo filed away. At some point, I pass out head first on his desk. But then I pick up where I left off.

It's seven AM before I climb out of this dark fucking rabbit hole of a mess my father has made. My eyes burn and my neck is kinked, but I've got a list of names and an idea of where to start.

All this time, I blamed Rich Rose for killing my mother and sister, for obliterating everything this family could've been—but it was my father the whole time.

He ruined us.

And now, I'm going to ruin him.

CHAPTER FORTY-TWO

AUGUST

"ROUGH NIGHT?" Sheridan meets me at the gate the next afternoon.

I rub my eyes, which are probably red as fuck. And I don't remember the last time I ate or drank a glass of water for that matter. My hair could use a comb and my five o'clock shadow is coming in by the second.

I look like shit.

I feel like shit.

"Yeah, didn't sleep much," I shove my paper cut-covered hands into my pockets.

"It's kind of cold out here ..." She eyes the house behind me and rocks on her feet. "We going to head in or we going to just stand around and hope we don't turn into human icicles?"

"I don't think it's a good idea," I say. "Not tonight."

"Oo .. kay?" Her brows lift. "You told me to come here today at three o'clock. Did I miss something?"

"There's some stuff I have to deal with." I'm so exhausted, I don't know if the words coming out of my mouth make sense or if they're gibberish. It's like being drunk without touching a drop of liquor. "I really need to focus on this right now."

"Focus on what, August? I'm confused ..."

"Family stuff."

"Can you be more specific?"

"I just think we need to cool off for a second," I say. "Lay low."

Her pretty mouth forms an 'O' and she takes a step back. "Yesterday you asked me to marry you, and today you're saying we should cool off? What's going on?"

I can't tell her what I know. I can't risk her running off to her parents and telling them before I have a chance to talk to any of the people in that drawer. I need to get to them first, assure them it's safe for them to start talking, and put together a plan to get my father behind bars where he belongs.

It's a delicate, intricate process—and I can't risk a single misstep. My father has sharks for lawyers, and they can sniff out red flags and loopholes like chum.

"Please, Sher. Trust me. I can't get into this right now, but I'll tell you everything as soon as I can."

"Is it a deeply personal and complicated matter?" She lifts a hand to her hip, using the line her father used on her when she tried to confront him about the supposed affair.

If I say yes, I'm fucked because she'll think I'm cheating.

If I say no, I'm lying.

"It's a private family matter," I say.

"Are you in trouble?"

If my father finds out what I'm doing, yes. I'll be a dead man.

"No," I say. "Not if I keep my mouth shut."

"You can tell me anything, August. Why can't you tell me this?"

"Believe me, I want to. And I will. Just not now."

Glancing at the black pavement at our feet, her lower lip trembles. But she doesn't cry. She sucks in an icy December breath and lets her hands fall to her sides.

"I can't believe I fell for this," she says. "You're no different than any other guy who thinks he knows what he wants until it gets serious, and then he freaks out and needs space."

"I can see how it might look that way."

"Did you, or did you not just tell me I couldn't come inside and that we need to cool off, i.e., spend less time together." She cocks her head to the side. "Wait, are you high right now? Are you on something?"

She sniffs, eyes wide and mouth half agape, as if she's waiting for me to tell her this is all some sick and twisted joke.

She doesn't want to believe this, but to be fair, neither do it.

I never thought we'd come this far, just to have to turn back around—but it's only temporary.

"You've got to be fucking kidding me." Her tone changes, flat and broken at the same time. "God, I'm stupid. I really am. To believe you meant all those things? To fall for your stupid act?"

She pretends to smack herself on the side of the head, and then she turns away as thick tears fall in rivulets down her cheeks.

I have to steel myself. This is for her safety. For our future.

It's the way it has to be—but only for now.

"I know how this sounds." I move toward her, reaching for her arm but she yanks it away with one violent, angry pull. "I'm a man of my word, Sheridan. I'm not going anywhere. But I need to take care of something first. I love you, and I have every intention of marrying you someday. But that'll never happen if I don't take care of this first."

"You're a sick bastard, August. I hope you know that." She returns to her car, slams the door, and reverses out of the gate.

She's mad now, but all of this is for her—to clear her family name, to keep her safe, and to ensure I can spend the rest of my life never having to worry if she's in danger.

CHAPTER FORTY-THREE

Sheridan

"HOW THE HELL does a guy go from asking to marry you one night to telling you he needs space the very next day?" Adriana paces across her room.

"Your guess is as good as mine." I page through one of her millions of magazines. "Maybe I'll go back to campus for the rest of break. Some of my friends are still there. No point in hanging around here."

"There's got to be something else going on. I just don't buy the cold feet thing. If it were anyone else, yeah. One hundred percent. But not him. Guy's obsessed with you. To the nth degree. No way he'd try to lock you down and suddenly change his mind."

"Do you think there's someone else? An ex-girlfriend maybe?"

"All the people I talked to that know him say he doesn't date—unless maybe he met someone at school this fall? But when he came into work that day before Thanksgiving and wrote that note ... that doesn't sound like a guy with a girl-friend back at school, you know?"

I lean back against her headboard. "I don't know what to think anymore."

"What are you going to do?"

I slink a shoulder up to my ear. "I don't know. I don't even know if we're broken up? It was all so strange. I'd never seen him like that before ... kind of frantic and messy, with this far-off look on his face. He looked like he hadn't slept or showered since the last time I saw him."

"Maybe he's having a nervous breakdown."

"Over what?"

She shrugs. "He said it was a private family matter. Monreauxs do messed-up shit all the time. Maybe he feels like he has to clean up someone's mess before he brings you into it?"

"Maybe," I say. "Maybe not. Who knows?"

"I don't think you should go back to campus."

"Why not?"

"Because right now you're assuming the worst—and remember when you did that with your dad? And how upset you were? You make rash decisions when you're upset, Sher. You always do. All I'm saying is maybe he's not lying to you, maybe he's trying to protect you, and maybe you shouldn't run back to campus in case he needs you?" She throws her hands in the air. "Just my two cents."

She's right.

Sliding out my phone, I send him a quick text now that I have his number again.

ME—I'm really unsettled by our conversation earlier. Are we still together, August? Or was that you breaking up with me? Should I stay or go back to school?

He doesn't text me back until 1 AM that night.

ENEMY DEAREST—I didn't break up with you.

Sitting up in bed, I tap out a laser-quick response, only before I'm finished, he sends a second message.

ENEMY DEAREST—Trust me and wait for me. That's all I ask.

ENEMY DEAREST—I love you.

I toss my phone aside, stare at the wall, and remind myself he's never let me down before. And Adriana was right—I do sometimes assume the worst.

Now that he's back in my life, the thought of losing him all over again is terrifying.

CHAPTER FORTY-FOUR

I HAVEN'T SEEN Sheridan in two weeks, and I'm fucking dying. But it's all about to be over. My obsession with justice, relentless determination, and weeks' worth of interviews and working with the local police means all of this is about to be over. Even if most of them live comfortably in my father's back pocket, their day in the sun is about to come to an end. They won't be able to argue the mountain of evidence I've collected. The proof of corruption. Either they get on the right side, or they'll be just as fucked as him in the end.

It's a deep, dark web. A nightmare to untangle.

But when it's over, it'll all have been worth it.

I'll be able to sleep at night knowing she's safe, forever out of harm's way.

I told my father I'd lost interest in her, hoping his radar would cool and whatever scheme he was cooking in the back of his twisted little head would fizzle out. And he bought it. He hasn't asked about her once. But if he were ever to see us together, it'd be game on. He'd put whatever plan he had in motion before she lived to see her next birthday, I'm certain.

"You ready?" Detective Zimmerman asks.

Another police officer inspects my wires. We're three blocks from the house, parked in an unmarked van. A minute from now, I'll head home and confront my father, tell him I know all about the evidence and what he's really done, and hopefully he'll talk enough to incriminate himself.

We head to the house, and they park behind a wall of hedges. At the gate, I punch the code, and let myself in. Hands in my pockets, I keep a casual stride, and once inside, I find my father in his study, sipping his nightly Scotch and shouting at someone on his work phone.

I rap three times on the open door. He shoots me a look and points to his phone.

"It's important," I mouth.

"Gil, listen, I'll have to call you back," Dad says, ending the call. "What? What do you need?"

"I wanted to talk to you about a few things," I say. "Disturbing things that have recently come to light."

He folds his hands on his desk, and I take the seat across from him.

The concerned expression on his face morphs into amusement, eyes sparkling and full grin on display.

"All right, son. Tell me, what rumors have you heard this week?"

"I wish I could say they were rumors. Unfortunately I've been able to confirm every last one of them."

"What are you talking about? Quit being so vague. Cut to the chase." He waves me on.

"Your top drawer," I say. "Your blackmail drawer. I've seen everything inside. I've taken pictures. I've copied the thumb drives. I've spoken to the people whose names are on those folders."

Color drains from his face, though he keeps his posture rigid.

"I actually spoke with Harold Munson, the retired chief of police who ran the department back when Cynthia Rose was murdered. And again when Mom was killed," I say. "He's actually battling Stage IV pancreatic cancer. Not much time left. Also, dying men tend to want a clean conscience before they go. They also want to make sure their family is provided for. I took care of that last part for him—all he had to do was give me a confession." I pick at my nail. "And damn. Let's just say it was worth every penny."

My father leans back in his creaky wooden chair, examining me from a different angle.

Or maybe he's thinking about Monreaux Corporation, what's going to become of it when he's rotting in a jail cell. I'm not sure what'll happen to it. If it'll get liquidated to pay off all the lawsuits that'll be thrown his way in the near future. But I don't care.

I don't need his dirty money.

It can't buy any of the things I'm interested in—love, happiness, true contentment, peace of mind.

Those things are priceless.

Mary Beth made the right choice marrying for love and not money.

"Do you have anything to say or would you like me to keep going?" I ask.

"You need to be very careful, August," he says.

"Is that a threat?"

"Clearly you know what I'm capable of. You've seen the evidence. Tread lightly. You're my son, but at the end of the day, a man's got to look out for number one."

"Don't you ever feel bad? About all the lives you've destroyed? The lives you've *taken*?"

"Bad things only happen to bad people, August." He clucks his tongue.

I always knew my father was different, but now I know exactly what he is: a narcissistic megalomaniac with a God complex.

"So help me, August, if you take me down, I'm taking you down with me," he says. "Stay out of my way, and you'll have the world eating from the palm of your hand. The choice is yours."

"How could you do that to your own wife and daughter?" Any minute the police will be busting through here. This could be the last chance I get to ask the question that's been keeping me up at night these last couple of weeks.

"Your mother was planning to leave me," he says with a shrug. "I strongly advised her not to, told her it wouldn't be *safe*. She didn't listen. If you've an ounce of intelligence in that thick skull of yours, you'll do the same."

"So you'll kill me too?"

"I'll do what I have to do."

"All right." I head to the hall. "I think I've heard enough."

A second later, the main entrance doors swing open, slamming against the walls, and foyer fills with uniformed officers. I point them toward the study, and I stand back, blending into the dark fixtures and furnishings as I watch them place him in cuffs.

He shoots me a smug glare on his way out, and he walks with the confidence of someone with a whole team of lawyers on speed dial. But even the best of the best won't be able to get him out of this.

We have a fucking mountain of evidence on him.

As soon as they're gone, I call Uncle Rod and share the good news. Then I shoot a text to Soren, letting him know Dad got arrested so he hears it from me before he sees it on TV. I don't give Gannon the same courtesy—he'll find out soon enough from one of his minions at the corporation. Nor do I let Cassandra know. For starters, I don't know where she is. And second, she's not my concern.

I help myself to my father's closet, punching in the code to his safe, which he told me once several years ago when he was drunk. Astoundingly, it still works. The door beeps and pops open. I sort through the watches, jewelry, and cash, until I find my mother's diamond engagement ring, and I tuck it in my pocket.

Someday, when the time is right, I'll have the stone reset into a new design for Sheridan.

I lock the safe and head downstairs, swiping my keys off the counter before heading to my car. Fifteen minutes later, I pull into the Roses' driveway, making my way up the front walk, my heart in my throat.

Sheridan's car is here.

Her parents' car too.

I ring the doorbell, clear my throat, and wait.

A second later, a tall, thin man stands behind the storm door.

He steps onto the porch. "Can I help you?"

"Yes, hi. I'm August Monreaux," I say. "And I am deeply in love with your daughter."

"Rich? Who's out there?" A woman's voice calls from inside. A moment later, she steps out from behind him.

"August Monreaux, ma'am. It's nice to finally meet you." I extend my hand.

"He came to tell us he's in love with Sheridan," he says to her. I don't know them enough to read their expressions or interpret the glances they exchange.

"I'd also like you to know, that my father is currently under arrest for the murders of Cynthia Rose and Elisabeth Monreaux," I add.

Mary Beth braces herself against her husband, her jaw slack.

Rich stands, unblinking, unmoving.

"On behalf of the Monreaux name, I'd like to apologize for any hardships that have been put upon your family as a result of my father's acts. We're in the process of setting up a victim compensation account, and I'd be happy to direct you to our attorney for further information."

"Mama?" Sheridan's angelic voice trails from behind them as she steps out, barefoot, cheeks flushed and hair wild like she just got up from a nap. Fucking adorable, as always. "August ... what's going on?"

"It's cold out here," Mary Beth says. "Why don't we all go inside and talk a little more?"

Sheridan's big blue gaze widens, as if she didn't expect the gesture.

"If you don't mind, I'd like a few minutes alone with Sheridan," I say.

Her father hesitates, studying me before offering a single nod. "All right."

I follow her to her room, shutting the door behind us.

"August, what's going on? These last two weeks—" she says, until I quiet her mouth with mine.

And then I tell her *everything*.

Every last damned detail.

I tell her about my father's obsession with her mother, the steps he took to frame her father for Cynthia's murder. I tell her about my mother's "accident," and every life he's ruined, destroyed, and annihilated since.

"He would've used you as a pawn," I say. "When he told me he'd forgiven your father, he was lying. There was nothing to forgive because your father was innocent. He was just hellbent on getting back at him from all those years ago."

"Do you think he would've … hurt me?"

"He would've done something. Hard to say exactly what that would've been. But I wasn't going to chance it. That's why I had to keep you away. I told him I dumped you. I didn't want to risk us being seen together. It was the only way."

I kiss her forehead.

"It's over for him," I say when I'm done. Pulling her against me, I add, "He'll never be able to hurt anyone ever again."

Pressing her cheek against my chest, she closes her eyes and breathes me in.

"Tell me what you're thinking right now," I say.

Gazing up, her shiny eyes smile. "I think you're the most amazing person I've ever known, that's what I'm thinking."

"I want to take you out tonight. On a real date." I wrap my arms around her waist.

"I love you," she says with an exhausted hum in her tone.

"I love you the most, Rose girl."

EPILOGUE

Sheridan

FIVE YEARS Later

THERE'S a cool breeze in Charleston today, which is a blessing because at eight months pregnant, the whole world feels like a sauna some days.

I fix a glass of iced blackberry tea and head for the front porch, getting comfortable on the wooden swing August built for us. Any minute now, my husband will be pulling up with my parents, who flew in to stay with us for a few weeks to help situate the nursery.

We just moved into this house a month ago. Found it on a whim. We'd been living in a charming two-bedroom historic townhouse downtown when we happened to take a drive one Sunday afternoon in the suburbs and spotted a realtor hammering a sign into the yard.

We pulled over and asked if we could take a quick tour.

The place was empty—the owners having just moved for a job. But as soon as we set foot inside, I knew.

It was home.

I pictured everything so clearly: the two of us making breakfast in the kitchen, the garden we'd plant in the back yard, where we'd put August's favorite chair in the study. The four bedrooms upstairs were perfect too. Not too big, not to small. There was even a small nursery suite off the master.

And the outside was to die for. Brick and stucco accents with wrought iron railings. Three stories. Piazzas on every level. Slate roof. There was even an outbuilding that was once a carriage house once upon a time—the perfect place for August to set up an office.

We made an offer that day, closed a month later, and we've been settling in ever since.

I sip my tea, close my eyes, and let the wind toy with my hair as our baby moves in my stretched belly.

I wish I could've captured the look on August's face when we found out we were having a boy. He had it in his head that he was going to have all girls. And for months he said he hoped it was a girl. I think a part of him is afraid to re-live his own childhood, a house full of boys who could never seem to get along. But I like to remind him that our family will be different. It'll be whatever we make it to be. It won't be perfect, but it'll be loving. Filled with memories and traditions. And maybe a few fights because that sort of thing is only natural ...

I rub my tummy, gently pressing against what I assume is his little foot. Or a fist. Hard to know.

Smiling, I whisper, "I can't wait to meet you, AJ."

When August told me his mother used to call him AJ

but that his father refused after she died, I insisted this would be the sweetest way to honor her.

What I wouldn't give to meet the woman who gave my husband life. I know she'd be immensely proud of the man he's become.

The last several years have been a magical blur. After I finished my nursing degree, I followed August to Portland, where he took a coveted job at a tech startup with one of his college friends. I finished my BSN out there, while he worked crazy hours to get his side project off the ground—an innovative app and software suite called Jogger Safe. When he branched off on his own, he had the freedom to work from anywhere in the world.

We spent a year traveling the country trying to figure out where we wanted to place our roots. A week in Savannah. A long weekend in Austin. A holiday in Chicago. We finally settled on Charleston after falling in love with its historic charm, agreeable winters, and sweet Southern drawls. It was the perfect place to settle in and kick off the rest of our life together. And while we thought about placing roots in our hometown, we decided it was better to leave the past alone and start fresh.

Besides, I don't think August would ever want to see his family home again. It only makes him think of his father, who rots away in a prison cell forty miles from there, and Gannon, who ran off with Cassandra after the trial—until they blazed through Gannon's bank account and she left him high and dry for some other rich asshole.

AJ kicks again, and my lips curl into a slow smile.

I haven't met him yet, but something tells me he's going to be intense like his daddy. All Monreaux men are intense in their own ways, I've come to learn. I told August he needs to think of it as a super power; that he needs to rein it in, control it, and use it to his advantage.

A car horn honks, and I glance up to find August's SUV inching into the driveway. A second later, my parents climb out of the passenger seats. It takes me a second to get out of the swing, but I head down the front steps and meet them halfway.

"Hi, sweetheart." Mom wraps her arms around me.

She looks good. The pink has returned to her cheeks and her eyes are brighter than ever. Ever since they won that settlement, their financial worries have ceased and they're no longer stressing, waiting for the bottom to drop out again. With Vincent behind bars, my father has been at his current job for five years—a record for him.

Life is truly good.

"Come in, come in. I can't wait to show you guys around," I tell them.

Dad gives me a side hug and helps me up the steps, and Mama gets the door. August follows with their luggage, wheeling it to the guest room upstairs.

Someday I hope to have little ones in every single bedroom. I told August I want a whole house of Monreauxs, and he laughed, but I meant it. I want to have all the babies with him. I want all of the laughter, all of the memories, all of the good and the bad, too.

My parents settle in and meet us in the hallway for a tour.

"So it was built in 1817." I claps my hands like a proper tour guide. "By General Leopold Renoir, for his wife and five children."

I point out the terra cotta chimney pots, original ornamental plaster details, and two hundred year old marble mantels.

"Back then, the men and women had separate drawing rooms," I say when we get to the first level. "And this house has two kitchens, a main kitchen and a prep space—because back then that's where the house staff prepared the meals and washed the dishes."

My mother oohs and aahs over every intricate detail, her gaze poring over every corner of every room as if she might miss something. Meanwhile, my father makes a beeline for a window overlooking our back yard. It's small. Maybe a third of an acre worth of space, but it's enough for a swing set. A pergola. Room for children to run around.

"You're going to need a vegetable garden," Dad says to August.

August smiles and nods. I don't think he's ever watered a plant in his life, but he humors my father nonetheless.

"This is a beautiful home, sweetheart." Mom rests her head on my shoulder. "And so filled with love already."

"It truly is."

"I'm so happy for you. And August, too," she says. "That you found each other, that you've created this life."

I once told August that our fate was written long before we were even born.

I stand by what I said.

I just know now that I had it all wrong.

Fate wasn't trying to keep us apart; it was trying to bring us together.

Chapter One

Trey

"So my cousin was at this party with Westcott a couple of years ago, and she claims he snorted pure Peruvian cocaine off a stripper using a ten thousand-dollar bill, and then, get this—he *lit the bill on fire*," a woman's nasally voice trails from the eighth-floor break room.

Never heard that one before ...

I stop outside the door and listen. I'm on my way to a conference call, but I can spare a few minutes for some cheap entertainment, especially on a monotonous Tuesday. Most people hate Mondays. I hate Tuesdays. Mondays are full of hope and ambition for the week. Wednesday's halfway to Friday, Thursday closer still. But Tuesdays? They're boring, tedious. Generally unexciting.

"That's nothing," a second woman says. Her voice holds

the desperate, youthful quality of a follower. A sheep who goes with the herd. I can sniff out those types a mile away. "I used to date this paralegal who worked for one of his attorneys. Said Westcott threw the most insane parties where everyone had to sign an NDA the second they walked in, and she was pretty sure everyone got roofied because the next day no one could remember what happened."

I stifle a snort.

Fake news ...

"I'd legit give an entire paycheck to be a fly on the wall at one of his parties," the first one says.

"Right?" the second one—the spineless disciple—counters. "Did you know his house is, like, two-hundred-thousand square feet? I tried to look up pictures of the inside of it, but all I could find is this book that was written in the nineties when his parents were still alive. Not going to lie, I was kind of disappointed. Reminded me of a castle-version of my Nana's house. Hope he's updated the place. God knows he can afford it."

The first one laughs. "Maybe he wants it to look old on purpose? Wasn't he screwing that woman twice his age a few years ago? Maybe he likes old things."

My jaw tightens. The woman to whom they're referring is my aunt. She accompanied me to a bevy of fundraisers one year when I was tired of the revolving door of desperate women sucking my dick for a chance to get a photo with me on a red carpet.

I throw up a little in my mouth.

Only an ignorant idiot would mistake my aunt for a lover.

They're lucky she isn't here to listen to this bullshit.

She's made grown men cry with her sweet smile and cutting tongue. These two would be minced meat.

"Eh, I doubt that," the other one says. "Did you see the last girl he dated? Freaking. Drop. Dead. Out. Of. This. World. Gorgeous."

She was easy on the eyes.

I'll give her that.

But that was about the extent of her admirable qualities.

"Didn't he date two girls at once before? Like a throuple kind of thing?" Number two asks.

Dated? No. Fucked until I grew bored of them? Absolutely.

"Probably," the other laughs.

"Do you guys actually believe all that?" A third woman interjects, her voice soft yet feminine but her tone direct, no-nonsense. "If he makes everyone sign NDAs at his parties, then couldn't your cousin get sued for sharing that? And if your friend and everyone at that party thought they were drugged, wouldn't they want to get tested? Also, they haven't made ten-thousand dollar bills in decades. That, and I highly doubt he does coke. Everyone knows he's vegan."

Silence.

"Also, what the inside of his home looks like is none of your business—that's extremely invasive," the third woman continues. "How would you feel if someone was Googling your address, trying to find pictures of where you slept? Where you ate dinner? And doesn't one of you have a sugar daddy right now? You were just talking about your 'allowance' a minute ago ..."

Silence.

"I kind of feel like when you're the richest person in the world, people are going to be curious," the second woman says, a little late on her defense. "It comes with the territory."

"Yeah," the first one chimes in. "It's not like we're being stalkers. It's different when you're famous."

"Ah, true," my fearless advocate sighs, a hint of sarcasm in her tone.

I lean closer to the door, just enough to catch a glimpse of her face – only to be met with the back of her head and the ice-blonde waves cascading over her shoulders. A pinstriped blouse is tied high on her waist and cuffed at her elbows, and a fitted skirt skims her hourglass curves.

She reminds me of one of those Old Hollywood pin-up girls my grandfather was obsessed with in his younger days. He kept a full file of photos in a desk drawer in his study, where my notoriously jealous grandmother would never see them.

I lean away before I'm spotted.

"My mistake, ladies," the modern-day Marilyn Monroe says. "I must have forgotten rich people aren't human. By all means, carry on."

I glance at my timepiece and make a mental note to have my right-hand man and personal attorney, Broderick, check the cameras in the break room so I can get the names of the two Gossiping Gabbys. And I take a hint of pleasure in imagining them commiserating at some God-awful trendy neighborhood bar, drinking sugary cocktails that match the pink slips they're about to receive.

I have zero tolerance for bullshit gossip—but I'll make an exception if it's flattering.

I have a business to run—biggest in the world, in fact. And I've had more than a few deals go south because of idiotic rumors.

The women's conversation pivots to the topic of "keto

friendly chocolate", and I take that as my cue to leave. Only the instant I take a step past the open doorway is the same instant the curvy blonde in the pinstripe blouse exits the break room.

We collide in passing, but it's a subtle collision.

My arm brushes hers just enough for a quick startle.

Palm splaying across her chest, she apologizes.

Our eyes lock, like she's realizing who I am. This happens on a daily basis. For whatever reason, I intimidate the fuck out of people with my mere presence.

The woman sucks in a breath before going silent, recognition widening her eyes, and then she brushes a flaxen wave from her forehead, chewing the inner corner of the juiciest rose-colored mouth I've ever seen.

Funny how a moment ago she was so brave, standing up for a man she'd never met and now she's a deer in the headlights. Doe-eyed and all.

"What's your name?" I ask. A work badge hangs from her neck, but I can't take my attention off her pleasing almond-shaped gaze with their spray of dark lashes and ocean-blue irises. A chorus of wild flowers, sun-dried cotton, and fresh air fills my lungs. She smells like a morning in the countryside, and for the briefest moment I'm transported to childhood summers at my grandparents' country home in Surrey.

She swallows, straightens her shoulders, and tips her chin upwards. "Sophie Bristol."

She doesn't ask my name. I imagine she doesn't need to.

"Thank you," My gaze skims past her delicate shoulders toward the break room doorway, "for ... *that*."

Her full lips press and she offers a slight nod. "You're welcome."

"I'm not vegan by the way," I add.

Her nose wrinkles. "I'm sorry?"

"You told them I was vegan. But you should know, I'm very much a carnivore." I give her a nuanced wink and earn a reserved smile from her pretty mouth in return.

With that, I'm gone.

I don't stick around—I don't have the time. I'm officially running late for a meeting with the board of Ames Oil and Steel, one in which I'm attempting to make a record-shattering, unheard-of offer. Not that I need it. As the richest man in the world, I don't need much of anything, personally, professionally, or otherwise. Acquiring businesses has become more of a sport in recent years. I'd compare it to climbing mountains. You start with the smaller ones and work your way up to the tallest.

Ames Oil and Steel is about to become the Mount Everest of my career.

I head to the elevator, press the button for my private floor, and swipe my key before heading to the private boardroom.

The second I stride through the door, Broderick greets me, throwing his hands in the air and mouthing something along the lines of, "What the hell?"

The projector screen behind him is filled with a bevy of middle-aged faces with impatient frowns, all of them video-conferencing from a stuffy-looking room in Philadelphia.

"Ladies, gentlemen, esteemed members of the board, I hope you weren't waiting long." I smile. I'm told I look halfway pleasant when I smile. When I'm not, I've been told I'm akin to an expressionless marble statue and people tend to grow uncomfortable when they think they can't 'read' you.

I take a seat at the head of my forty-foot mahogany table. Broderick slides me a legal pad emblazoned with the

Westcott Corporation logo, along with a pristine Caran d'Ache fountain pen—only the best for my note taking. It was my father's favorite brand. I'd hardly call myself sentimental or superstitious, but some things are worth an exception.

"Mr. Westcott, we assume you received the agenda for today's meeting?" Someone from their team breaks the east coast silence.

Broderick slides me a printed email.

"Have it right here." I give it a quick perusal, speed-reading the bullet points and identifying the words that matter. "And I can already tell you that half of these items are unnecessary. I know your time is valuable. As is mine. So I propose we both stop wasting it, and you tell me the number you want on the check. I can have my CFO authorize it before close of business today."

I'm met with a few chuffs, and a handful of them exchange unreadable stares.

Unprofessional, but I'm willing to turn the other cheek because once I buy them out, I'll never have to see their sour faces again.

"Mr. Westcott, as we all know, you're well aware of the legacy clause in our contract," Nolan Ames, the man at the head of the table with a 51% stake of his family's company, folds his hands.

"I'm well aware. Yes. Thank you." I bite my tongue and hope he doesn't pick up on the condescension in my tone. This absurd legacy clause is the only thing holding up the takeover and so far neither of us have been willing to budge. It's difficult to see eye-to-eye when your opposition is an incredulous asshole on a power trip. "But from one businessman to another, I'd like to remind you that everything is negotiable."

He leans forward in his oversized leather chair, head tilted, polite smile painting his aging face, and he clears his throat. "My great-grandfather founded this company."

I nod, as if I'd never heard the name Ames along the likes of Astors, Rockefellers, and Rothschilds. I listen, silent as if I've no idea what it's like to run a company founded by generations of familial predecessors.

"At the end of the day, it's a family business," Nolan says. "It can't switch hands unless I know for certain it'll continue to *stay* a family business."

The idea of an environment-demolishing corporation being a "family business" is laughable at best. But this man is the kind of delusional with whom one can't argue.

I shoot Broderick a look. He pinches the bridge of his nose. We both know this is bullshit. Likely a stall tactic. If Nolan really wanted to sell, he'd sell. We've had enough off-the-record conversations with board members to know they're ready to unload. Steel is holding steady but oil is at a twenty-year low. They can't compete with the Saudis in this market. They're ready to take their money to greener pastures and they'd have done it eight months ago when I initially offered, but I'm not interested in 49%.

I'm an all-or-nothing man.

"I'm willing to double my last offer," I say, "which, we can all agree, was remarkably generous."

One could even argue it was *stupid* generous.

Nolan peers at his folded hands. Still. Soundless. Either the conference call has glitched and they're frozen, or he's counting dollar signs. A second later, he finally moves, twisting the glinting platinum and diamond wedding band on his left ring finger, sliding it off then on again.

"Mr. Westcott, do you mind if we place you on mute for

a moment?" A woman in oversized pearls and a charcoal suit stands.

"Not at all," I say.

She reaches for the black device in the center of the table. The sound disappears and the screen goes dark. Nothing but a flashing icon that shows we're on hold.

"Can't wait to be done with this prick." I point my pen toward the screen. "At this point, I should make *him* pay *me* for wasting my fucking time."

Broderick exhales. "Just be patient. It's going to happen. You always get what you want."

I sink back into my chair.

He's right.

I *always* get what I want.

In fact, I don't recall a time when I haven't.

Glancing to my left, I take in a view of the somber Chicago skyline outside and contemplate my weekend plans. When I return my attention to my legal pad, I've jotted a name on the lower right corner of the first page. I don't remember doing it, but it's undeniably my handwriting.

Sophie Bristol.

I must have written it so I could remember. With over sixty thousand employees, I couldn't begin to remember anyone's names outside my tight-knit circle of trusted executives.

The screen fills with the Ames baker's dozen once more and the sound returns. A handful of indiscernible whispers. Shuffled papers. Cleared throats. Creaking chairs.

I circle Sophie's name to remind myself to check into her later—mostly out of curiosity. Her face—and body— suddenly adulterate my focus, and very rarely does something distract me to this degree.

"Have we reached a decision?" I ask.

Broderick gives me a subtle wink, as if he's certain this is the moment Nolan finally relents after eight agonizingly tortuous months of back-and-forth negotiations.

"Not quite. I have a proposition for you," Nolan says. "If you're open to hearing it."

"Of course." I sit up.

Broderick shifts in his seat, listening, taking notes as Nolan lays out an offer I never could have anticipated.

Nolan Ames is holding strong on the legacy clause. He wants me to "find someone," to "settle down," to get fucking *married* and start a family. He's also graciously giving me two years because according to him, "you're thirty-five and your best years are behind you anyway." He even had the audacity to say I'd thank him someday.

Thank him for *what*? For a money-hungry trophy wife? For a kid that'll inevitably be raised by a team of nannies? For a version of my life I've never wanted?

People like me don't do the marriage-and-family dance.

It's not who we are.

It's not who I am.

I'm aware of my strengths. I'm also aware of my weaknesses. I'd be a horrible husband and an even worse excuse for a father.

Nolan agreed to put everything in writing—that he wouldn't offer his shares to anyone else in the next two years, and the board agreed to do the same. I imagine there was an extensive amount of coaxing going on behind the scenes, hence the muting, but I don't have time to imagine what he could possibly hold over their heads because I'm too busy wrapping my mind around this preposterous, unprecedented stipulation.

"Who the hell does he think he is?" I all but spit my

words at Broderick when we disconnect a few minutes later. "He's insane."

Broderick rises, his chair groaning beneath his body-guard-esque frame, and he tosses his pen on the table. Pacing the windows, he inhales hard and heavy, always a man of few words.

"I'm going to need you to actually fucking say something." I exhale, my patience non-existent. Though my words are sharp, Broderick's got a chainmail ego. He can handle it, unlike the spineless trout before him. He puts up with my moods, whichever way they swing, and when necessary, he puts me in my place.

It's why I've yet to replace him in the ten years he's worked for me.

Most people tell me what I want to hear.

Broderick tells me what I *need* to hear—the truth.

A man can't make savvy business decisions based on sugarcoated lies.

"It's a power move," he says, eyes pointed yet unfocused. I don't like this side of him. I need my shark, not his shell-shocked alter.

"Obviously." I clench my jaw. "So what do you propose?"

He stops wearing a pattern into the carpet with his polished dress shoes and turns to me. "How badly do you want this?"

"Do I even have to answer that?"

His mouth forms a straight line, nostrils flaring. "Fine. This is the plan. We hire someone. We find a woman—one we can trust—and we pay her to marry you, have your child, and to do it all in Nolan's timeframe."

"Please tell me you're fucking joking."

He lifts a brow. "Eight months of this back-and-forth

bullshit and the man hasn't budged, Trey. Hasn't even come close. You heard what he wants. He's not wavering on that clause. And unfortunately, he knows he has the upper hand because anyone else would've walked by now."

"This is the most absurd thing I've ever heard." In my nearly fifteen years of negotiating acquisitions and takeovers, I've yet to hear of such a provision. If I didn't know better, I'd think I was being pranked. But Ames has a reputation. He's a family man. Wife of nearly ten years. Two kids. The bastard even wrote a book on "creating the ideal marriage in an anti-marriage world." Instant bestseller. He considers himself an expert in that—and many other —arenas.

In my experience, powerful men who think they're the smartest asshole in the room make some of the dumbest decisions ... sometimes simply because they can. The world doesn't tell men like Nolan Ames "no" just as it doesn't tell men like me "no."

I hunch over the table, staring down at the circled name. *Sophie Bristol.*

"All right. Plan B. We tell him we're going to pass," Broderick says, lifting a finger because he knows I'm about to protest. "If he knows you're willing to walk away and take your excessively generous offer off the table, maybe it'll light a little fire in him. Level the playing field a bit. Tip the scales in our favor—or at least equalize them."

"And if it doesn't?"

"Then we move on and find another company to buy."

I don't like the idea of moving on. I want *this* company. I've had my sights set on it for years, and when rumor had it he was looking to sell so he could retire early and focus on being a "family man," I jumped on the opportunity.

"No." I exhale. Perhaps I'm being petulant in this

moment, but I don't fucking care. There's a way to make this happen, I'm certain.

"Then we need to find someone," he says, "someone who's compatible with you, someone you find attractive, someone who would be an ideal mother, and like I said, someone you can trust. We could have them vetted by a psychologist if you want, a doctor as well to make sure she's capable of bearing—"

I lift a palm. He shuts up mid-sentence.

"—now you're getting too many people involved." I wave his words away, gaze focused on that name. *Sophie Bristol.* The syllables roll soft and sensual in my mind. I can only imagine the way they'd feel on my tongue. "I want you to look into her."

I rip the page from the legal pad and slide it toward him.

"She works here," I say. "No idea what department. I ran into her earlier. She might be a fit for ... this."

Broderick scans the name before folding the paper into fourths, and then he tucks it into the interior pocket of his suit jacket. "I'll see what I can find out."

Chapter Two

Sophie

I'm in the middle of running a Tuesday report for Miranda in Accounts Receivable when my office phone flashes with an unfamiliar extension.

It takes me three rings to process the name on the Caller ID.

It takes me an additional stomach-dropping ring to answer. "Sophie Bristol speaking."

In the three years I've worked at Westcott Corporation, Trey Westcott has *never* called me.

"Ms. Bristol, I need you to report to my office." The commanding tenor in my boss' voice sends actual chills down my spine—not an easy feat. "Immediately."

The number of times I've physically seen the unknowable powerhouse of a man, I could count on one hand, and all of those times have been in passing—with today being an exception.

From what I've heard, a person only gets called into his office when they're about to be fired. The man likes to dole out pink slips in person. He claims it's a respect thing, though I can't help but wonder if he simply gets off on it. Power changes people.

Then again, Westcott's been powerful his entire life. Born to one of the wealthiest families in the world and orphaned as a teenager, he's spent the past twenty years turning his $500 billion inheritance into a net worth that tops a trillion dollars.

A hundred times, I've tried to wrap my head around that kind of money, but I can't come close to fathoming it. They say if you were to count to a trillion, it would take two-hundred-thousand years. I don't think an ordinary person could stay sane with that kind of influence and authority.

Some of the most prominent people in existence are terrified of him—of his capabilities. And the shroud of mystery (and rumors) that surround him only add to his intimidating allure.

I log out of my computer and quickly calculate the odds of it being the last time I do so. He's got no reason to let me go, that I can think of, but I've lost track of how many times I've watched some poor, thankless company minion packing their belongings into a cardboard box while they attempt not to break down in tears in front of their staring colleagues. Once they load the elevator, they're never seen or heard from again.

I don't tend to fear anyone.

Trey Westcott is an exception.

For the past hour, I've replayed the break room incident in my mind on a loop, wondering what he heard and how much, if any, he attributed to me.

He stopped me in the hallway and said, "Thanks for ... *that*."

Was there sarcasm in his tone?

What if he thought I was the one spreading those ridiculous rumors?

Also, why is he calling me personally? He has half a dozen assistants to do this sort of thing ...

"Ms. Bristol?" His brusque voice in my ear tells me I don't have time to wonder.

"Yes." I keep my composure and swallow my concerns for now. "I'll be right there."

Westcott is my boss' boss' boss' boss' boss on a zig-zagged chart that makes me dizzy if I stare at it for too long. I didn't think the man knew I existed.

I've sat in on some meetings, amongst a hundred others, and we've passed in the hallway a time or two, never making eye contact. Other than that, nothing about our dealings have been remarkable or memorable, at least not for him.

I slip my work badge around my neck and lock up my office, mentally calculating how long it'll take to get from the eighth floor of the southwest corner of our extensive corporate campus to the northeast section where I'll hitch a ride on a private elevator to a penthouse office suite where Mr. Westcott spends no less than seventy hours a week.

Five minutes later, I check in at the desk outside his office where his number one assistant works behind a shiny black desk so gargantuan it nearly swallows her whole.

"Mr. Westcott wanted to see me," I say. "Sophie Bristol, from Payroll."

Spa-like music plays from hidden speakers but the air is particularly icy. I heard this is how he works. The hospital-grade air purifier combined with the frigid sixty-six degree thermostat keeps Westcott clear-headed and helps him do his best thinking.

The nameplate on the assistant's desk identifies her as Mona, and while I've seen hundreds of emails go out on his behalf—all with her name on them—I'd yet to put a face with it. She's stunning. Wide set hazel eyes. Inky dark hair that shines like lacquered glass. Pouty, matte-red lips. Lingerie model body. Baby face. Barely twenty-three if I had to guess.

She taps a button on her phone, lifts her fingers to the microphone of her headset, and mutters something low before pointing to the double doors behind her with the hand-carved Westcott monogram: a giant W flanked with a P on the left and an A on the right.

Pierce Ainsworth Westcott III.

The third in a line of successful, old-moneyed men, the world has only ever known him as Trey.

"You can head in," she says, gaze careful yet curious. "Mr. Westcott is ready for you."

I press my fingertips against the gold-plated door handle and give it a push.

It swings open and in a flash of a second, I know how Alice felt when she went down the rabbit hole.

Chapter Three

Trey

The doors glide open, presenting a beautiful bombshell of a woman backlit by the soft lighting of the reception area.

"Ms. Bristol." I check my watch. She isn't late. Quite the contrary. She came as soon as I called. But it's crucial she learns I don't like to be kept waiting. This will benefit her going forward.

She clasps her hands softly in front of her hips, drawing my eye toward her delicious hourglass frame, and pulls her shoulders back.

Clearing her throat, she accepts my gaze head on.

I like her already.

"What can I help you with, Mr. Westcott?" Her voice is smooth and unshaken. If I make her nervous, she's doing a superb job of hiding it.

"I'm told you work in Payroll." I come around the front of my desk, taking a seat on the edge and folding my arms across my chest.

She hasn't taken a single step closer, keeping a careful distance of ten, maybe twelve feet between us. Either she's quietly intimidated by me or she's got a thing for personal space. If it's the latter, we already share something in common.

"I do," she says. "Going on three years next month."

"And you love your job?" I ask.

Without pause, Sophie answers, "Of course."

I don't buy it.

Her brows meet. She's confused. Understandably so.

"Tell me, Ms. Bristol, what are your long-term goals here at Westcott Corporation? Where do you see yourself in five years? Ten?" My attention shifts to her glossy pale waves and the glistening lips that deliver her words on a breathy velvet cloud.

She's a walking, talking juxtaposition of vulnerability and confidence.

An enigma.

I'm too distracted by the way she carries herself to listen to the words coming out of her mouth. Besides, her answers don't matter. I've already chosen her. Once my mind is set, there's no changing it.

Sophie is in the middle of waxing on how long it took her just to get an interview here when I lift a palm to silence her.

"Thank you for that information, Ms. Bristol," I say. "I've heard enough."

She half-squints before righting her posture.

"I'm going to cut to the chase," I say, drinking in her Coke-bottle figure. The subtle nip at her waist, the elegant way her heels lift her calf muscles, the shiny, flawless set of teeth I've yet to see overtaken with a full smile, the regal posture—either she's pedigreed and hailing from a respectable family or incredibly self-assured and disciplined.

Either way, I'll take her—she's perfect for what I need.

"I'm relieving you from your current position," I say, the way I've said to countless souls who've stood in her very position. I never apologize. I never break eye contact. I never sugarcoat.

The only difference now is I'm about to dump the opportunity of a lifetime into her lap, and she hasn't the slightest.

I resist a smirk.

A sharp intake of breath passes between her open lips, but her expression is impossible to read. Her eyes—a steely Atlantic blue—don't show a hint of emotion. Still as a statue, she lingers. Or maybe she's hardening herself. This is a girl in complete control of her emotions. So much more than a pretty face and a marathon-sex worthy body.

"May I ask why?" she finally speaks, voice unbroken.

"Because I have another job for you. One I believe will suit you better," I say. "Not to mention the pay and benefits will beat anything you could ever make on your current track."

She winces. "I'm sorry. I don't understand. Are you firing me or promoting me?"

"Both."

I reach for the stack of papers on Westcott Legal Department letterhead and slide them toward her, along with a pen. "Before I get into the details of this new position, I'm going to need you to sign this NDA. It's a standard, boilerplate contract. I just need to know that the offer I'm about to make you won't be shared outside this room, beyond the two of us."

Her inquiring gaze dances over the fine print, and a moment later, she reaches for the pen —albeit reluctantly, makes a few elegant loops, and signs on the line.

"This would be a personal position," I say. "You'd work for me. With me. And only me."

"Like a personal assistant?"

"No. I have five of those already." I roll my eyes, realizing how fucking ridiculous this proposition is going to sound. The words haven't so much as left my mouth and already I'm cringing on the inside. "Before I elaborate, I'd like you to know that I've had my personal attorney dig up your file, and I have to say I'm impressed with your background. Four years at Princeton. Dual degrees in international business and accounting. President of three collegiate clubs. Founder of two charities. Fluent in multiple languages. A laundry list of remarkable references ... All of this by the age of twenty-seven? I have to ask: why are you wasting your time working in payroll here?"

"As I said earlier, Mr. Westcott, it was quite difficult to get an interview at your company and, when I finally did—I took what I could get. I've actually received two promotions since I've been here. From what I understand, the opportunity to move up is worth the wait."

It's true. It's a steep climb but the view is incredible. Many will try. Few will reach the pinnacle of Westcott success. That's the secret to maintaining a ball-busting team that comprises the core of my company.

"There are a few blanks I need to fill in—mostly concerning your familial history—but given your extraordinary background, your work ethic and loyalty, I'm confident I've made the right decision, and I believe you'll be much happier in this new position."

"Which is ...?"

"I'm in need of a," my mouth curls, as if I can't help but laugh at what I'm about to say, "personal partner. Or to put it in black and white ... a wife."

"Wait—what?" She tilts her head and a hand lifts to her angled hip. A moment ago she was stoic and composed, but something tells me I'm about to see a different side of her—

and I hope I do. I need to know everything about her, familiarize myself with the facets of her personality. "Did you just say you need a *wife*? Is this a joke?"

She peers from left to right, as if inspecting her surroundings for a hidden camera or two.

"I wish it were. Believe me. I fully understand the outlandishness of my request."

"Why me?" she asks after an endless pause.

I drag a hard, cold breath into my lungs. "I believe I already explained that to you."

She folds her delicate hands in front of her again, this time her fingers twisting into a gridlock.

"Respectfully, I have to pass."

I almost choke on my spit, but I contain my reaction. "My attorney will send you the offer, in writing, as soon as we're finished. I behoove you to take it home, read it over, and reconsider."

Her full lips press together. "I'm sorry, but my answer is still no."

"I was under the impression you were single. Am I wrong?" There was no husband or common law spouse listed on her medical insurance paperwork. From what Broderick could find, she lived alone in a fifth-floor, one-bedroom apartment approximately four blocks from here.

"I am," she says.

"Allow me to paint a picture for you. We could start with six months together," I say. "And a tastefully publicized whirlwind engagement. At the end of those six months, you would receive a sum of two million dollars. Another six months after that, we would make everything official—a wedding. Could be a grand affair if you'd like, or we could hold a private ceremony anywhere you'd like. After the wedding, you would receive a payment of five million dollars. If, within the year that follows, our marriage produces a child, you would receive an additional ten million."

It's a drop of water in the vast ocean that is my wealth, but to someone making Sophie's humble salary, it's a Powerball jackpot.

Her iridescent irises flash.

But she says nothing.

"You and my child would forever be financially cared for. You'd want for nothing. And if you'd like to legally go our own ways, I would grant you a divorce as well as primary custody, and we would come to a fair co-parenting agreement. I would never expect you to stay in a loveless marriage or sacrifice your long-term happiness."

It's imperative that I be upfront about this.

I can promise her all the money in the world, but I could never promise her my heart.

"I'm not a pawn, Mr. Westcott," she says, spoken like a woman who knows her worth. "And I'm not for sale."

"Of course you aren't," I say with the careful negotiating tone I use with anyone sitting on the other end of a business deal. "I'm not buying you, Ms. Bristol. I'm buying into a partnership with you."

"You're a good salesman, Mr. Westcott," she says. "You paint a lovely picture. But things like that—they can never be that simple. Contract or not."

I chuff. "It's not like there's a precedent for this sort of thing. I assure you, anything you want from me will be put in writing. It'll be a fair agreement. And I'm nothing if not a man of my word."

She begins to speak but stops.

"I'm in a situation, and I need your help. No, I *want* your help. And I would help you in return. It's as simple as that." And then I add, "I think we can both agree it's the opportunity of a lifetime."

"I'm sorry, but no, thank you." Short and sweet, as if she's slipping back into her graceful, poised demeanor like a satin jacket.

She doesn't stick around to even consider the generous offer I've made, the easy money, the lifetime of financial freedom with a side of luxury. While the contract would guarantee her seventeen million dollars over the course of two years, the mother of my child would live a life afforded to royalty. I could add a house. Ongoing child support. Every resource she could possibly need or want to maintain a high standard of living.

She'd be set until her dying day.

"Again, Broderick will send you the contract," I say. "As you read it over, please bear in mind that everything is negotiable."

Chin tipped forward and gaze locked on me, she asks, "Do I still have a job here or am I fired?"

She doesn't so much as hint at considering it.

I contemplate the legal ramifications of threatening someone's job in exchange for a relationship, and I think better of it.

"Of course not," I say.

Besides, it'll give us more opportunities to see one another. From here forward, I'll be making extra trips to her section of the Westcott campus.

My future wife shows herself out without any fanfare, her heels padding silent on the lush carpeting.

I'm sure, once she peruses the paperwork later over a glass of twist-cap five-dollar wine in her humble apartment, she'll reconsider.

And tonight as she lies in bed, she'll imagine a life with

me. The gravity of my offer will hit her like a wall of regret. Come morning, my phone will ring. And if it doesn't? I'll find a way to change her mind.

I always get what I want.

And I want Sophie Bristol.

Available Now!

Wall Street Journal and #1 Amazon bestselling author Winter Renshaw is a bona fide daydream believer. She lives somewhere in the middle of the USA and can rarely be seen without her trusty Mead notebook and laptop. When she's not writing, she's living the American Dream with her husband, three kids, the laziest puggle this side of the Mississippi, and a busy pug pup that officially owes her three pairs of shoes, one lamp cord, and an office chair.

Winter also writes psychological suspense under the pseudonym of Minka Kent. Her debut novel, THE MEMORY WATCHER, was optioned by NBC Universal in January 2018 and her book, THE THINNEST AIR, was a #1 Amazon Kindle bestseller and a Washington Post best seller five weeks in a row.

Winter is represented by Jill Marsal of Marsal Lyon Literary Agency.

Join the private mailing list. <- HIGHLY RECOMMENDED!

Follow Winter on Instagram!

Like Winter on Facebook.

Join Winter's Facebook reader group/discussion group/street team, CAMP WINTER.